# THE WORDS WE LEAVE
## Unspoken

ALSO BY L. D. CEDERGREEN

*Ripple*
*Gravity*

# THE WORDS WE LEAVE
## Unspoken

L.D. CEDERGREEN

This book is a work of fiction. Any references to historical events, real people, or real places are used fictitiously. Other names, characters, places, and events are products of the author's imagination, and any resemblance to actual events or places or persons, living or dead, is entirely coincidental.

Interior Design by Penoaks Publishing, http://penoaks.com
Cover Design by Robin Ludwig Design Inc. at
http://www.gobookcoverdesign.com/

ISBN: 978-0-9893783-5-2

To my sister, Christina

*Of two sisters one is always the watcher, one the dancer.*

*— Louise Glück*

# 1

## *Gwen*

I can almost hear each second tick by from the round clock on the wall that I stare at over Dr. Rand's shiny bald head. He's speaking to me, his mouth is moving and yet his words, words like *cancer*, *stage four*, and *terminal* are beating a distant drum in my head, almost in time with the second hand of the clock. *Or is that my heart?*

"Gwen? Gwen? Do you understand what I'm telling you?" Dr. Rand asks as he stands, leaving his chair and moving around his desk to kneel in front of me.

"Gwen? Are you alright?" he asks again, this time his voice is loud, like a beacon penetrating the dense fog that I am lost in. My eyes venture from the clock to his kind, weathered face that is now only inches from mine.

"What?" I whisper through the knot sitting in the back of my throat.

"Do you understand what I'm telling you? We're dealing with more then one tumor this time. I'm sorry, but the cancer's back. Only now it has metastasized."

"So what's the plan *this* time? More surgery? More chemo?" The thought alone of more chemotherapy makes the room spin and I instantly feel queasy. But I'll do it again, if that's what it takes.

"Well, we can try an aggressive approach if you want, but I'm not going to lie. It will be hell and the chances of beating this, at this stage, aren't likely."

"So what then? What are you saying?"

He stands and leans back on his desk, crossing his ankles. I watch him remove his wire-rim glasses and rub his eyes, waiting for him to tell me the plan, the treatment, the solution.

"I'm saying, Gwen, that there's not much we can do. We wait. We monitor your condition and, in the meantime, you spend time at home with your family. I'm sorry. We just didn't catch it in time."

*Time.* After the first cancer diagnosis, I told myself that I would never take another day for granted. That I would wake each morning and remember how precious time is, that I would truly live my life to the fullest. And I did just that, for a while, but I realize now as if I'm stuck in a very bad déjà vu moment, that I have once again allowed myself to get swept away in the rat race, relying on the "later" in life, as if my existence had no expiration date. I had underestimated just how fleeting life could be. *Time.* That word resonates in my head, louder and louder as my mind flashes to Olivia and Max. To John.

Olivia, my sweet girl, is ten years old, but when I think of her, I still picture her round toddler face framed by short wispy strands of blonde hair. Her eyes were so big for her tiny face back then. She was born stubborn and strong-willed, much like me, but with pure tenderness on the inside. She has ruled our world since the day she was born, a princess in her own mind. But she needs me the most, even though she is the oldest and fights me tooth and nail for her independence, hell-bent on doing everything herself. Deep inside she needs me. And Max, my baby boy, just barely turned five. He still has those big, chubby hands and pudgy cheeks, not quite rid of his baby softness. I know that it is only a matter of months before it will be gone, lost to the leanness of boyhood. He is the one who relies on my snuggles, always in demand of a physical closeness, a mama's boy through and through. John often accuses me of liking Max more, but I deny it. It's not that I like him more; he's just easier to love – if that makes any sense. And yet, I have loved Olivia longer and possibly more fiercely, as if she needs me to fight for her affection in order to prove my love for her. In contrast, Max is completely uncomplicated. He is more like his daddy; he even resembles John with his blond curls and big blue eyes. And then there's John. My one, *my only*, true love. Not many people are fortunate enough to have what we have. It's the real deal. He's the one person, the only person, I want sitting in the empty chair beside me. But he's also the one person I didn't want to burden with worry until I knew for sure.

*And now I know.*

Recently celebrating thirteen years of marriage, I can't imagine my life without him. And I can't begin to picture *his* life without me. On the occasion, thirteen years had seemed like such a big chunk of time, but now, in this moment, it feels like so little. *Time.* How much time will I have left with them? How much time is enough? Why is this happening to me?

"Of course, the choice is yours. If you want to try an aggressive approach, we can start immediately."

"Choice? I have a choice? Like what kind of choice? Make myself so sick that I actually *want* to die or pretend like everything is fine until the cancer eventually kills me? Either way I'm dead, right? Is that what you're saying?" Tears make their way down my cheeks as I try to keep myself from shouting. I am suddenly so angry. I did everything right the first time around. I survived the lumpectomy, the chemotherapy, the radiation. I went to my follow-up appointments. I ate healthy, I exercised, I even prayed. I'm a good person, a faithful wife, a devoted mother. I think of all the numerous selfless things that I do, ticking them off one-by-one in my mind. I volunteer on the PTA at the kids' school not because I am desperate to be involved but because I took over from my best friend Lucy when she gave birth to twin boys; her third pregnancy she labeled a "whoopsy" that overwhelmed her to the point of near insanity. I drive carpool nearly every day of the week for my two neighbors who have children in separate schools, feeling grateful to be able to lighten their morning chaos. I coach Max's soccer team, having no soccer experience myself but mainly because no one would step up to fill this role, not even John with his busy work schedule, and let's face it, someone has to do it. I bake six extra items each year for the school bake sale, excusing the working moms in Olivia's class from this annual fundraiser. And I am happy to do it. And yet as I scroll through this do-gooder list in my head, I know that this will not help my case. I know that it will not matter how many cakes I bake or teams I coach or kind gestures I perform; it won't change the fact that I have cancer and that I am very likely going to die. This isn't supposed to happen to me. I'm only thirty-six years old.

Wiping the tears from my eyes, I stand and thank Dr. Rand, although I really want to punch him in the face.

"Are you okay, Gwen? Can I call someone for you?" he asks, empathy written all over his face. I know that he's trying to be nice. I know that he really *is* sorry this is happening to me. But for some reason, the look of pity in his eyes makes me even angrier.

"I'm fine," I say a little too harshly, as I sling my designer handbag over my shoulder and march out the door.

I reach my car in the parking garage before the dam breaks and the floodgates open. I rest my forehead on the cold, leather steering wheel and sob. I feel guilty for feeling sorry for myself and then I instantly feel angry for being so damn selfless at a time like this. I'm overcome with so many different emotions, so many different worries, but I keep coming back to the same fear. Telling John. How am I going to tell John? How do you tell your partner in life, your soul mate, that you won't be growing old together after all?

I am suddenly afraid to go home. I can't go home and pretend that everything is okay and yet I can't bring myself to tell John this devastating news. Telling him will make it all real and I'm just not ready for it to be real. *Not yet.*

I'm not ready to die.

# 2
## *Charley*

I hit the Bluetooth button on my steering wheel console as I weave through Friday morning traffic. I'm late, again.

"Hello?" I yell into the car's interior, fighting against the noise of the rain beating on the windshield and the Seattle traffic that encompasses my small car.

"Charley?" I hear my sister's voice. I am stunned that Gwen's calling me. We haven't spoken in over three months, which is the longest we have ever gone without talking.

"To what do I owe the honor of this call?" I ask.

"Look, I know that I haven't been returning any of your calls, and I'm sorry about... you know... the incident," she says. "I'm in the city and thought maybe we could spend some time together. I could ask John to deal with the kids for a night or two and we could... I don't know... go out to dinner or something. Have some fun? Just you and me. What do you think?"

This doesn't sound like Gwen. She doesn't just make plans on the fly. These things were scheduled weeks ahead of time, methodically outlined on the family calendar that hangs on the side of her refrigerator. And she hardly *ever* leaves Olivia and Max overnight. But, just hearing the sound of her voice now reminds me of how much I miss her and so I snatch up her offer like a ravenous dog chomping at a dangling piece of meat.

"Okay, sure. Do you want to stay at my place? I mean, it's not much, but you're welcome to stay."

"That would be great," she says. "I might need to borrow some clothes and maybe a toothbrush. This was kind of spur-of-the-moment."

Just as I am about to speak, some guy in an SUV cuts me off.

"Asshole," I yell while I flip him off. Gwen is silent on her end of the phone and so I mumble an apology. "You can borrow whatever you need." I glance at the time on the dash of the car. *Damn, I'm so late.* "I'm on my way to work now, but I'll be home by five."

"Works for me. See you at five," she answers quickly and a little too upbeat. Something is definitely off, but I push it aside and say goodbye, feeling genuinely excited about spending time with my sister.

Minutes later, after paying a hefty twenty-five dollars to park in the garage across the street from the office building where I work as an assistant in a top-notch financial firm, I collapse into my desk chair and boot up my computer.

"Charley?" I hear his stern voice through the intercom and immediately my heart starts to race.

"Yes, Mr. Preston?" I respond, my breath still short from my morning rush.

"Can you come into my office, please?"

"Yes." The way he says "please" makes me worry that he's angry.

I grab my iPad from my desk drawer and hit the power button with my index finger as I walk gracefully to his corner office, straightening my black pencil skirt along the way.

I knock softly before opening the door and stepping inside.

"Close the door behind you," he says.

I do as he asks and move to the leather chair near his desk as I look out the wall of windows that are slightly fogged and streaked with rain.

"Charley, you're late again," he says with disappointment.

"I know, I'm sorry. Traffic was a bitch." I smile and shift my attention to his face, where I watch his furrowed brow soften. Anyone else might be intimidated by Grey Preston.

He pushes his chair back from his desk and stands. "I thought you took the bus," he questions with suspicion and I suddenly feel like I'm in the principal's office. I usually do take the bus, but I was running late. I am about to say this out loud, but as he walks slowly toward me, his brown eyes darken and I know without question that he is not mad. My breath hitches in my chest as I take in his perfect, masculine features. His freshly shaven jawline, his glistening dark hair cut short around his neck and ears, but still a little long on top. The way his body fills out his dress shirt, giving just a hint of the sharp definition that hides beneath the fabric. His dark slacks hang just right from his hips, shaping his perfect rear-end.

When he is standing directly in front of me, he leans over and grips the arms of the chair on either side of me, bringing his lips just inches from the side of my face.

"I didn't wear you out too much last night, did I?" he whispers against my ear, leaving a wave of goosebumps down my spine as I close my eyes for a brief moment.

A smile stretches across my face as I think of last night and what he did to my body. This man is going to be the death of me, I swear.

"No," I drawl, moving my head to the side, away from him, and gently pushing his face from my neck with my fingertips. He's too close. He shouldn't be this close to me in the office.

He sneaks in a subtle peck on my cheek before standing to his full six-foot-three height and walks back to his desk.

"Good, because I'm already anticipating what I'm going to do to you tonight," he says with his back to me and my body already heats at his words. And then in the same moment, I remember Gwen.

"About that," I say, already regretting making plans with my sister. "I can't come over tonight. I have plans with my sister."

"That's too bad," he says, cocking his head to the side in disappointment as he takes a seat behind his large mahogany desk.

I suck in a deep breath, remembering the day this whole affair started, right here in this office, on his desk. The tension had built up between us for weeks until Grey finally made the first move. It was late, the office quiet and I couldn't help myself. He's just too much sexy all wrapped up with a pretty bow. The truth is, I couldn't remember ever wanting something more than I wanted him that night.

"Yeah... well," I agree with a sigh as I compose myself and switch into my work mode, erasing the images of what Grey looks like underneath his shirt and tie. I wake up the screen on my iPad and clear my throat. "You have a lunch meeting with Harold Lidman today and Tom Snyder called after you left yesterday, you should call him. He's feeling anxious about the new strategy."

"Typical," he mumbles, deliberately tapping his keyboard with his index finger. "Can you pull up the Tripp account and get Scott on the phone for me? I've got to go over these numbers with him before close today."

"On it," I assure him as I stand to leave.

Before I reach the door, he asks, "You didn't tell Gwen about us, did you?"

I turn back to face him and smile. "I never kiss and tell, Grey."

As I'm leaving his office, he yells out, "Try not to be late again, Miss Brant." I ignore him and continue back to my desk, trying to hide the ridiculous grin on my face. And in the same moment, I attempt to shake off the feeling that what I'm doing is wrong. I shouldn't be sleeping with my boss. I shouldn't be jeopardizing the best job I've ever had. A job that I have, I might add, because Grey is an old friend of John's – Gwen's husband. And because John happened to put in a good word for me. Because Gwen was tired of seeing me screw up my life. And now, I'm screwing my boss.

# 3

## *Gwen*

I fill my day with distractions. I manage to call John and work out the details of missing the weekend with the kids without giving him any reason to suspect that I'm keeping something from him. He seems pleased, happy even, that I'm making an effort with Charley. Despite the number of times we have opened our home to her, or our wallet for that matter, or helped her in some way, and despite the number of times helping Charley has come back to bite us in the ass, John has still managed to love her, like I love her. The way that you love a sister in spite of her faults. And even when I am so mad at her that I could spit fire, John always has a way of putting it all into perspective. He'll say things like, "Gwen, at least your sister's not a drug addict who stole your identity to score her next fix," or, "Come on Gwen, it's not like she would intentionally hurt anyone." He, without fail, helps me to see the bright side of things, but that's just his way. John invariably sees the good in life, in people. Which is why he probably can't detect the hitch in my voice or my overly-wordy explanation – something I only do when I'm nervous. It wouldn't occur to him that something is wrong or that I'm lying to him. He believes in me, unconditionally. Guilt floods my heart at the thought.

Just as I assured John I would, I call my neighbor, Kristin, and ask her to pick the kids up from school. I call Jen Moore, Deklin's mom, and ask her to fill in as head coach for Max's soccer game tomorrow. I ask for all the favors that are owed to me, tenfold, and then I call the spa and fill my day with last minute appointments. After a pedicure, a massage, a facial, a body buff with a seaweed wrap – whatever that is – after I rack up a six hundred dollar bill, I sit in the relaxation room wrapped in a fluffy white robe, mindlessly numb, and try to wrap my head around my new found fate. I won't allow my mind to wander to the future, to think about everything that I will miss. It's too painful, too real. Instead I think of the present, right now, and how I go about my life with this massive dark cloud hanging over my head. How do I wake up tomorrow morning and start my day? Will I do anything differently? And with these thoughts comes the fear again. The fear is like this big, heavy boulder sitting in my chest threatening to rip me apart. It hurts, this weight on my heart; it hurts like hell. And I know that the source of this fear – this pain – all begins with telling John.

I think back to all the times I was nervous to tell John something big. Although, nothing seems quite as consequential as telling someone that you have cancer. That you are going to die. How does one even announce such a thing?

I remember the first time I told John that I loved him. I was a nervous wreck. I was barely a day over twenty and had never really been in love before. Not in that ceremonious way that you love when you're old enough to make good on your dreams and your promises. When you can look into someone's eyes and know that this could be it, this could be your future.

It wasn't happenstance or serendipity that brought John and I together. Unless you want to call a semi-secret set-up a fateful event. It was your typical college introduction; my roommate was dating John's roommate and both said roommates thought it would be somewhat harmonious if John and I were dating as well. Lucky for Mike and Susanne, John and I hit it off. I was a virgin until I met John. So I guess my declaration of love held a little more weight than the usual terms of endearment that college coeds toss around like coins in a fountain.

I realized it early on in our relationship but felt the need to play the cat and mouse game that so many of my friends swore by. So for weeks, I agonized over it. Said the words aloud in the mirror whenever I was alone in my room. The scenario on repeat in my head whenever I was with him. It almost slipped out a few times, but I held back, kept my secret a little while longer. Playing hard to get was not easy, especially when John had become my last conscious thought each night and the first thing I thought of each morning. But afraid of losing him, I played along.

One night as our eager hands fumbled with buttons and our kisses became more intense, I knew that I was ready to take things to the next level. We were in my dorm room. Susanne had gone home for the weekend, and knowing that we had the room to ourselves for two whole days filled me with a confidence and boldness that I had not felt before that night. Between heavy breaths, as John and I were standing in the dark, removing our clothes with nervous anticipation, I had blurted out "I love you," and without missing a beat, John had wrapped his hand around the back of my head, pulling me closer before devouring my mouth with his own. My heart was thrumming in my chest and I feared that he didn't feel the same way, that I had said it too soon.

But then he pulled away, tucked a loose strand of my hair behind my ear– an endearing gesture that would later become noteworthy, almost poetic, looked me straight in the eye and said, "I love you too, Gwen." The way my name passed through his lips, slow and seductive, was the most beautiful thing that I had ever heard. I silently scolded myself for being so nervous, for keeping my thoughts and feelings to myself for so long, for doubting myself – doubting John.

A stray tear trails down my cheek at the memory and I wipe it away with the terrycloth sleeve of my robe. That moment feels like a lifetime ago and yet, here I am juggling that familiar fear again as if I'm still that girl. Terrified of the vulnerability that comes with just a few simple words.

Hopefully a night with Charley will be the escape I need. The pause from reality I need to gather my strength before facing John with the news.

# 4

## *Charley*

I park my car alongside the curb in front of my one-bedroom bungalow that I rent near Green Lake. It isn't much, but it's cute and within walking distance to all my favorite bars and restaurants. It's home.

As I walk up the path that leads to my door, I spot Gwen sitting on the front step, lost in thought, waiting for me. It is only drizzling now, the heavy rain from earlier dissolved with the light of the day. Darkness looms, as it always does this time of year, but there's still enough daylight to see that Gwen is soaking wet.

"Gwen? How long have you been waiting here?" I ask, glancing at my watch to confirm that it was only a few minutes after five.

She doesn't move at the sound of my voice, not even to look up at me.

"Gwen," I say her name louder, an unsettling feeling rising in my gut.

She looks up and immediately smiles, returning from wherever her mind was a moment before.

"Charley, you're here," she chimes as she stands and hugs me. I hug her back, aware of how cold she feels, how damp her overcoat is.

"You're freezing. Come inside," I say as I step away from her and unlock the door. We both move into my small living room. I set my purse down and begin to move magazines from the red-slipcovered sofa, placing them on the coffee table instead.

"It's so good to see you. I missed you," Gwen admits as she removes her coat and sits on the worn leather chair in the corner of the room.

"I was surprised to hear from you today, but I'm glad you're here." It's no lie. I *am* excited that she's here. She lives only an hour's drive north, but typically I go to see her. It just makes more sense with the kids and their hectic schedules. So the idea that she's on my own turf and that I have her all to myself, feels nice. I take off my coat and lay it across the wooden bench just inside the door.

"So what do you want to do tonight?" I ask.

"Let's go out to dinner. I'm feeling sushi, but I'm flexible." She smiles but it doesn't reach her eyes. My senses are on high alert and I know that something isn't right. But I also know that she'll tell me when she's ready. If I have learned one thing over the years it's that you don't push Gwen. She does everything in her own time. I always think of her like a tightly wrapped present, beautiful on the outside, so contained and poised – perfect. But inside, something wonderful and boisterous awaits. Only a select few are privy to what's inside, the real Gwen hidden behind all the tightly wound packaging.

"Sushi sounds good. We could walk to Fusion down the street. If we hurry, we might even make happy hour," I say glancing at my watch again. "Do you want a change of clothes?"

Gwen looks down at her damp slacks and says, "Yeah, I should probably change."

Walking the few short steps to my bedroom, I grab a stretchy pair of leggings out of a dresser drawer and pull a long knit sweater from a hanger in the closet and throw them at Gwen. "Thanks," she calls out.

"I have boots to go with that, if you want," I yell from the bedroom as I undress down to my purple lace thong and matching bra that I chose to wear this morning when I thought that Grey would be ripping them off me this very minute. A sigh escapes me. *This is better. This is healthier, better for my soul*, I think to myself.

I pull on a pair of worn jeans and a sweater and grab a pair of taupe suede booties for me and a pair of black leather riding boots for Gwen, making my way back to the living room. Gwen steps out of the small bathroom across from my bedroom, her eyes scanning my new attire.

"I swear, you look good in anything. And look at me," she says as she motions toward her body with both hands. "I'm lucky I could stuff myself into these leggings."

I laugh. "You look great, Gwen. They're suppose to be snug."

"Snug? These couldn't be any tighter if you painted them on," she says with a smile.

"Here. Put on the boots, it will finish off the look just right." I hand her the boots.

"Well, at least we share the same size in something," she says as she sits down and pulls them on one at a time.

We both step into the bathroom where I run a brush through my long, brown hair and Gwen paints her lips with a mauve gloss. I watch her face in the mirror, comparing her round shaped face to my oval one, the way her short, thick blonde hair, cut in a stylish bob makes my light brown hair seem unusually dark. Her hairstyle and overall look screams perfection while my hair and makeup seem wild, untamed. But the one thing that connects us, the one feature that gives away our shared DNA, our relatedness, is our hazel eyes. Big and green with strong flecks of gold that could appear a muddy shade of blue with the right color of shirt. Eyes that link us both to our father, at least that's what I've been told. Other than that, one would never know we're sisters.

"Ready?" I ask.

"Yep."

We slip back on our coats and step into the cool night air. Gwen and I walk swiftly down the street, shivering slightly from the damp cold, chatting about my mundane day at work and the fall weather that has come early this year.

The trendy sushi restaurant is bustling when we arrive, but Sara, the manager, sees me and motions to an empty two-top near the back. Gwen and I bypass the crowd waiting at the door and find our coveted seats.

"Wow, that's what I call service," Gwen whispers as we sit.

"I come here a lot," I admit with a shrug.

We order a couple of beers and Gwen surprises me when she orders a bottle of sake. She's not much of a drinker.

By the time our miso soup arrives, we are both feeling a little more relaxed and our stiff conversation flows with ease, as if we never missed a beat.

My cell phone buzzes in my purse and I absentmindedly retrieve it. And just as I do, I see the name "Grey Preston" light up the screen. Unfortunately, so does Gwen.

Without answering the call, I stuff my phone back into my purse, sheepishly.

"Why's Grey calling you on a Friday night? Everything's going okay with your job, right?"

I fumble for words. I never was a good liar. "Uh, I probably just forgot something. I'm sure it's nothing." I brush it off, desperate to change the subject.

"Shouldn't you answer his call? It could be important."

"It's fine. Besides I'm off duty," I say, waving my hand in the air. My cheeks blush just the slightest bit pink, I know from the subtle heat that warms my face.

"Oh. My. God. You're sleeping with him, aren't you?" she asks me, her hazel eyes wide.

"Sshh. Geez, settle down. I am not sleeping with him," I say quietly, averting my gaze, unable to look her in the eye. A dead giveaway, I'm sure.

"Charlotte Brant," she says, sounding just like my mother, narrowing her eyes at me. "You're lying. You're sleeping with him."

I take a deep breath, preparing myself for the lecture, the disappointment.

"Do you have any sense in that head of yours?" she asks in her motherly tone. "I mean, seriously, he's your boss. John's friend." She shakes her head at me but I refuse to feel guilty at her words. I refuse to let her scold me.

"I like him. It just happened," I say defensively.

"You like him? Since when do you *like* anyone? Is it serious?" she asks, knowing as well as I do that I don't do serious. I never stick around that long.

"I like him," I repeat, shrugging my shoulders.

"So, you like him? Just like you liked my neighbor's son?"

"Oh here we go," I say with full sarcasm. I should have known that we couldn't go one night without her bringing it up. The incident that came between us three months ago, the night that ended with her screaming at me to get my priorities straight, to grow up. Ranting about how selfish I was and how she was tired of taking care of me, tired of worrying about me. I had slammed her front door and walked away but not before spouting, "Fuck you," at her from the top of my lungs. I had called her to apologize weeks later, knowing that she was right. She's always right. But Gwen was angry and she can hold a grudge like none other. I was beginning to worry that I had pushed her too far, that I had really lost her for good this time. I couldn't imagine my life without Gwen. She's all I have, besides my mother. But Connie and I aren't exactly close.

"Let's set aside the fact you were watching my kids for the night and they could have walked in on you at any moment. Which is completely irresponsible, if you ask me. But besides that, Aidan is only twenty, not even old enough to legally drink. I've known him since before puberty, Charley. He's just a kid. And I have to live next door to these people."

"First of all," I say, holding up one finger. "Trust me when I say that Aidan is most definitely an adult. A pretty hot one in fact."

Gwen shakes her head at me. I hold up two fingers.

"Second of all, the kids were passed out cold. And we were being discreet."

"Discreet? I have images in my head that should never be in my head, Charley." She places her fingertips on her temples, thrusting her big eyes at me. "And trust me, these images are not appropriate for children. Not to mention my couch. Eww." Her face contorts in disgust. "One night. You couldn't go just one night without sex?"

"Sorry. I don't know what else to say. It was impulsive and crazy, I admit, but it was hot. Or at least, it would have been hot if you hadn't interrupted us."

"I swear, you're worse than a guy," she says, shaking her head again but smiling. And then she giggles. I can't remember the last time I heard her laugh like this.

And then I start to laugh too. And before we know it we're both laughing so hard that tears are running down our faces.

We recover, wiping the tears from our eyes and she says, "I love you, I do. But I stopped trying to understand you a long time ago." She says this out of love and her words are endearing in their own way.

Changing the subject, I ask, "So what's going on with you anyway? You're acting weird. What's up with the last minute weekend visit?"

I see her tense, but her tone is contradicting, easy.

"I'm not acting weird," she says defensively. "I just needed a weekend away and I missed you."

"A weekend away? Since when?"

"Since now," she says, picking up her chopsticks and stuffing a spicy tuna roll in her mouth. She chews slowly as I eye her with suspicious curiosity.

"Is John having an affair?" I ask.

Without a second thought she rolls her eyes and replies, "Oh please. It wouldn't occur to John to have an affair."

She's right. He's as loyal as they come. He doesn't have a cheating bone in his whole body and he adores Gwen, practically gushes over her, even after all these years. Theirs is a relationship to be envied.

I change tactics. "Oh my God. It's you. You're having an affair," I say, shocked at my own idea, trying to imagine Gwen having sex with someone besides her husband. The idea is too far-fetched and absurd, and yet I wonder.

"No, I'm not having an affair. I would never do that to John."

"Okay, so what is it?"

"Nothing. Can't a girl just want to see her sister?" She brushes off my interrogation but it's hard to miss the way her face falls or the way the breath she takes is so deep, that her shoulders raise at least three inches before her entire body shudders on exhale. And my gut is so twisted that I can't imagine eating another bite of sushi.

# 5

## *Gwen*

I know I should tell Charley. I know this as I watch her, ready to pounce at the first sign of admittance. I evaded her questions gracefully, but I can tell from her sudden silence that she knows I'm keeping something from her. She doesn't push, she never does. She knows me too well.

We finish our dinner in almost complete silence except for the random comments about the food or the weather. We walk back to Charley's in complete darkness, the damp cold seeping into my bones with each step. We both comment on how exhausted we are, so I wash my face and change into a pair of Charley's pajamas. I crawl into her queen-size bed with my Kindle and stare at the ceiling while I wait for Charley to do the same.

"Are you going to read for awhile?" she asks, pulling the covers back and sitting next to me with her back against the wooden headboard.

"Yeah, how about you?"

"I have a few issues of *Vogue* I could catch up on," she says, applying a lavender scented hand cream to her palm and rubbing her hands together.

"Okay." I prop my Kindle on my torso and wake the screen. I attempt to read a book I started in the doctor's office earlier, but not one word is registering in my mind. I am consumed with thoughts of my appointment earlier today, my prognosis, and my family. And once again I am filled with fear, fear of telling John. Do I just go home, sit him down and tell him that I'm going to die? Just like that? It reminds me of when I told him that I was pregnant the first time. Much different circumstances, with far more optimism. But I was scared to death, nonetheless.

I can remember the exact moment that I found out I was pregnant with Olivia. I remember pacing the worn wooden floors of our first apartment we rented as a married couple. It was small and old; it smelled of mildew like most apartments in Seattle. I can remember lighting scented candles in every room in an attempt to obscure the damp smell. The scent of cinnamon still conjured memories of the early years in that old apartment.

John and I had just barely graduated from college. John's next step was a master's degree in business. I had just started a job as the manager at the Hotel Belmont, working crazy hours, but it was all part of my initiation into the world of hotel management. We were barely scrapping by on my measly salary.

At twenty-four years old, we were the youngest newlyweds I knew, but we were in love and determined to start our life together. We knew it would be hard work with our opposing schedules and our limited income, but that didn't hinder our relationship one bit.

*Until now*, I remember thinking as I stared at the positive pregnancy test. The one I had taken after one missed period and a week of nausea that I wouldn't label "morning sickness" because it lasted the entire day and into the evening. It was more like, "morning-noon-and-night sickness.".

The test was positive; I was officially pregnant. I remember thinking, *I shouldn't be crying. I shouldn't be upset. I shouldn't be scared. Scared to tell John. We were married. We were adults. This should be happy news. I should be rejoicing. I was going to be a mother. I was going to have a baby.* But instead, I paced the length of the small apartment, biting my lip until it bled, thinking about how this would change our life, change it in a bad way. I was the only one working. Would John be able to continue his degree? What would he think? What will he say? We didn't plan for this. We had just barely registered for health insurance. We could hardly afford to feed ourselves. We lived in a one-bedroom apartment, stretching our monthly income as far as it would go. All these thoughts swirled in my head as I waited for John to come home. I said those two words over and over to myself, "I'm pregnant," but no matter how I tried to spin it – I couldn't imagine a positive reaction from John. My fear and anxiety was building each minute that I waited for him.

When he finally did appear at the door, soaking wet from the unrelenting rain, I immediately broke down at the sight of him. He took one look at me and rushed to my side, pulling me into his lap on that old worn leather couch. I sobbed against his shoulder, unable to say the words that I had rehearsed for nearly an hour.

"It's okay, Gwen. Whatever it is, we'll work it out," he assured me. And in that moment, the fear of telling him, the fear of the unknown, the fear of what was to come melted away as I was reminded of why I loved this man so much. We were a team and everything would be okay.

"I'm pregnant," I whispered against the side of his face.

He pulled back and held me by the shoulders, looking into my eyes.

"What?" he asked in shock.

And so I said it again, my voice barely a whisper, "I'm pregnant."

I saw the realization hit him in the expression on his face, moisture filling his eyes. "We're having a baby?" he asked, wide-eyed. I nodded. He crushed his lips against mine, so intensely, as he held me close with his hands wrapped around my back.

"Oh my God, we're having a baby," he said, pulling back just enough to say the words before kissing me again. It might not have been planned, the timing may not have been right, but it didn't matter. John and I were going to have a baby, a family of our own and despite all of the above, it was meant to be. And once again I had felt silly for being so nervous, for being afraid to tell John.

"Fall fashion sucks this year." Charley's voice breaks through the silence, bringing me back to my crushing reality and the fact that I'm not alone. As I hear her drone on about plaid and feathers and platforms, exhaustion seeps in from every angle. I feel it in every single muscle in my body. I'm ready for this day to be over.

# 6

## *Charley*

I see Gwen in my peripheral vision rub at her face and abruptly sit up. She reaches over and pulls at the chain of the bedside lamp, and then lies back down on her side, facing away from me. I sigh and set my magazine down, switch off my own lamp and lie down on my back, staring into the darkness. I can feel her body shake and hear her muffled sobs as she cries silently into her pillow. This is not the Gwen I know. I can count on one hand the number of times I have seen Gwen cry, including the times she cried tears of joy, like when she said her vows to John or the moments following the births of Olivia and Max. Gwen was the strong one, she faced the hard things head-on with a head full of optimism and a heart made of steel. She was indestructible. She had held my hand through every step of life, literally since I took my first steps. She was five when I was born, six by the time I learned to walk. My mother loves to tell the story of Gwen holding my hand and teaching me how to walk. And that's the way it has always been. Gwen the strong one, the nurturing one. And Charley, poor little Charley, the one who needs reassurance with each step in life.

I'm not sure what to do. Watching Gwen silently crumble before me. I'm the one who falls apart and Gwen's the reassuring voice, the comforting pat on the back. I'm not good at this. Fear rushes through me, causing my heart to pound in my chest.

"Gwen?" I say her name so quietly that I can barely hear my own voice.

She slowly rolls to her back and stares up at the ceiling. I turn my head and look over at her, her face highlighted by the street lights that stream in around the closed blinds. I see tears slide from the corner of her eye and trickle slowly down her cheek until they spill onto the pillow, leaving a darkened, wet circle on beige cotton. I reach over above the covers and grab her hand. I take her cold hand in mine and squeeze, just a light squeeze to let her know that I'm here. I'm afraid to ask what's wrong, afraid of what she's going to say next. So we both lay in silence and I feel her squeeze my hand back before her quiet sobs break through the silence, filling the room and fracturing my heart. She completely breaks down and I resist the urge to pull her against me and hold her like she would do for me. But I know Gwen. She needs her space; she needs time to work through whatever is breaking her apart in this moment before she can talk to me. And so I just lay still and squeeze her hand so tight that I can barely feel my fingertips while my own tears fall gently against my pillow. I brace myself for what's to come because I know it will be big, life changing. Nothing small or simple would warrant such an emotional response, such a silent confession from Gwen. My mind races through the possibilities. *Is it Olivia? Max? Is it John?*

Before my mind even settles on Gwen, she whispers quietly into the silent darkness, "I'm going to die."

*I'm going to die.* Her words echo through my mind before I have the sense to absorb them. I sit up abruptly without letting go of her hand. "What?" I ask, now feeling frantic, desperate for answers, an explanation.

Gwen swipes at her eyes, one at a time. "I saw my oncologist today. The cancer is back. I felt another lump in my armpit and so I had a bunch of tests done. I got my results today and it's not good. He said that it spread and I don't have much time left. I'm going to die. And it's like I can feel it. Like this is it."

She says it so matter-of-factly, she's so calm. But her words punch me right in the gut, hurt me so deep inside that I feel like I might throw up.

"I'm scared, Charley. I'm scared to tell John. I'm scared for the kids. I'm scared of feeling sick, of what it will feel like in the end. I've never been so scared in my life and I don't know what to do. I don't know..." Her voice trails off as she sobs so hard that her body shakes. I don't know what to say. I lie down next to her and wrap my arms around her and squeeze. I feel her relax into me and roll to her side. And I hold her as we both cry, the way she has done for me so many times before. Like the day that Dad left, or the day Jennifer Holt – my best friend in third grade – moved away, and especially after my first real broken heart. She was there, holding me just like this and I remember feeling as if she was holding every broken piece of myself together, afraid that if she let go I would crumble into a million pieces. I hold her like this now until I feel her heartbeat slow and her breathing even out. When I'm sure that she's asleep, I roll away from her knowing that sleep will not come to me tonight. I can't stop the thoughts that circle in the deep crevices of my mind, the thoughts that scream, *It should be me.* Gwen is full of too much life, too much love and has too many people that depend on her, love her. *She can't die. It should be me. Why isn't it me?* And my heart ruptures, breaks completely wide open at the thought of my life without Gwen, at the image of the two little faces that will have to experience the world without their mother.

The pitter-patter of rain on the roof echoes in the quiet room, and I match my breath to its beat to distract my mind from what lies ahead, to ebb the unbearable pain that has taken root inside me.

I am up early, cracking eggs into a bowl, plopping bread in the toaster. I couldn't sleep, instead my mind drifted away from the desperation and settled into a better place. I'm on a mission. I refuse to give in, to let Gwen give up so easily. I will help her through this; I will be strong for her. There has to be another way, some other option. And so my mind is as busy as my body in the early morning hours as I make Gwen breakfast and contemplate what I am going to say to her.

As if on cue, Gwen pads softly into the small galley kitchen, rubbing the sleep from her eyes. "Since when do you get up this early?" she asks, her words drawn out as she yawns and stretches her arms above her head.

"Sit," I tell her as I pull a bar stool out from the counter that separates the kitchen from the living room. I plop a plate down on the counter in front of her and pour her a cup of coffee. And then I lean over the counter, resting my elbows on the cool granite and launch into my spiel that I rehearsed in my head all night.

"Tell me exactly what the doctor said. We need to figure out your options, get a second opinion. We'll fly to Switzerland if we have to, Gwen. You're not going to die. I won't let that happen."

Her shoulders sink as she sighs. "Charley, I appreciate your fight, I do. But Dr. Rand doesn't feel like treatment will be effective and I shouldn't spend the time I have left sick and hospitalized. I should spend it with Olivia and Max and John. And you. I don't know if I have it in me to fight this. The first time around was so hard on John. I just don't know if it's worth it. I don't know what the kids would do while I went through treatments and surgeries. They were too young to know what was going on last time. This time it would be different. I don't know. I honestly don't know." She wraps her hands around her coffee mug, bringing it hesitantly to her lips before taking a sip. Her eyes are glazed over, filled to the brim with unshed tears.

I slam my fist down on the counter, startling her. "The Gwen I know wouldn't give in. She wouldn't give up without a fight. Listen to yourself, Gwen. 'I don't know what the kids will do while I'm getting treatments,'" I imitate her voice, adding a little whine for effect. "Well what are they going to do when you're dead, Gwen? What will John and Olivia and Max do when you're gone? How about then?" She jumps at my words, too harsh coming from my mouth. I don't stop there.

"We need a second opinion. I never liked that doctor. What kind of respectable man wears a plaid bow tie anyway? There has to be more options. I refuse to accept this, and so should you." I feel anger move through me, filling the spaces that were filled with sadness just hours ago. I'm angry at Gwen, angry at her Pee-wee Herman of an oncologist for stripping her of hope, but I'm mostly angry at God.

33

Gwen sets her coffee cup down on the counter and folds her arms across her chest. "Charley. I..."

"Don't say it, Gwen," I insist, holding my hand up to stop her from speaking. "Don't tell me to listen to you. I won't."

I watch her sigh and reach for her coffee cup again, a quiet acceptance that I take as my cue to keep talking. I grab my laptop from the small desk in the corner of the living room and take a seat on the empty barstool next to Gwen. And we spend the next hour searching the Internet for treatments and procedures. I even make the awkward phone call to Phillip Nash, a well-renowned cardio-thoracic surgeon who I dated for a few months last year. He gives me the name of three oncologists that are known for treating the untreatable and are heading up several trials for cancer research. He wishes me luck and it's hard not to detect the regretful tone of his voice. As if he knows how hard Gwen's journey is going to be, how hard she will have to fight. At least he didn't comment on how things had ended between us last year. He had wanted more, as they always do, but I just didn't have anything else to give. He's a great catch and any girl would be lucky to have him, if they can tolerate interrupted dinners and middle-of-the-night wake-up calls. The man is undoubtedly married to his job, but even I have to admit that there's definitely something noble about a man who spends his time saving lives.

Gwen and I make a plan. She agrees to call all three oncologists that Phillip suggested and I agree to watch Olivia and Max next weekend while she goes away with John for one night, alone. We both agree that telling John now when they both will have to dive back into their routines, moments later, is too unbearable. She wants to tell him alone, when John will have time to digest the news before having to face the kids or work. Gwen seems more determined once we make a plan and I feel like maybe, just maybe, everything will be okay.

We watch a movie in our pajamas, an old Sandra Bullock film that Gwen and I used to watch together years ago. When the movie is over – after Gwen and I both shower and dress –we say goodbye at my door before she runs to her car, dodging the heavy rain. I watch her drive away, down my narrow street until I can no longer see her car. I look up into the dark, stormy sky from my doorstep where I stand sheltered from the rain, and wonder why this is happening to Gwen of all people.

"Please don't let her die," I say quietly, my voice lost to the thunderous roar of the heavy rain beating down on the pavement. "Please."

# 7

## *Gwen*

With a heavy heart, I drive home in complete silence. The rhythmic drone of the windshield wipers lulls me into a deep and thoughtless trance. I follow the traffic, mindlessly, letting my subconscious lead me home.

The sixty-mile drive to Seaport goes by in the blink of an eye and I find myself inching down the long driveway and parking in my spot in the garage next to John's sleek black sedan before sunset. I take a deep breath before exiting the car. *I can do this*, I think to myself. It's only six days. Six days of living a lie, six days of pretending that my life is the same as it was yesterday morning.

I open the door that connects the garage to the kitchen and before I can even set my purse down, Max runs straight into my legs and wraps his chubby little arms around my knees, nearly knocking me to the ground.

"Mommy's home," he squeals. And my heart soars. I kneel down and embrace him, pulling his small frame into my arms and kissing the side of his face and then the top of his head, inhaling his sweet scent. He smells like peanut butter and baby lotion and I squeeze him tighter against me.

"Hey Bubs," I say when he wiggles out of my arms. I fight the emotions that rock through me, pushing aside the thought of Max's life without me. It's too painful.

"Daddy said I could have a treat if I ate all my dinner," he beams. His face is covered in peanut butter.

"Let me guess, you had peanut butter and jelly for dinner?" I ask with a smile stretched across my face.

"Yup," he answers, proudly. "And apples and cheese too."

"Wow, sounds like a good dinner." I stand and run my fingers through his blond curls. "Come here, let me clean your face little man." Opening a drawer, I remove a washcloth and wet it under the faucet. "Let me see that sweet face," I say as I hold him by the chin and gently wipe the peanut butter from his mouth and round cheeks.

"Thanks Mommy," he yells as he runs away toward the family room.

I sigh. *One down, two to go*, I think as I make my way into the family room in search of John and Olivia.

"Hey honey," John calls out from where he's seated on the cream-colored sectional couch, his feet propped up on the matching ottoman. He's wearing a faded pair of jeans and an old Seahawks T-shirt. His face is covered in stubble and he's wearing his glasses. I smile, thinking how young he looks without his suit and tie, when his blond hair is unruly and his face unshaven. He probably didn't have time to shower let alone shave or put in his contacts. A phenomenon that still baffles him after spending any length of time alone with the kids and usually earns me a little more appreciation for my full-time role.

"Hi Mom," Olivia says as she looks up from her book that she's reading. I sit down next to her on the couch, pulling her against my side and kissing her cheek.

"Hey Love Bug," I mumble against her ear quietly, so only she can hear. I have learned to tread lightly with Olivia. She's growing up and stuck in that middle ground between a little girl and a young teen. She's over the mushy stuff, including the pet name that I gave her when she was only a bundle of cells in my womb. I know she still needs me in the same way she always has, even if she refuses to accept it.

"How's Charley?" John asks as he leans over Olivia's head and kisses me on the temple.

"She's great, actually." I realize that I can't look him in the eyes. I have never kept a secret like this from John and I suddenly feel nervous and guilty. Instead, I fix my eyes on the television where John is watching a football game with the volume muted.

"What did you guys do?" he asks.

"We went out for sushi last night and then just lounged around today," I say, mindlessly running my fingers through Olivia's long blonde strands, my gaze still focused on the football game. But all I can picture is Charley and I researching cancer treatments on her computer, and planning the rest of my life, so to speak. Whatever's left of it anyway.

After putting the kids to bed, I retreat to the kitchen and pour myself a glass of red wine. John is in the shower and I take a minute to catch my breath. I walk to the French doors that lead out to the deck and look out at the dark bay. The rain has stopped and the blanket of clouds have opened up, revealing a large, yellow gibbous of a moon that glows low in the sky, a soft contrast to the dark and inky, flawless surface of the water. A sailboat inches across the bay, its mast lit up with white lights. I open the door and step out onto the deck. A chill runs over me from the cold air but I don't mind. I can smell the salty sea of Puget Sound and hear the water lapping softly against the rocky shore, and I'm reminded of all the reasons why John and I bought this house six years ago. I was pregnant with Max and Olivia was getting ready to start kindergarten. Money wasn't an issue really, John's growing success would have allowed us a beautiful home anywhere, but we both wanted to escape the city, to raise our kids in a smaller community with good schools. Having grown up in Seaport, I knew everything that this small seaside town had to offer and John fell in love with this house the instant he saw it. The house itself was stunning but it was the acre of lush landscape situated right on the water that sold us. The view was breathtaking and the peace and quiet a welcomed retreat. We have been so happy here. I want to hope that we will all be happy here for years to come. I want to dream about our future in this house. Taking pictures of Olivia and her prom date in front of the marble hearth of the fireplace, Max and his friends tearing up the yard at elaborate birthday parties that I plan down to the tiniest detail, the kids returning here during their college breaks, and the pitter-patter of little feet from the grandchildren that will one day grace this house. I want to picture all these moments and yet, it is only a reminder of what I will miss if this disease wins. It's too painful to dream or plan for a life that I may not get to experience.

I wipe a stray tear from my cheek just as I hear John enter the room.

"What are you doing?" he asks as he steps into the kitchen.

I turn and step back inside, closing the door behind me. I clear my throat, trying to erase the emotion stuck in my chest.

"Just thinking," I say vaguely.

John retrieves a wine glass from the cabinet and pours himself a glass of wine from the open bottle on the counter.

"Oh, yeah? About what?" he asks as he walks over to me. I turn away to take in the view once more, avoiding his eyes.

"About how much I love this house," I sigh. It's as much truth as I can muster.

I feel him behind me as he wraps his free hand around my waist and kisses the side of my neck.

"What is it Gwen? You seem a million miles away. Come back to me."

His words fill me with guilt as I feel my conscience slowly build a wall between us, one lie at a time. I can't answer his question honestly, so I evade, changing the subject.

"Did you know Charley's sleeping with Grey?" I hate to throw Charley under the bus but I need to derail the conversation.

John chuckles and I turn to face him. "What? Did you know?"

He tips his head back and then shakes it side to side. "I'm not surprised is all."

"What does that mean?" I ask defensively, although we are so far past me having to defend Charley.

"Nothing. It's just Grey is an attractive man and Charley isn't exactly hard on the eyes. It was only a matter of time. They're both single."

"Doesn't that bother you? I mean he's her boss, your friend."

He brushes a stray hair from my cheek and looks into my eyes.

"Gwen, Charley's an adult. And besides, it might be good for both of them. Actually Grey is perfect for Charley, now that I think about it. They both avoid relationships like the plague." He smiles and takes a sip of his wine.

"We're talking about Charley here, John. This could end badly for Grey. And for Charley's job."

"Nah, Grey's a big boy. Besides it's none of our business."

He leans in and kisses me gently on the lips. I close my eyes, savoring this predictable and mundane gesture, something that I suddenly realize I have taken for granted, along with so many other things. And without another thought, I bring my hand up and spread my fingers through his hair at the back of his head, pulling him closer to me. I deepen the kiss, moaning against his mouth as I feel him part his lips, letting me in. We kiss like this for a moment longer, our breath coming in deep, long pulls.

John pulls away first and mutters under his breath, "What in the world?"

My mind tries to recall the last time that I initiated sex – initiated anything for that matter. Surely our sex life is spontaneous enough that a heated kiss alone would not warrant such a comment. But as much as I hate to admit it, sex has become somewhat of a chore for me. Another check mark on the list to complete by day's end. Dinner, check. Baths, check. Homework, check. Sex with John, check. With this realization plus the pressing matter of my numbered days, I take John's hand, ditch our wine glasses on the counter, and practically drag him upstairs to our bedroom where I lock the door and strip my clothes off in one fluid motion. The smile on his face, as if this show of hunger on my part is amusing, empowers me and so I undress him as well. When he is standing completely nude in front of me, I step back and take a minute to admire him. He runs nearly every day and it shows; his body is lean and sculpted. He looks nothing like other men his age, most who haven't aged nearly as well, something that I do notice but probably don't assure him of often enough. I pull him to me and devour his mouth once again, until I feel his throbbing erection between us and I push him back until he's sitting on the edge of the bed. I kneel before him and glide my hands up his bare thighs as I close my mouth around his length. A low hiss escapes him and I wonder how long it has been since I have done this for him. Probably years, too long to remember. In the beginning, John and I had sex at least once every day. I had discovered a new side to myself that first night in my dorm room, a pleasure that I had never known existed. After that, I was insatiable, hungry for more. There wasn't anything that I wouldn't do for him or with him. I was a willing participant, an eager student. But years and two needy children later, as well as the tiresome daily grind, had eventually tamed that side of me.

I wrap one hand around the base of his shaft, stroking him as I glide my mouth up and down in the same rhythm. He kneads his hands in my hair and applies gentle pressure, encouraging me to take him deeper into the back of my throat. I feel an ache stir in my core, my own need escalating at the sound of John's pleasure. I take him to the brink before pushing him onto his back on the bed, where I straddle him, lowering myself onto his erection, moaning as he fills me to the brim. I grind up and down, back and forth, finding my rhythm. His hands are on my hips, urging me to ride him faster as our movements become rough and desperate, a far cry from our usual more-controlled encounters. There is nothing controlled about this at all.

Our breath is heavy, his loud grunts only interrupted by the words he speaks to me in a strained voice, "Yes," and, "Oh, God," and, "Faster." I match him breath for breath, my uninhibited moans and whimpers pouring out of me as every fiber of my being is centered in my core, the need building so intensely I can think of nothing but my release. And then I cry out as white light flashes behind my closed lids, my body pulsating again and again. John grips my hips tighter and moves me against him one more time before spilling into me and I collapse on top of him, completely spent and fading fast.

Once he catches his breath, John kisses my temple, the rest of my face is buried in the crook of his neck, where I can taste the salt of his sweaty skin. "I love you," he whispers into my ear.

All I can manage is a muffled, "Mmhmm." He rolls me to the side and slowly pulls out of me, before walking to the en suite bathroom to clean up. He returns with a warm washcloth for me, something he always thinks of. I clean myself and then use the restroom, and before thinking better of it, decide to sleep naked next to my husband. Something I haven't done since college.

John lays on his back and tucks me into his side, moaning his approval of my sleeping attire, or lack of. Within minutes he is snoring softly beside me and I am wide awake, my exhaustion from my orgasm long gone. I roll away from him and decide that I can't sleep without my pajamas after all, it feels too foreign. After pulling on a pair of lounge pants and a soft cotton tank top, I quietly unlock the bedroom door – just in case the kids need something – and crawl back into bed where I lay awake for hours, thinking about all the moments I want to share with my family before I die.

# 8
## *Charley*

Once Gwen leaves, I busy myself with cleaning up the house. When all 800 square feet of my bungalow is as clean and organized as I have ever seen it, I fill the bath with hot water and lavender sea salt and submerge myself in the scented warmth. I close my eyes and replay the last twenty-four hours in my head. All I can do is repeat a prayer, my new mantra, over and over again in my mind. *Please let her be okay. Please let her be okay.* I fight back the tears that fill my eyes, unwilling to let them fall, unwilling to believe that there is reason to be sad. Not yet.

Wrapped in my white terrycloth robe, I plop down on the sofa and pull back the curtain covering the large front window that faces the street. I notice that the rain has stopped for the time being and admire the large, not-quite-full moon that casts light on the dark, fall night.

Before my own thoughts eat away at me, I text Grey with a simple *Hey*. To my surprise he texts back immediately. *Just thinking of you, want to come over?* His invitation is exactly what I need. To lose myself in him for a few hours, to numb the pain, to take away the helplessness I feel for Gwen. I text back a simple, *Yes.*

*I'll be waiting.* His words send a thrill through me and I quickly get dressed, needing to be in his arms as soon as possible.

I park down the street from Grey's condo, thankful that the rain has stopped. My breath releases into the night in visible white puffs, as if to prove that the air is bone cold. Pulling my jacket tighter around me, I increase my pace toward the entrance to Grey's building.

He buzzes me in without a moment's pause and I ride the elevator to the twentieth floor with thoughts only for Grey.

His door is slightly ajar when I arrive and so I knock softly and step inside, closing the door behind me. Grey walks toward me, barefoot in jeans slung low on his hips and a long sleeve black shirt that clings to his arms and chest, showcasing his perfect physique. His casual look, slight stubble covering his jaw and the hunger in his eyes, increases my need for him as I feel a knot form in my chest.

"Hey, how was your—" he begins to say, but I cut him off when I pull his face to mine and plant my cold lips on the warmth of his. He slides my jacket off my shoulders and down my arms and draws my body flush against his. I tangle my fingers in his hair, claiming more of him with my mouth. I can feel his need pressed against me and I frantically work the buttons of his jeans to free him, bringing me closer to what I came here for, closer to what I need in this moment. When his jeans fall to his ankles, Grey wastes no time stepping out of them and peeling my shirt from my body along with his own. I wrap my legs around his waist, grinding against him as his tongue invades my mouth, possessively. I can feel his hands on the skin of my back as he grips me tightly, holding me against him. *I need this so much,* I think to myself as heat gathers within me, driving away the cold. Our bodies are so close that I feel, rather than hear, the deep sound of his groan as it thunders in his chest.

"Please," I beg against his lips, needing to feel him inside me. He sets my feet on the floor just long enough to remove my jeans and lace thong, as well as his boxers. My thoughts are screaming, *Take it away, please Grey, take it all away.* He backs me up slowly with his body – lifting my legs around his waist once again – until I feel the cold, hard surface of the wall against my bare skin. He fills me with one strong thrust, slamming me up against the wall, knocking all the air from my lungs. I feel him everywhere, his breath hot on my cheek, my neck, my chest as his tongue explores my skin. His hands grip my backside tightly as his thrusts continue, punishing in their intensity but I don't want it any other way. He consumes me and I welcome it. Grey finds his rhythm and I lose myself completely in him until we both reach our climax, and I soar so high that I actually fear the crash that follows, afraid that it will pull me so deep that I may never recover.

Later after Grey has taken me on nearly every surface of his condo and I am completely spent, we lay naked on the plush rug in his living room, basking in the afterglow. My mind is completely numb, the amazing sex bleeding all emotion from me just as I had anticipated.

"How was your night with Gwen?" Grey asks as he traces circles on my stomach with the tip of his finger.

I tense. And just like that my reality comes crashing down all around me, the emotions swirling like a brewing storm cell. And I can't push them away.

I turn to face Grey. "Can I tell you something without it ever leaving this room?" I ask, wanting to tell him about Gwen, needing to tell somebody, to say it out loud.

"Okay," he says hesitantly. This isn't us. We don't confide in each other. We don't talk much at all. We just fuck. We give in to this insane attraction, selfishly take what we want. We leave everything else outside the door and focus on the flirty, spontaneous fun. And we do this because it's all I want from him and I made that clear from the start. But right now, I want to forget my own rules.

"It's about Gwen. She's..." I start to say but I can't finish my sentence for fear that the swirling emotions will surface, exposing too much. Grey's dark eyes question mine, waiting for my words that never come. I can't do it; I can't cross that line with him. And this realization leaves a hollow pit in my stomach, a sense of loneliness that I haven't felt in a long time.

"What about Gwen?" Grey asks, concern etched in his eyes.

I stare at him for a moment longer and then look away, taking in the angled cuts of his bare chest and say, "Gwen knows about us. I tried to deny it but... well... she can see right through me." I had to say *something*.

"Well, I guess it was only a matter of time," Grey says as he props his head up on his bent arm.

I don't want to talk about Gwen or us or anything else for that matter. I close my eyes, bringing my lips to his, wanting to chase it all away again. Grey doesn't hesitate as he wraps his arms around me and pulls me on top of him.

"God, Charley. I could never get enough of you," he mumbles as I lower myself onto his already hard length and take control, spreading my wings and taking flight. Desperate to get my fix, yet not wanting it to end.

It is nearing midnight when we are done and I stand slowly on shaky legs and make my way to the bathroom. When I emerge a few minutes later, fully dressed, Grey is sitting on the edge of his bed wearing only his boxers.

"Come here," he says, a quiet demand. I walk to him and he reaches out and pulls me to stand between his legs as he rests his forehead against my chest. I run my fingers through his unruly hair and hold him there as he breathes me in.

"Stay the night with me, Charley." It is more of a request than a question, but he's quiet as he waits for my response.

I sigh and he looks up at me. His warm eyes lock with mine, searching for an answer and I nearly lose myself in his gaze. We both know I won't stay. I lean down and kiss him softly on the mouth but he pulls away. "Please. Don't make me beg." His hands are on my ass, holding me tight against him as if he's afraid to let me go. The tenderness in his eyes fills me with a vague sense of fear.

"I can't," I whisper, shaking my head.

"Break your rules, just this once. Stay with me." His long arms wrap around me tighter as he buries his face in my cleavage.

"I can't," I say again as I reach behind me and pull at his hands until he releases me.

"I'll see you on Monday," I say as I turn toward the door, leaving him there, alone, his brown eyes filled with defeat.

*Walk away Charley*, I tell myself. Part of me wants to stay. But most of me knows what will happen if I do. Nearly all of me knows how vulnerable I become if I stay. *People always leave. It might as well be me.*

I pull the door closed behind me and walk swiftly to the elevator, pushing the down arrow, begging for a quick escape. "Come on," I say to myself as I hit the button several more times, looking up at the floor numbers as they light up one by one until the elevator dings and the doors slide open. A middle-aged woman is inside wearing navy velour sweat pants and a shiny, red raincoat, holding a small, brown long-haired dog in her arms. She flashes me a fleeting smile as I step inside and I only nod, moving to the back corner of the elevator where I lean against the wall as if I need its support to hold me up. As the doors slide closed, I feel the tension drain from my body and let out a loud breath - one that I didn't realize I'd been holding.

# 9

*Gwen*

I open my small suitcase and begin to pack for the weekend, wondering what I should wear when I tell my husband that the cancer is back and maybe for good this time. We're taking the ferry to San Juan Island for a night away. I booked a room at our favorite bed and breakfast near the harbor. I'm filled with worry when I think of leaving the children with Charley but I know that this weekend is a necessity and there's no backing out. I have texted Charley numerous times over the past few days to make sure that she's prepared to stay the night alone with the kids. I normally wouldn't leave them with her for that long, but I'm not about to add my mother to the mix. I can't deal with her when I'm barely holding myself together.

The week flew by unexpectedly as I buried myself in my daily routine. The house has never been so clean. It was almost as if I could forget what was happening, until the still of night when I lay awake and could practically feel the cancer eating away my insides. The painful lump in my armpit, pulsating with life. I called all three oncologists that Charley's ex recommended, but after speaking to Dr. Sheldan over the phone, I knew he was the only one I wanted to meet. He seemed optimistic and knowledgeable, granting me a small measure of hope; which is more than I can say about the others. My appointment is on Monday morning and, to be honest, I'm more nervous about telling John the news than I am about meeting with Dr. Sheldan.

I pack for cold weather and rain, adding John's things as well and join John and the kids in the kitchen where the smell of toaster waffles wafts in the air.

"All set?" John asks as he swats my behind playfully with a kitchen towel.

"Yep. I just hope the kids are," I mumble under my breath while I glance at Olivia and Max sitting at the counter, shoveling bits of waffle in their mouths as if they haven't eaten in weeks. Their waffles are drowning in maple syrup. No matter how many times I remind John not to let the kids pour their own, it happens anyway and now I find myself mentally calculating how many grams of sugar are pooled on their plates. But it's not worth mentioning now when my mind is full of so many other concerns.

"They'll be fine, Gwen. Charley will be fine," John assures me and then places a gentle peck on my cheek, running his thumb over my furrowed brow. This small gesture reminds me to take a breath and relax, an unspoken message that John has mastered over the years.

As if on cue, the doorbell chimes and Max squeals, "Aunt Charley's here," as he barrels out of the kitchen toward the front door. A moment later, Max is pulling Charley back into the room with a huge grin on his face.

"Hi," she says, her cheeks flushed from the cold. She's wearing ripped jeans rolled at the ankle with worn black booties and a sweatshirt. Her dark hair is down and windblown into a frenzy around her face that bares no makeup. And still it's hard to ignore her beauty.

"Hey," I say, giving her a hug while John kisses her on the cheek and mumbles, "Good to see you."

It's hard to miss the way Charley avoids looking John in the eyes as she says, "Great to see you too, John." And then she quickly focuses on Olivia.

"Hey Olivia, how's my favorite niece?" Charley asks, making her way around the kitchen island to hug Olivia.

"I'm your *only* niece," Olivia reminds her in a tone that instantly fills me with shame.

"Right, you got me there," Charley frowns. "But still my favorite," she says in a sing-song voice.

"Okay so here's the kids' schedule and some ideas for meals and snacks," I say, wasting no time as I slide a stack of papers across the counter. "Also, the number to the place we're staying and our emergency contacts. You know our neighbor Kristin, and my friend Colleen. Also the number to the..." my voice trails off as I suddenly think of the pediatrician. I look at John and he gives me a nudge. I have to leave the number to the pediatrician's office in case of an emergency. I send out a silent wish that Charley will never need to call this number for all our sakes. I pull myself together while Charley stares at me, completely puzzled. "Um, the number to the pediatrician's office and the hospital."

"Jeez, Gwen, I think you forgot poison control and the police department," Charley teases.

"Very funny," I smirk.

"Gwen, we'll be fine. I got this," Charley says confidently, lowering her chin and looking me straight in the eye.

I try to relax. I try not to think about the last few times that I left Charley with the kids. The time Max wandered through the woods to the neighbor's house during a game of hide-n-seek. Max was missing for two hours before Charley called me in a panic. When I told her that the Gentrys had called my cell phone to let me know that Max was at their house, all she said was, "Whoops." Or the time Charley took Olivia to get her ears pierced, both fully aware of my rule. I had firmly denied Olivia for years, making her wait until she was nine. I had been furious at Charley but she had waved off my anger, saying, "It's not that big of a deal, Gwen." To be honest, it wasn't that Olivia was too young that upset me. What bothered me the most was that it was supposed to be something special that Olivia and I did together, and Charley had taken that moment from me. It was always like that though. My whole life, I was the responsible one, and Charley was the life of the party. Beautiful, fun Charley.

"Alright, let's get out of here so we can make the ferry," John says as he lifts a giggling Max and throws him up in the air, catching him just in time. "Be good, my little man," John says as he sets Max back on his feet and gives him a high-five.

"Okay. Bye sweetheart," I say, wrapping my arms around Olivia and kissing her cheek before she can move out of my reach.

When all our goodbyes are said, John grabs our suitcase and disappears into the garage. Charley winks at me and mumbles quietly, "You can do this, Gwen. We're all going to get through this, you'll see."

"I hope you're right," I whisper and hug Charley before joining John in the car.

We drive in silence to the ferry terminal, arriving just in time to board. The sky is dark, filled with endless gray, rolling clouds, but without the usual rain. The clouds shelter the coast from the cold, warming the air to the point where I almost don't need a jacket. Even in the gloom of fall and winter, Puget Sound boasts beauty, and John and I both admire the view from the slow-moving ferry as it glides across the dark water toward the islands.

I rest my head on John's shoulder as we lean against the railing of the ferry.

"I can't believe we have an entire night away from the kids," John says.

"I know. I'm looking forward to sleeping in."

John places his lips against my ear and I feel his warm breath on my cheek as he says, "Don't plan on getting too much sleep. You nearly killed me the other night, but I'm hoping for a repeat." I bump his hip with mine and shake my head, smiling at his suggestion. His breath on my face as he kisses me shoots chills down my spine and I suddenly don't want to face my reality. I don't want John to look at me any other way than the way he's looking at me right now.

The first time I was diagnosed with breast cancer – over four years ago, John was sitting right next to me, his clammy hand holding mine, squeezing my palm so tightly that I lost feeling in my fingertips. I didn't have to tell him; I didn't have to say the words to his face. I remember the exact moment I felt the lump in my breast. I was nursing Max in the middle of the night, who was just a tiny baby at the time, when I noticed it. I considered waking John that minute to show him, to ask if it was worth mentioning to the doctor. But instead, I waited until the appointment was scheduled before confiding in John. John had been there every step of the way from my initial mammogram to the biopsy, even though I kept telling myself that it was nothing, assuring John that there was no reason to worry. It was just precautionary, routine. And despite my protests, he was also by my side when I met with my doctor to discuss the results of the biopsy. Deep inside I think I knew it was bad news, why else would they not tell me over the phone. I think John predicted bad news as well. And so we were given the life-changing news at the same time, we faced it together from the very beginning, from the moment my doctor told me I had cancer. They had found it early. The best possible scenario. A lumpectomy, a few rounds of radiation and chemotherapy and I should be fine. Just like that. I felt nothing but determination at the time. I focused on the solution, not the problem. I felt strong, as I always do, maybe even stronger given the circumstances. My mantra, *That which does not kill us, only makes us stronger*, sang in my head through the thick of it, urging me forward, keeping me focused. John, however, was a mess. For months he fussed over me, worried himself sick over my diagnosis. He looked at me with pity and worry written in his eyes, and at the worst of the side effects from the chemo I could hear him crying quietly in the next room. And I remember thinking as I was hunched over the toilet, my own tears spilling from my eyes, desperately wishing the pain to end, *I'll be strong for both of us. I'll be strong for all of us and this will all be over soon.* When it *was* all over and I reached the coveted "remission" status, I worked hard to regain my place in John's eyes. I needed him to see me as his wife, a woman that he loved and hungered for, rather then a cancer-stricken patient. But most importantly, I needed him to see my strength once again. I had beat cancer. That had to count for something. And with time, John stopped treating me as if I was a fragile piece of glass that would shatter at the slightest touch.

Pulling me closer to him, bringing me back to this moment, John wraps his arm around my shoulders and I think, *Later. I'll tell him later.*

# 10

## Charley

*Okay. Now what?* I think to myself while I stare at Max and Olivia, the reality that I'm alone with them for over 24 hours finally sinking in. And then I think of the things I used to do in this town when I was little.

"Okay, kids. Bundle up, we're going out for a bit," I proclaim, clapping my hands together to rally the troops.

"Where we going, Aunt Charley?" Max asks, craning his neck up at me.

"We're going to the harbor before it starts raining and we're stuck inside." I brush my hand through his hair, admiring his adorable chubby cheeks.

"Can we get hot cocoa?" he asks, his blue eyes wide with excitement.

"Sure," I say.

"Yes," Max says as he pumps his fist in the air and runs off to get his coat and shoes.

"You in, Olivia?"

"Do I have a choice?" Olivia snarls, catching me completely off guard.

"Whoa. Where's the attitude coming from?" I ask, throwing my hands in the air, adding my own flair of drama. "That's not going to fly with me, young lady. Do we understand each other?"

"Whatever."

"Okay, this can be easy and fun or this can be hard and ugly. What's it gonna be?"

"Fine," she concedes and slips off the barstool slowly. I stand in front of her and place my fingers on her cheeks, gently lifting her mouth into a forced smile as I flash her one of my own. She rewards me with a small grin, ducks around me and trudges up the stairs. I might have my work cut out for me. What happened to my sweet little niece?

Once everyone is bundled in coats and rain boots, and Olivia has helped me secure Max's booster seat in the backseat of my small car, we climb in and head toward the harbor.

I once loved walking up and down the docks, looking at all the fishing boats and upscale yachts. My dad had been a fisherman and I can remember sitting on the docks, watching him unload bin after bin of fresh fish. When I was finally old enough to go out on the water with him, bundled in my rain coat and bright orange life preserver, I puked all over the deck of the boat. Without a moment's pause, my dad had grabbed a bucket attached by a thin rope, leaned over the edge of the boat and scooped it full of water which he poured across the deck, washing away my breakfast.

When I started to cry, he patted my back and said, "Sorry Charley, you just weren't born with sea legs is all." I wasn't sure, exactly, what he meant or what my legs had to do with it, but I stuck to the docks after that, inserting myself in my father's life in any way I could.

I swallow the lump in my throat and shake off the memories that come flooding back as I drive the familiar route to the harbor. We park the car and decide to hit the café first. The café sits at the birth of the docks, a popular place for breakfast or lunch and known for its fresh pastries. Usually in the late morning, after first catch, the red vinyl booths are filled with fishermen desperate for a cup of hot coffee. Although, today the place is practically empty. Olivia and I follow Max into a corner booth next to the window that faces the water. The kids order a hot chocolate with whipped cream and cinnamon rolls and I order a cup of coffee.

When we're done, we stroll out to the docks where Olivia and I follow Max up and down each row, admiring the boats, calling out the names of each one. The Blue Fin, Crabby Lady, The Office, The Cod Father, and my personal favorite, Rosalita. Something about it leads me to believe that love exists somewhere, even if that love is only for a boat.

The cold air fills my nostrils with the thick scent of salt and fish, the smell of Puget Sound arousing scenes of my past. Standing on the dock, beneath a sky of rolling dark clouds, I feel the weight of a thousand moments spent here. I imagine a life where no matter the problems my parents were having, my mother loved my father, loved our family. I imagine a life with my father, a life that he never left. A life where my days continued to be filled by moments here at the dock, counting fish and learning how to tie a slipknot. I imagine coming here when I had a bad day or needed advice. And my father would make it all better in the way he always seemed to, spinning the scenario until it didn't hurt so bad. I can almost hear his voice on the breeze now. I imagine he would say something like, *Sorry Charley, it's not fair,*

*what's happening to Gwen. But life's not always fair, and neither is death.*
He was a simple man with a simple explanation for everything.

We stop and watch as silvery salmon and crates of snapping crab are unloaded off the boats. And when we pass slip 21, I pause. I kneel down and trace my initials that are etched into the wood slats. CB. Right next to Gwen's initials. I remember the day we carved them.

"What's that Aunt Charley?" I hear Max ask.

"See these letters?" I ask. Max kneels down next to me. "These are your mom and I's initials. Your mom and I used to spend a lot of time here when we were your age."

"I didn't know that," Olivia says.

It doesn't surprise me. Gwen closed the door on that part of our life. It's a wonder that she can live in this town and not fall prisoner to the memories, but Gwen's strong like that. She can close herself off to things. I've always envied her ability to keep things simple. My life always feels messy and complicated. When I try to close the door on things, I end up feeling as if the walls are closing in all around me. Like right now in this moment. I close my eyes and I can see it all like an old movie, an old reel projecting on a screen, as it plays in my mind. I can hear the soundtrack, my desperate cries as I run down the tree-lined street, chasing his old pick-up truck like an abandoned dog. *No, Daddy don't leave. Don't leave me.* My voice growing hoarse the longer I scream and the harder I run, until his tailgate is out of sight, never to be seen again. Endless tears pouring down my little face. Gwen had watched it all from the porch, her eyes dry as dust, before she came and picked me up where I had finally collapsed in the middle of the street, crying hysterically. That empty, hollow pain in the pit of my stomach carving out a place where it would live for decades to come. Gwen had stroked my hair away from my damp face and held me for hours and all the while my mother was locked away in her room.

"Aunt Charley?" Max's voice pulls me back from the past as I look at his face and realize that I was exactly his age when my father left.

"Yeah," I whisper, suddenly breathless from the thought of Gwen leaving Max. Or leaving me for that matter.

"Can we go look at that big boat over there?" he asks, pointing to a huge cabin cruiser at the end of the dock.

"Sure." I stand up, glancing at my initials one last time before taking Max's hand as he leads us toward the big boat that caught his eye.

When we have seen nearly every boat docked in the harbor, I take the kids home. We decide on a movie and settle down on the big couch in the family room. Halfway through the movie, I receive a text from Grey. *How's it going, Aunt Charley? Surviving?* I smile at his playful words. He's been calling and texting more and more lately. I'd be lying if I said that I didn't like it, but it also unnerved me. The lines are beginning to blur as they inevitably do, but I'm not ready to end whatever this is between Grey and I. I text him back.

*Surviving. The hours are dragging by. What are you doing?*

I wait for his response as I try to sift through what I'm feeling.

*Just hanging out. Missing you. Counting the hours (yes they are dragging) until I can see you!*

I stare at my phone, reading his words over and over again as fear settles into the pit of my stomach. I don't even know how to respond to that. My phone chimes again with a new message.

*Too much?*

I smile, thinking that he knows me too well. I decide to be playful and not read too much into it.

*Depends?*

*On what?*

*What part of me you miss...*

*Every. Single. Part.*

His words send a chill over me as I imagine him saying them as his breath teases the bare skin just below my ear. He throws me completely off balance. I suddenly miss him too, although I'm not sure exactly what it is that I miss. I most certainly just got caught up in the moment. And I miss sex. I miss sex with Grey.

*I miss parts of you too. See you soon.* I stand and pocket my phone, ending this conversation before it gets out of my control.

"Time for lunch," I call out and make my way into the kitchen.

I make peanut butter sandwiches, a suggestion from Gwen's list.

"I'm not hungry," Max says. I bribe him with a chocolate chip cookie as a reward if he eats all his lunch. But he doesn't budge.

"My tummy hurts," he whines. And before I can ask him what's wrong, he throws up all over the kitchen floor. It all happens in slow motion and the sudden smell of sour milk assaults my senses. *Great. This is not happening.*

"Gross, Max," Olivia yells, snapping me into motion. I grab the trashcan just as he starts to heave again. He's crying and I feel terrible for him, wishing Gwen was here. Gwen would know what to do. I try to console him, while I lead him to the couch with the trashcan perched in front of him.

"I want my mommy," he cries.

*Shit.*

I can't call her. Gwen needs this weekend. *I can do this.*

"It's okay Max. Mommy will be home soon enough," I say, trying to console the both of us. I rub slow circles on his back as

Olivia plops down on the other end of the couch and unpauses the movie.

After a while, Max starts to drift off to sleep and I feel like the vomiting has stopped, *for now*. When the movie ends Olivia retreats to her room after uttering, "Gross," nearly fifty times. I don't blame her; my mind is screaming the same thing, although I don't say it out loud. I clean the kitchen floor, the whole time wondering how Gwen does this kind of stuff every day.

When Max starts moaning, I go to him. I'm poised and ready with the trashcan and when I place my hand on his back, I realize that he's burning up. He definitely has a fever. I'm suddenly scared. *What if he's having an appendicitis attack? What if something is really wrong?* I can't let Gwen down. Nothing can go wrong this time, not on my watch. I run to the stack of papers Gwen left and call the pediatrician's office, only to speak to an after-hours operator for Seaport Pediatrics who refers me to an Urgent Care Clinic where the on-call pediatrician is on staff. I bundle Max, call Olivia to come downstairs and take Max to the car with the trashcan in hand.

We drive to the clinic and wait in the waiting room for nearly an hour while Max sleeps on my lap. His little fevered body heating me like a space heater as my anxiety swells and what little patience I have grows thinner by the minute.

When a nurse finally calls Max's name and we are led back into an exam room, Max wakes up and starts to vomit again, although hardly anything is coming up. *Poor little thing*, I think to myself as we settle into the exam room and he falls limp in my lap again. As the nurse takes Max's blood pressure and checks his temperature, I am trying hard to stay calm but inside I'm freaking out, worried sick about Max and what Gwen is going to think. The nurse leaves the three of us alone in the quiet room, waiting for the doctor. I hold Max in my lap while Olivia silently reads her book and with nothing else to do, I watch the minutes tick by on the clock.

After what seems like an eternity, the exam room door opens and I look up, slammed hard with recognition as I stare into the piercing, transparent eyes of someone I haven't seen in years. I know him though, those brooding blue eyes full of mystery that dare to draw you in. And I also know that when he laughs, gone is the mystery and like a window to his soul, those eyes let you in and swallow you whole. Snapshots of my youth flash through my mind, one at a time, as I see the girl that I once was, falling for a boy with complete and reckless abandon. My heart begins to drum in my chest as I take in his face. He still looks young and kind, like the boy next door that I remember. Like the boy that I once loved. It's like staring into the face of a ghost, one that has haunted me over the years.

"Ben," I whisper, completely shocked and blindsided. My eyes leave his to glance at his name badge that hangs from the chest pocket of his dark blue scrub top. *Benjamin Roth, M.D.* As if there was any doubt, his badge confirms it. For a moment, sick little Max lies in my lap forgotten, as our eyes find each other again. He tilts his head to the side and his eyes bore into mine as if he can see straight through me.

"Wow. Charley?" he says as a question, as if he doesn't believe it's really me. Searing heat flushes my cheeks at the wonder in his voice and it's like time stills, barring the steady beat of the drum in my chest.

And then Max moans and we are both pulled from the moment, focusing on the patient. Ben goes into doctor mode.

"Hey buddy. Let's get you up on the exam table," he says as he washes his hands in the small sink in the corner of the room. I glance at Olivia. Her book is resting face down on her lap and for the first time, she looks worried about Max. I reach over and pat her leg, flashing her the most reassuring smile I can muster when she looks up at me.

I stand with Max in my arms and lie him down on his back on the exam table, straining under his dead weight.

"Max, can you tell me what's wrong?" he asks as if he's known Max his whole life.

Max only moans and so I find my voice, "He's been throwing up for a few hours and now he's burning up. I was afraid that he might have appendicitis or something—" I ramble when I'm nervous and Ben interrupts me.

"Let me do a quick exam and we'll see what's going on, okay," he says to me calmly.

I nod and sit back down in the chair next to Olivia.

Ben pokes around on Max's abdomen, listens to his chest and back with his stethoscope, and checks his neck and inside his throat.

"Well, he seems fine. I think we're looking at the stomach flu. He needs to rest and make sure he gets plenty of fluids. He's really dehydrated. I'd give him IV fluids but I don't want to traumatize him with needles if it's not necessary. He should be fine in twenty-four hours, but if not just call me." He reaches into his pocket and pulls out a business card, and when I reach for it our hands slightly touch and I flinch. He writes a few things down on Max's chart and I suddenly feel nervous about taking Max home.

"His mom's away until tomorrow. I'm not really sure what I'm supposed to do," I admit as I stare at Ben's name in embossed print on the thick white card in my hand.

"There's not much to do really. But I'll write down a few things for you, like something for his fever and what type of fluids to give him," Ben says as he takes out a prescription pad and jots a few things down. He hands me that as well and I avoid his hand like the plague.

"Thanks," I say, feeling sheepish as I slip both his card and the prescription in the back pocket of my jeans.

"No problem. I take it you don't have kids of your own?" he asks with a small smile splayed on his lips.

I shake my head, staring into his eyes, trying to wrap my mind around this bizarre, coincidental moment. Ben. Here in this room. After all these years.

After a long, drawn-out beat of silence, Ben turns toward Max. "Okay buddy. You're going to be good as new in a few hours." Ben helps Max sit up and then starts to leave the room. He stops in the doorway and turns around, resting his hand on the doorframe.

"It's good to see you Charley," he says, looking deep into my eyes. He hesitates, tapping his fingers twice on the doorframe and then walks away. I stare at the space that Ben just vacated and take a deep breath. It feels like my first real breath since Ben walked into the room. My mind is swirling with questions and all the things that I wish I would've said.

"Can we go home now?" Olivia says, bringing me back to the here and now.

"Yeah," I mutter, still dazed as I grab Max's jacket off the chair and pull his arms through the sleeves one at a time.

"You're lucky Dr. Roth was here. Mom doesn't like the other doctor," Olivia says nonchalantly, but her words hit me in the gut as confusion settles in.

"You know Dr. Roth?" I ask, turning to look at her.

She shrugs. "Yeah, he's our doctor," she says so matter-of-factly, as if everyone should know this fact. Except I don't. Anger flares at the realization that Ben is Max and Olivia's doctor and Gwen has never mentioned it to me. I push all the questions running through my mind aside, hand Olivia the trashcan we brought from home and take Max into my arms. I need to focus on my nephew right now.

# 11

## *Gwen*

The sky grows darker and darker while John and I enjoy a quiet seafood lunch where we share a bottle of white wine and talk about how nice it is to get away. We agree that we should do this more often. Especially now that the kids are older. For two years, Max had the worst case of separation anxiety and I refused to leave him with anyone but John. I could never enjoy myself knowing that he was home sobbing, desperately needing me. He's moved past that phase, thank God, but I still don't feel comfortable being away from the kids for long.

After lunch, John and I browse the shops that line the cobble streets of the island village. We buy little gifts for the kids and a few knickknacks for the fireplace mantel. As we stroll along the vacant streets, laughing with mild intoxication, John holds my hand, interlacing our fingers like a young couple madly in love. Like a couple who hasn't been married for over a decade, worn out from two children that consume every minute of their day.

Like a couple whose lives are not about to be torn apart by *cancer*. I squeeze John's hand a little tighter, holding on to this moment for as long as I can, my mind snapping a photograph that I can store away for a rainy day when I need to remember this moment, a *before* moment.

It starts to rain, big heavy drops, the dark sky finally unleashing the fury that it has threatened all day. The water gushes at our feet and the sound of the rain fills the once quiet street like the roar of an awe-inspiring waterfall. We run like school kids back to the bed and breakfast, straight to our cozy room, where we strip off our wet clothes and make love in front of a warm fire. And I think, *I remember this, this passion. How could I forget?* And when I am overcome with my release, my toes curling and my heart nearly pounding out of my chest, I'm hit with a wave of emotions. Overwhelmed to the point of tears, I bury my face in John's chest while he shudders his own release. When his breath evens out, he pulls back and looks deep into my eyes, stirring up feelings of guilt once again.

"Sometimes I love you so much that I can't breathe," he whispers, as he tucks a strand of my hair behind my ear, a gesture that conjures so many emotions within me. A stray tear slowly trickles down my cheek. And all I can think of is the unfairness of it all. I am so happy. My life is perfect in so many ways. I have survived so much already. *Why can't I just have this one thing? Is it too much to ask?*

And as if reading my mind, John says, "Sometimes I'm so happy that I find myself holding my breath, waiting for the other shoe to drop. Like a person can't possibly deserve this much happiness, ya know?" He gently wipes away my tear with the pad of his thumb and I suddenly can't breathe. I stare at him so intently, it's like I'm willing him to hear my thoughts so that I don't have to say the words aloud. And in the same moment, I know that I *can't* say the words aloud. I love him so much that I can't break his heart. I can't take this moment from him. I would do anything to protect him from this pain.

I close my eyes, breaking the laser focus of our gaze and whisper, "I love you too, John. So much." I kiss him on the lips, pushing it all aside and think, *Later. I'll tell him later.* And then I take a breath. Because that's all I can do for now.

# 12
## *Charley*

Both kids are in bed asleep, finally, and I lay quietly on the floor in Max's room. I'm afraid that he might need me and I won't hear him. He had a few more vomiting episodes but I feel like we have seen the worst of it. Even his fever has receded. I stare up at his ceiling where fifty or more glow-in-the-dark star stickers shine above. If I stare long enough, they almost look real.

I can't erase the image of Ben from my mind. He looked so good. His dark hair was shaved close to his scalp, accentuating the muscles along his jawline and neck. And those blue eyes, almost transparent, that can pin you in place with one look. He hadn't changed a bit and yet there was something more seasoned about him, the way he held his shoulders, the depth to his gaze. He had been more of a boy when I saw him last, at our high school graduation nearly twelve years ago, and now he's every bit a man. I hadn't known he was back in Seaport, never mind that he's Max and Olivia's pediatrician.

I think back to what happened all those years ago, the events that spiraled out of control until I was left completely broken. It was my own undoing though, as if I had broken my own heart when all I really wanted was to protect myself from that very thing. Looking back, I see how fragile I was. How the slightest sense of insecurity or distress could break me. But I knew what was coming then, I knew that Ben was leaving. It had to end at some point. But, still, I can't help but think of how things could've been, if I had been stronger. If I had been strong enough to love him. How it could have been, if it would have worked out the way we had planned.

I close my eyes and push the images away, reminding myself that nothing works out the way you plan. It was all for the best. I tell myself this as my heart clenches around what is buried deep inside, the regret and the guilt of what I did. How I pushed Ben away and then immediately wanted to take it all back. But it had been too late. It was too late. What's done is done.

I wake with a start, the glow-in-the-dark stars barely visible. Nausea steamrolls me and I leap up, making a dash for the hall bathroom. I hunch over the cold toilet bowl as my stomach unloads. My head feels as if someone split it down the middle with an ax. I can't remember the last time I felt this sick. I cough and sputter before rinsing my mouth in the sink and slinking down the wall until I'm sitting on the bathroom floor with my arms wrapped around my bent knees. I rest my forehead on my knees when the shaking begins.

*Ugh.* Max's flu. *Thanks Max.* The cycle continues as dawn comes and goes. Max wakes up feeling good as new, shedding a small measure of light on my situation. Barely able to stand upright, I set Max and Olivia up in the family room downstairs with a movie, a handful of granola bars, and juice before I hunker down in the bathroom just off the entryway, held prisoner for hours by this stinking flu. My only hope is that John and Gwen are home soon.

I hear the doorbell ring, which I plan to ignore, but I hear Olivia call out, "Who is it?" I try to tell her not to open the door, but my words come out only a hoarse whisper.

"It's Doctor Roth," I hear Ben say. My only thought, *Oh, God, not now.* How mortifying. I look and feel like death. And even more horrifying, I hear the bolt lock slide open as Olivia opens the door and lets him in. I sit stone still in the bathroom, eavesdropping on their conversation, wondering what he's doing here and hoping that he leaves before he discovers me in the bathroom.

"Where's your Aunt Charley?" I hear him ask.

"She's in there. She's sick now too."

"I thought that might be the case. Where's Max?"

"We're watching a movie."

"How's Max feeling this morning?"

"I think he's better."

"How about you? How are you feeling?"

"I feel fine, I guess."

Their voices fade as they move further into the house. *Great. No chance of him going away anytime soon.*

A few minutes later, I hear a knock on the bathroom door. I moan.

"Charley, you okay in there?" Ben asks.

"Yeah. What are you doing here, Ben?" I groan. I'm on my knees with my cheek resting on the cold toilet seat, my arms literally hugging the porcelain bowl.

"I came to check on you. I had a feeling you were next. I brought you some Gatorade and crackers and breakfast for the kids."

"You didn't have to do that. But thank you. We'll be fine." I wipe my nose and eyes on my shirt sleeve and lay my cheek back down against the cold.

"I'm coming in, Charley."

I abruptly sit up, my head spinning from the sudden movement. "No, don't come in," I call out, but he's already stepping inside the small bathroom. His presence filling the cramped space until I feel like I can't breathe. I bury my face in my hands and mumble, "Seriously, this is so embarrassing, Ben."

He kneels down next to me and I can smell his masculine scent. "I'm a doctor. I've seen worse, trust me."

I peek out between my fingers to see him smiling.

"But really Charley, are you okay?" he asks with tenderness in his tone.

"I've felt better. I didn't realize that doctors made house calls anymore."

"Well, only for you." His words reach me somewhere deep inside but I push them away.

"I'm taking you to bed," he says while reaching his arm around my shoulders and gently helping me to my feet.

"Confident much," I mumble but too tired to fight him, I lean my weight into him, feeling so weak and dizzy that I'm afraid I might pass out.

"Stop it. You know what I mean."

"Yes. I know what you mean," I whisper. And then I direct him to the guest bedroom across the hall, where he pulls back the bedding and tucks me in. He leaves me in bed, in the dark, my body shaking in spasms before returning a few minutes later with a bottle of Gatorade and a plate of crackers.

"Do you mind if I stay and hang out with Max and Olivia so you can rest?" he asks quietly.

"Be my guest," I reply, suddenly feeling so tired that I can hardly keep my eyes open. He starts for the door when I am barely still conscious, but I still feel his hand as it threads through my tangled hair and his finger as it trails down my cheek. I hear his breath release as he sighs. And before I have time to process it or sift through the emotions his tenderness evokes, I am gone, held captive by sleep.

# 13

## *Gwen*

John turns the car off after parking in the garage and we both sit in silence. "Re-entry," as we like to call it, is hard after a weekend away and we both savor our last moment of peace and quiet. The entire drive from the ferry I was focused on the failure of my mission. The sole purpose of the weekend alone that I had planned. I didn't tell him. Instead, the weekend evolved into something magical. A reconnection that I hadn't even realized we'd needed until there it was, all around us, pulling us closer together. And maybe we needed this weekend to be about us; maybe we needed this weekend *before* I tell him. At least that's what I'm telling myself now, desperately trying to justify my dishonesty, my failure to confide in my husband. The worst part is that I have to face Charley. The one person who knows the truth.

John leans over and kisses me on the cheek, and I turn toward him, kissing him on the mouth.

"What a great night away," he says and then leans back in his seat with a heavy sigh. "Think they'll notice if we hide out in here for a bit longer," he asks.

I smile, picturing us making out in the car like teenagers, hiding from our children.

"I miss them, I do. But why is it so hard to go back in there?" I ask, turning to John for an answer.

He only laughs and says, "Because it's a jungle in there. The kids are probably fighting and you know the house is a mess."

"Oh for sure the house is a mess," I agree. We both laugh.

"And because once you walk in that door, you become their mom again, instead of my beautiful, incredibly sexy wife," he says tenderly as he lifts my hand to his lips, placing a gentle kiss there as he looks into my eyes.

"Careful John," I chide. "Am I not always beautiful and sexy?"

"You are. But can you blame me for wanting you all to myself a little bit longer?" His sulking eyes warm me and make me smile, reminding me of how much I love him.

"I suppose not," I tease and then more solemnly I add, "I love you, John."

"I love you too, Gwen," he says and kisses me on the forehead.

I sigh. "Let's do this."

We walk into the house, calling out for Olivia and Max when we are met with silence. And as we move through the kitchen, approaching the family room, we finally hear quiet voices.

I am shocked to find Ben Roth sitting on the floor of the family room playing cards with Olivia and Max, and Charley nowhere to be found. A million thoughts run through my mind. First, I'm feeling guilt and anxiety about the obvious fact that Charley knows about Ben, something that I've been keeping from her for sometime. Feeling immediately defensive, my mind runs through all the reasons why I kept this from her. But then another thought jumps into my head. Why is Dr. Roth here? Did something happen to Olivia or Max? My eyes frantically scan their faces. They look fine and in one piece. But surely, Charley had called him for a reason. And finally, I am left wondering why Charley is not here.

"Hi Mom. Hi Dad," Olivia finally says, waving at us from where she is seated on the floor.

"Hi Love Bug," I manage to say. "Where's Aunt Charley?" I ask.

Ben stands and faces John and I. "Hi Gwen. John," he nods our way. "Um, sorry to catch you off guard. Max had the stomach flu yesterday and Charley brought him into the clinic, just to be sure that he was okay. And he's fine," he assures me and then says, "I stopped by this morning, worried that Charley or Olivia could be sick. And Charley was pretty ill. She's sleeping now. I hung around to keep an eye on these two." He ticks his head to the side, motioning toward the kids and Max giggles.

"Oh my God," I say, running to Max. I kneel down beside him and instinctively feel his forehead. "Are you okay, sweetie?"

"I threw up," he said. "But I was so brave, Mommy."

"I'm sure you were, Bubs." My heart clenches at the thought of Max being sick without me here to take care of him. *Why didn't Charley call me?*

"Well thank you, Ben. I appreciate you being here," John says, as he steps forward and shakes Ben's hand.

"No problem. Glad I could help," he says in response. "Max seems completely fine today. I've been trying to get fluids in him and food as well, but he's pretty stubborn. He hasn't eaten much."

I run my fingers through Max's hair. "Thanks. I'll work on it."

"Well I should get going. Tell Charley that I hope she feels better soon." He grabs his jacket off the back of the couch. "Bye Olivia. Bye Max," he says and then adds with his finger pointing at Max, "Keep working on that strategy I taught you. You'll be beating your sister in no time." Max gives him a salute, nearly poking his own eye out and Ben smiles at him before facing John and I, holding his hand up in a subtle wave. "Bye. See you around," he says, in that casual way you say to people who aren't necessarily your friends but rather people you see fairly often for one reason or another.

"Thank you Ben, really. You didn't have to stick around, but we're so grateful that you did," I tell him as he simply nods, smiles and leaves the room, letting himself out the front door.

I take a deep breath and look at John as he raises his eyebrows, knowing that Charley is likely to be pissed at me. I hug Olivia and go in search of Charley, hoping that she's okay.

As I slowly push open the door to the guest room, I can barely make out Charley's figure huddled under the bedding in the cover of darkness.

"Charley," I whisper as I make my way to the bed.

"Hey," she croaks. "You're home."

"How are you feeling?" I ask as I feel her forehead and brush her hair back from her face, which I can see clearly from the light pouring in from the hallway. Her cheeks are pale and hollow and she looks so young, reminding me of all the times she was sick as a child and I took care of her. All the times I would heat soup from the can in the microwave and then spoon it in her mouth while she lay in her bed, wiping the steady stream of broth from her chin with a paper towel. I would console her, rub her back and whisper words of encouragement, in the same way I did when she was sad or upset. I did these things knowing that my mother couldn't get out of bed to do them herself. It was clear that she was suffering in a way that I couldn't understand at the time. When our dad left, she became bitter and depressed. In my mother's emotional absence, and given that I was the oldest by five years, I had assumed the role of Charley's caretaker. Always with mixed feelings. I could never quite settle on feeling compassion or a bit of resentment toward Charley. Compassion because she was my younger sister and I loved her dearly and wanted desperately for her to feel safe and loved but resentful simply *because* she was my younger sister. And rather than spending my time playing with the other girls my age, fretting over petty matters like clothes and boys, I was wiping the tears of a five-year-old girl and making sure that she was clothed and fed.

"I think I'm better. How was it? How are you?" she asks and I can see her eyes grow wide as she searches my face waiting for an answer.

"It was fine. We had a great weekend, actually."

"It was fine," she repeats. "What do you mean it was fine? What did John say?"

"Well, I didn't actually tell him," I whisper as I look over my shoulder toward the open door like someone who has something to hide.

"You didn't tell him," Charley raises her voice.

"Shh, be quiet," I scold as I sit on the edge of the bed. "I just couldn't tell him. We were having so much fun and connecting in a way that we haven't in a long time. I'll tell him soon. I will." I say this to reassure Charley as much as myself.

"Oh Gwen. You have to tell him. You can't keep this from him."

"I know. I will."

Charley sits up and wraps her arms around me and the weight of the truth envelops me as much as her embrace. I just wish it would all go away. All of it.

I hear Charley groan and then she bolts out of bed, nearly knocking me to the ground, as she runs for the bathroom across the hall. I follow her when I hear her retch repeatedly, the bathroom door left wide open. Her slim figure is bent over the toilet and I feel awful for her.

"Are you okay? Can I get you anything?" I ask when she finally collapses onto her knees with her head resting on the toilet.

"Oh God. This is the worst. Children are evil," she mumbles into the arm that her face is buried in.

"Sorry about that. But thank you for taking care of Max. You could have called me, ya know?" I lean against the doorway and fold my arms over my chest, watching her.

"I know. But I also knew you needed the time alone. We survived, though." And then she lifts her head and turns to look at me, "Please tell me that Ben left?"

"Yeah, he left. He said to tell you that he hopes you feel better."

"Which reminds me. I'm pissed at you," she says, narrowing her eyes at me before dropping her face back down in the crook of her arm.

"I can only imagine," I deadpan, taking a deep breath and exhaling slowly, waiting for her to lay into me.

"I'm so mad that you didn't tell me."

"I have my reasons, ya know."

"Ugh. I can't talk about this right now. I feel like shit," she says with her face pressed into her arm, her words so muffled I can hardly comprehend what she's saying. "Shut the door. I'm just gonna lay here for awhile."

"Okay. Just yell if you need anything. I take it you're spending the night?"

"Obviously."

I close the bathroom door and lean against it, taking a moment's pause. I didn't tell John that I have cancer. I didn't tell Charley that Ben was back in town or that he was our pediatrician. I've been avoiding my mother for weeks. I know that it's time to face it all, but I just want to crawl under a rock and hide. Life feels too complicated at the moment. I think of the appointment that I have the following day with the new oncologist. Maybe after I have more information it will be easier to talk to John. Maybe when they can offer a solution, the truth won't be so hard to divulge.

"Mommy," I hear Max call out from the family room. I smile and think how predictable this part of my life is. And predictable is exactly what I need right now.

"Be right there," I answer as I push off the bathroom door and walk swiftly toward my son, all at once needing to feel his small frame in my arms.

# 14

## *Charley*

I open my eyes to sunlight streaming in around closed blinds, the brightness causing an unbearable pain in my head. I can hear dishes clanking from the kitchen and muffled voices signaling the chaos of Gwen's Monday morning. I really don't know how she does this shit every day. I sit up slowly, rubbing the sleep from my eyes before gulping down a warm glass of water from the nightstand, feeling completely parched. I am suddenly starving, a good sign that I'm over the flu.

I glance at my phone on the nightstand, noting the time, and decide to text Grey to let him know that I won't be at the office today. I may be late often but I have never missed a day of work.

His response comes immediately. *Are you okay?*

*Yes. Max shared the stomach flu with me, but I feel much better. I'm still in Seaport though.*

*Okay. Call me later. Feel better and drive safe.*

I stumble into the kitchen to find Gwen frantically packing lunch boxes while at the same time flipping pancakes on the stovetop.

"She's alive," she says before calling Olivia and Max to the kitchen. In an instant it sounds as if a herd of elephants are coming down the stairs and my head pounds with each thunderous thud.

I grab a warm pancake from the impressive stack that Gwen has prepared and slowly nibble on it.

"What's your plan today?" Gwen asks. "Going in to work?"

"No way. Still recovering. I think I'll take a shower and head home. How about you?"

Max and Olivia plop down simultaneously in barstools at the kitchen island and Gwen places their plates on the counter in front of them.

She leans in close and whispers in my ear, "I've got my appointment with Dr. Sheldan at eleven."

I nod as she turns and starts to tell the kids that Kristin is picking them up from school today. Max pumps his fist in the air, and yells, "Yes, I get to play Carter's new Xbox."

I cringe at the peak of his voice as it rattles my brain.

Olivia whines, "Seriously Mom? It's so boring. I'm the oldest one there."

"Well just start on your homework and I'll be there to pick you up as soon as I can," Gwen says.

I look at Gwen and ask if she wants me to go with her. She just shrugs and says, "Only if you feel up to it."

"Of course, I feel up to it. You shouldn't have to go alone," I say quietly, leaning closer to her.

"Okay, that would be nice actually. I've gotta get these little buggers to school and then I'm driving into the city."

"How about this… meet me at my place at ten-thirty. It's on the way and we can drive to the medical center together."

She nods. "Thank you," she says after a bloated pause. I watch as she places a lunchbox into Olivia's pink backpack and zips it closed wondering how long we can keep this from John.

I finish my pancake and the herd exits just as abruptly as it entered, leaving the house eerily quiet. I shower, throw on some yoga clothes and drive through steady traffic back to the city, all the while lost in dangerous thoughts of Gwen, my past with Ben, and all the uncertainty that swarms around me.

Gwen's knee is bouncing up and down as she thumbs through a celebrity gossip magazine. I look around the waiting room. There are ten or so other people sitting in the same beige leather seats, nervously waiting. Most are women. I note that two women have scarves wrapped around their bald heads, their eyes big and shadowed. It reminds me of Gwen when she was battling cancer before. The bald head, beady eyes underlined with dark circles, rosy cheeks, and that frail, thin look about her. She was so sick. I swallow the lump in my throat and place a firm hand on Gwen's bouncing knee to reassure her. She looks up from her magazine and I can see the fear in her eyes.

"Talk to me about something, I'm going crazy here," she whispers.

"Gwen, everything's going to be okay," I assure her.

"Just distract me. Tell me about Grey." She waves her hand through the air, encouraging me to start talking.

And so I ask, "Why didn't you tell me about Ben?"

She sighs and looks down, smoothing her slacks with her hands.

"Charley..." she hesitates.

"Tell me. Why the lie?"

"I never lied to you. I just didn't tell you. There's a difference."

I look at her, waiting for an explanation, with my arms folded across my chest.

"You have to understand that he's the best pediatrician in town. Dr. Shultz is old and frankly, gives me the creeps. I was lucky that the kids were accepted by Ben's practice. He's totally booked. I mean, not only is he the best but just look at him, every mom in Seaport flocks to him based on his looks alone."

I hold my hand up. "Okay I didn't need to hear that."

"Anyway, I was afraid if I told you he was back, something might happen between you two and, if it went to hell, we could lose our spot. And I was worried about you. He broke your heart. And I feel like you've never really gotten over it, even after all these years."

"Gwen, what are you talking about?"

"Charley, you were devastated when you broke up and he left town. And you haven't genuinely cared for someone since."

"Gwen, it's not what you think." I frown, remembering it all too well.

"Okay. I'm listening."

I rest my face in my hands gathering my thoughts and then look up. "I can't believe we're talking about this here, right now." My eyes scan the waiting room.

"You're helping to distract me, remember. Just tell me." Gwen bumps her elbow against my arm and tosses her magazine on the table in front of us, where it lands on a pile of other magazines and medical brochures.

I take a deep breath. "Well... I kind of slept with Brody Knight a few weeks before graduation."

"What the..." she starts to say a little too loudly, before lowering her voice. I glance around the room to find several people looking our way.

"What the hell, Charley?" she says, now more of a whisper.

I shrug, not really wanting to go into the details. But of course Gwen won't leave it alone.

"Why would you do that? Brody Knight? Seaport's very own football star? That guy was such a... such an egomaniac," she scowls.

"I know. It was horrible and I wanted to take it back immediately but of course it was too late."

Gwen sits forward and turns to look at me, where I'm slouched down in my chair with my arms folded across my chest, feeling a mixture of shame and remorse. It all happened years ago but seeing Ben brought back an arsenal of emotions that I suddenly feel completely defenseless against.

"Wait. Was he your first?" she asks me, her big eyes jutting out of their sockets.

"I just thought... I just thought... I don't know *what* I was thinking." I moan and bury my face in my hands again, leaning forward until my elbows come to rest on my knees.

But deep down I remember exactly what I had been thinking. Ben was leaving. He had been accepted to his dream school on the other side of the country. He was brilliant and he had this incredible plan for his future which all started at Harvard University. We had been inseparable for three years, crazy in love. Both of us virgins, we had been saving ourselves for graduation night, when we would finally have sex for the first time. Ben knew everything about me, and yet he still loved me anyway. He was the only one who really seemed to get me, the real me. He assured me that I was part of his plan. That the distance would not come between us. He argued that four years was nothing in the grand scheme of things, in comparison to the rest of our lives. I knew better. I wanted to believe in him, in us. But even at eighteen I was no naive little girl. The idea of not being with him made my chest hurt, and caused real, physical pain. It was as if I needed him to breathe. The notion that I had let myself depend on someone so much that life without them seemed unbearable was a terrifying realization. Ben was leaving me and there was nothing I could do to change that. I remember desperately wanting to end things with him on my own terms, to have some semblance of control over the situation. I pleaded with him, throwing out every reason in the book why we should break up; he was leaving and we should end it now, that long distance relationships never worked out. But he wouldn't listen, refused to let me push him away. But that was exactly what I did when he found me in the backseat of Brody Knight's car with my skirt pushed up around my waist just weeks before graduation. Sealing our fate. Ben had accepted early admission the following week and left the day after graduation. I stayed behind and attended community college in Seattle that fall, with a shattered heart, never hearing from him again.

"Gwen Porter," a voice calls from across the waiting room and I sit up abruptly and squeeze Gwen's hand.

"Here we go," I hear her mumble as we both stand and make our way across the waiting room.

# 15

*Gwen*

Charley and I are led into an office rather than an exam room, where we both sit in matching dark leather chairs that face a large tidy desk. My thoughts are racing as we wait for Dr. Sheldan.

A dreadful ten minutes later, he enters the room apologizing for the wait. He introduces himself as he shakes my hand and I introduce Charley.

Dr. Sheldan is younger than I expected and shorter, but he has a handsome face and kind smile, putting me at ease immediately.

He addresses me once he is seated behind his desk.

"Gwen. I've reviewed your history, blood work, scans and your biopsy results and I'm not going to lie. I can't offer you a different prognosis than Dr. Rand. However, I can offer you a treatment. We're dealing with metastatic breast cancer that has spread to your lymph nodes as well as your bones. Unfortunately there is no cure, but we can design a treatment plan specifically for you that would focus on the length and quality of your life. We have a variety of treatment plans and studies show that any one of these treatments could prolong your life by five years..."

"Five years," I choke out, interrupting him. My mind fast-forwards five years as I envision Olivia as a teenager, feisty and independent as she tries to find herself in this cruel world. And Max, he would be the same age that Olivia is now. Tears sting my eyes. It's not enough time. It's not enough. I wipe my tears away with my fingers and clear my throat as Dr. Sheldan continues.

"But Gwen, I've had hundreds of patients make it past the ten-year mark, some even longer."

"Will I have to have chemotherapy again?" I ask him.

"Well sometimes we use chemotherapy to slow down tumor growth or shrink the size of the tumors, but in your case I don't feel that the benefits of chemotherapy would outweigh the risks, so I'm going to suggest a cancer medication that we'll inject intravenously coupled with a handful of oral medications to promote healthy cells, healthy kidneys, and such. You'll also be on a very strict diet to optimize the treatment. You'll have monthly scans to make sure that the treatment is effective. It's not uncommon to change your therapy if we're not getting positive results. Sometimes the tumors can develop a resistance to the drugs, in which case we would need to try something else. But other than that, you can live a normal daily life, the emphasis on *live*, Gwen. Do you have any questions?"

"I don't know. My head is kind of spinning right now," I say as I try to absorb everything he has just told me.

I hear Charley ask, "So there's nothing else to do? What about surgery? Does she need to have the tumors removed?"

"That is an option that we can certainly explore but generally at this stage the cancer cells are already present and growing, so the need to remove the tumors isn't imperative."

"So that's it? We treat the cancer, basically to keep it from getting worse but we can't get rid of it?" I hear Charley ask.

"Yes. Unfortunately we can't get rid of it. I'm sorry."

I am a messy pile of tears and snot as I listen to them speak back and forth as if I'm not sitting right here in this room. My heart pounds in my head and I feel as if I'm in a tunnel, their voices becoming muffled and distant. After a few moments of silence, Charley hands me a tissue and the simple touch of her hand, grounds me, pulls me back into the room. I blow my nose loudly as Dr. Sheldan and Charley both watch me in utter silence. I close my eyes, take a deep breath, straighten my shoulders and resolve to be strong.

Finding my voice I ask, "So when do we start?"

"We can set up an appointment for your first treatment this week. The sooner, the better."

"Okay," I say, nodding my head up and down, reassuring myself as much as everyone else.

"Okay," Charley repeats, placing her hand on top of mine where it rests in my lap.

"Okay," Dr. Sheldan says, nodding his head as well.

I feel as if the three of us are all in on one giant secret, a pact, each with a common goal. And it's hard not to feel the weight of the absence of the one person who should be in this room, who should be part of the pact. *What have I done? Keeping this from him.*

Once Charley and I shake hands with Dr. Sheldan and I have set up my appointment for my first cancer treatment, we leave the medical center. As I step out of the building into the thick drizzle of rain sheeting down at a slant, I stop and turn back to look at the heavy glass doors as they shift closed. A distorted image of myself stares back in the reflection of the glass. My once perfect blonde bob is wet and matted against my face, my black mascara smeared under my eyes. I look a mess. *I am a mess*, I think. The glass doors slide open as an elderly couple steps outside, their hands held up to shield their aged faces from the rain, and the mirrored image of myself is gone. I turn to Charley, who is standing in the mist watching me with pity in her eyes, but I can see the underlying fear in the depth of her gaze. She says nothing which, for someone who hides behind her quick wit and sarcasm, says too much. Charley reaches for my hand so I take a step toward her and in a flash we are darting across the street toward the parking garage, holding hands in the rain.

And that's it. I am officially dying of cancer. I am going to die. Maybe not today or tomorrow or next week but someday soon. Someday that will come sooner than it should, sooner than I planned. I know, though, as sure as the Seattle rain, I will fight for every one-more-day.

I try to hold on to this brief moment of strength, but as my thoughts shift to John, the reality sinks in, the fear takes hold and my strength crumbles to the ground where it is washed away in a steady stream of rain. I am left vacant, knowing what lies ahead; I have to tell John.

# 16

## *Charley*

I hear a knock, startling me as I wipe the tears from my eyes and go to the door. I've been sitting in a pool of pity, thinking only of Gwen for hours. The tears haven't stopped falling since she dropped me off. I am suddenly aware of my disheveled appearance, but really after the day I've had, I don't care as much as I should.

I open the door to find Grey standing on the top step, leaning in under the eaves to keep dry, holding up a white paper bag from Sam's Deli. He's still dressed in his office attire, although his suit jacket and tie are missing. My breath catches in my throat as I look into his warm eyes. His looks never cease to amaze me, but there is something else, like a small nudge to the heart that I can't seem to put my finger on.

"Grey, what are you doing here?" I ask, completely taken by surprise.

"I wanted to check on you. And I brought you some soup. Your favorite, lemon chicken from Sam's." He hands me the bag and I look at him in awe.

"How'd you know that was my favorite?" I ask him.

Grey taps his temple with his index finger and says, "I know a few things." And then he sinks his hands into the pockets of his dress slacks and shrugs. "And I pay attention."

And another unidentifiable nudge. This simple gesture sends a ripple of warmth through me.

I run my hand through my wild hair, nervously, and step aside, a subtle invitation for him to come inside.

He steps through the doorway and looks around. He has never been inside my place; we always go to his condo.

"This is cute," he says as I close the door. It's a far cry from his expensive high-rise condo downtown, but I have to agree, it *is* cute.

"Thanks. I wasn't expecting you, I'm kind of a mess," I say, placing my hand on my forehead, feeling a bit flushed suddenly. I feel so vulnerable in the moment. Something I don't like to feel. I like to be in control and Grey has caught me completely off guard.

"Are you still feeling sick?" he asks with concern etched in his eyes.

I had almost forgotten that I was sick, it seems like days ago. My stomach rumbles loudly, filling the silence and Grey's concerned expression morphs into a full grin.

I cringe. "Apparently I'm feeling better, and starving for that matter," I say. Holding the open bag up to my face, I inhale and add, "This soup smells so good, mind if I eat?"

"Not at all. Please eat."

"Do you want some?" I ask as I step into the kitchen to grab a spoon from the utensil drawer.

"Nah. I just came from an early business dinner." Grey sits down on the sofa, his hands clasped in his lap. He seems nervous as he rubs the inside of his left palm with the thumb of his right hand. I don't blame him. This feels a little awkward. This isn't what we do.

"Would you like something to drink?" I ask while I remove the container of soup from the bag and lift off the lid. The soup really does smell heavenly and I realize that I haven't eaten anything since the dry pancake I nibbled on at Gwen's early this morning.

"I'm good," he replies.

I take my soup and sit down on the sofa next to him, curling my legs up underneath me. We sit in silence, as I shovel spoonfuls of warm soup into my mouth. I look up when I feel Grey's eyes on me. I stop eating, feeling completely unnerved and flash him a subtle smile.

"Thank you. For the soup. It's so good," I say, averting my eyes from his intense gaze.

Grey reaches over and places his hand on my leg. "Is everything okay, Charley?" he asks.

I set my half-empty soup container on the coffee table as I feel the tears bubble to the surface. I try to fight them as I start to say, "Everything's fine," but my words get caught in my throat. The tears fill my eyes and spill down my cheeks before I can stop them and I feel so very vulnerable and scared, but at the same time I don't care. I can't hold it in another moment or I might combust. These are emotions that I save only for Gwen. Gwen is the only one who I confide in, who comforts me, but I can't talk to her about this. I have to be strong for her. I can't let her see me fall apart.

I feel strong arms around me as Grey pulls me into his lap and holds me tight. The fear and uncertainty unleashes,

101

practically bursts out of me and I sob onto his shoulder, shaking in despair. And Grey just holds me, rubbing his hand up and down my back in a soothing motion. I feel so small and fragile in his arms, wrapped against his large, strong frame. I can't remember the last time someone held me like this. Or rather that I allowed someone to hold me like this.

When the sobs begin to ebb and I can breathe once again, I pull back and wipe my face with the bottom of my T-shirt.

I look at Grey through bleary eyes and suddenly feel so embarrassed.

"Oh God, I'm so sorry," I say, wiping my fingers under my eyes, removing the last trace of my tears.

"Don't apologize, Charley," he whispers, showing all his cards in his eyes. "Talk to me. What's going on?"

"I can't," I say as I start to shift off his lap, removing myself from his embrace. Fear seizes my heart, holding my words, my emotions prisoner.

"Charley, please, don't push me away. Talk to me," Grey pleads as he holds me tighter, but I can't. I just can't. I try to pull away again, but he won't let me go. I suddenly can't breathe. I need some space; he's too close. I push at his chest and try to stand. He releases me, although reluctantly.

I step away until I am in the middle of the room, keeping my back to him as my heartbeat slows and I feel a sense of calm wash over me.

"Why can't you talk to me, Charley? We can be more than this. I *want* to be more than this. If you'll just let me. Just let me in." Grey's voice is laced with frustration and understanding at the same time. It's as if he knows me. His words a testament to that fact, because he's right. I won't let him in. I *can't* let him in.

I hear him move behind me seconds before I feel him pull me against him, my back to his front. He wraps his arms around me and dips his head down to my shoulder, kissing me lightly on the neck. His lips trace an imaginary line to the space behind my ear and I close my eyes, reveling in the feel of him. I turn slowly and move my hands to his hair as I pull his lips to mine, all at once needing to be with him in the only way I know.

Grey must feel the same way as he pulls me tighter into his arms, his tongue wrapping around mine in a seductive dance. I can feel him grow hard against me and it only fuels the fire ignited in my core. Scooping me up in one swift move, Grey walks through my bungalow slowly, unsure of where to go, until he finds my bedroom and lies me gently on the bed. He slowly peels my yoga pants and lace panties from my body, followed by my T-shirt and bra. When I am completely naked, lying bare and vulnerable before him, he steps back and looks at me while he undoes his belt and pushes his slacks and boxer briefs to the ground. I meet his gaze until my eyes shift lower where he strokes his throbbing erection in his hand. The air feels thick and charged with a new intensity that I can't explain, my need to feel him inside me just as strong as ever but shadowed by a sense of fear as if this is our first time together. I reach for him and close my eyes when I feel the weight of his body against mine. I can feel his gaze as if it is burning through my closed lids but I can't look at him now – not when he's this close.

His hand finds my folds with a gentle yet potent caress, bringing me to the brink as my breath escalates until I am practically panting. And then with one slow, strong thrust he is inside me, and I melt around him as if he was made just for me. My fingers claw at his back as I pull him closer, his lips at my neck moving in the same slow, punishing rhythm as his hips. As he moves in and out of me, in complete control, I can't help but feel something different from before. Swirled with the usual and intense heat in my belly, the frenzied need building in my core, is a sense of longing, an almost emptiness and fulfillment braided together as one. Grey never once changes his speed or his intensity, despite my pleas, as we move together until we both find what we are in search of. I explode around him just as he fills me with his release and I lay completely satiated in his arms. Emotions boil just below the surface, the debilitating fear threatens to take hold but I push it away. I feel tired, weary. As if Grey is my weakness, crumbling what little strength I have to keep the wall around my heart intact. I just want to lie here and relish in this feeling for a while. I want to feel something for just a moment longer, before it all evaporates into thin air and I'm left to deal with the consequences.

I slowly open my eyes and feel Grey's strong arms wrapped around me, the heat from his bare skin almost suffocating. The soft orange glow of dawn leaks in through the cracks in the blinds, alerting me that it's morning and my body turns rigid at the realization that Grey and I slept together. He stayed the night. I turn slowly in his arms to wake him but I feel that little nudge again when I see the soft innocence of his features, the vulnerability captured by sleep. He stirs and pulls me tighter against him, a lazy smile appears on his face and I know that he's awake even though his eyes are still closed.

"Grey?" I whisper.

"Mmm. Yeah," he says, his voice scratchy from sleep.

"Grey, get up, it's morning," I say, digging my finger into his shoulder.

He smiles bigger and nuzzles in even closer.

"Yes it is," he says, kissing my cheek. "Let's have morning sex." I feel his erection digging into my hip.

"We both have to be at work soon," I say, unable to keep the anxiety from my voice.

"Then let's have *quick* morning sex," he says, flipping me on top of him in one swift move.

I try to push away from him, "Grey, I'm serious. You need to go."

"I'm serious too. And I need to come," he says as he tries to kiss me. He's laughing now. He thinks this is funny. He runs his hand down between us and I feel my body slowly begin to betray me. I don't do morning sex. I don't do sleepovers. But the feel of Grey's hand in all the right places makes me feel at ease, it feels familiar. I moan and ease myself onto Grey, forgetting all about the fact that it's morning, forgetting the way Grey unravels me, forgetting myself completely. I move slowly at first, finding a rhythm that works for both of us, and before long we are both panting and frantic with need until I am trembling above him, searching for breath. At the same time, I hear Grey grunt as he empties into me.

I pause for a moment as my heart rate slows before peeling myself off of Grey, begging him to get dressed as he rolls over and buries his face in the pillow with a groan.

I dash to the bathroom to clean up and when I return to the bedroom, I realize that it's nearly time for us both to be at the office. Grey's sitting on the end of my unmade bed in last night's clothes. I stand across the room and cinch the tie on my silk robe as I watch him slip on his dress shoes and I can't help but feel frazzled. *How do I walk into the office and act as if I didn't just kick him out of my bed?*

In a quiet command, he says, "Come here."

I walk slowly to him and he pulls me down on his lap, his hand grazing my bare thigh where my robe is split open. "Have dinner with me tonight," he says, looking deep into my eyes.

I close my eyes for a quick second and take a deep breath before meeting his gaze. "Dinner? I can't..."

"It's just two people sharing a meal, Charley. Don't freak out," he smirks.

"Dinner," I repeat with my lips pursed, trying it on for size.

"Yes, dinner. With me. In public. Can you handle it?" He's challenging me, something he has only done in the bedroom, but he knows me well enough to know that I never back down from a challenge.

"I can handle it," I retort with a smile.

"Good," he says, weaving his fingers in my hair and pulling my face to his. He places a gentle kiss on my lips, taking my breath away in an instant. It's too much all at once.

"Grey?" I open my eyes slowly.

"Yeah?"

"I want to have dinner with you. I do. But I can't tonight. Can I take a rain check?"

His face is inches from mine as he stares at me for a beat.

"Okay, not tonight. Saturday night then. I'll pick you up at seven."

I nod. "Okay, Saturday night."

He kisses me once more and as I start to stand, he smacks me on the ass, startling me.

"Get your hot ass to work, Miss Brant. You're late. Again."

I turn and catch his wicked grin. My thighs clench. *I want this man too much*, I think. And that thought makes my heart clench.

# 17

## Gwen

I sit at the kitchen counter, staring aimlessly out the glass doors with my hand wrapped around a full mug of coffee that I can't seem to muster enough strength to lift to my lips. I can see the green grass glistening with dew in the back yard and beyond that, the island ferry inching across the sound, leaving behind a subtle v-shaped wake. The sun is shining today, lighting up the glasslike surface of the water with a fiery glare. It's a beautiful day, and yet I can't seem to snap out of my dark mood. I feel depressed. Tired. A feeling that I'm not familiar with.

Last night I laid in bed just staring at John while he slept soundly, completely oblivious to the ticking time bomb wedged between us. I wanted to wake him so many times and just confess, whisper it all quietly in the dark. But in the end, I couldn't wrangle enough nerve.

Earlier this morning I had mindlessly slipped on a pair of sweatpants and a sweatshirt, pulled my hair into a ponytail and finished off my disheveled look with a pair of camel-colored Uggs. I can't remember the last time I didn't bother with my appearance, regardless of whether or not my day consisted only of carpool and housework. I dropped the kids off in the turnabout, something I have never done, and asked Olivia to walk Max to his classroom. Olivia had rolled her eyes at my request, but rather than pitch a fit, she had grabbed her brother's hand and marched him across campus toward the kindergarten wing. It broke my heart to ask her to do something for Max, when it should have been my responsibility. With their five-year age gap – the same as Charley and I – I try hard not to burden Olivia with taking care of Max.

I hear the doorbell ring, startling me, and I slowly make my way to the front entry. I open the door to find my mother standing on the front porch in a straw visor, her short wavy blonde hair spilling out the top. She's dressed in her usual attire of loose fitting leggings and a draped, cotton sweater, all in neutral shades. Her oversized, black vegan-leather handbag is hanging from one shoulder and a Whole Foods reusable shopping bag is dangling on the other.

She pulls her tortoise-shaped sunglasses from her face and smiles at me.

"Mother, what are you doing here?" I ask her.

"Well, you haven't returned any of my calls, so I thought I'd come check on you." She looks me up and down with a frown and asks, "Are you sick?"

I take a deep breath and give her a closed-lip smile. My mother is the last person I want to see right now. She's pushy and talks too much and I just want to spend the day alone. I'm not in the mood for her interrogations or her opinions.

"Yeah, just feeling a little under the weather today," I reply. She pushes her way past me.

"You poor thing. You need to take better care of yourself, Gwen. You do too much. Sometimes it's okay to take a break," she says, making her way down the hallway toward the kitchen.

*Here we go*, I think as I push the door closed and follow her to the kitchen. She has the shopping bag on the counter as she unloads its contents one at a time. Cellophane wrapped boxes of tea, a jar of rainbow-colored gummy vitamins, a bottle of apple-cider vinegar, cranberry juice and several tiny dark bottles of essential oil line the dark marble countertop.

"Mom, I can buy my own groceries, ya know?"

"I know, but you don't have a Whole Foods in Seaport. And Felicity just told me about this new tea that's suppose to energize you *and* build-up your immune system. And of course, you can never have too many vitamins for the kids."

I just stare at my mother with my signature closed-lip smile that I use only for her. She has recently become a vegan and is obsessed with her new lifestyle, not to mention her obsession with her spiritual advisor, Felicity. My mother has had several obsessions over the years. At one time it was knitting and Charley and I were showered with scarves, hats, sweaters, and an assortment of Barbie clothes made entirely of yarn. When she finally gave that up it was yoga and meditation, which led her to Buddhism. Our house looked like a shrine for eight months until she gave that up and moved on to something else. It was always something though. After my dad left, it had been men. Luckily, that phase had lasted only a year or so. My mother started out the perfect homemaker and mother, but once my father left, she crumbled. Most days she locked herself in her room, barely able to take care of Charley and I, let alone hold down a job. We got by on what little we had but I slowly grew to hate her. I can remember my anger building each day, resentment taking root as I watched her wallow in her weakness, while her daughters fought to be strong. But then one day, three years after my dad left, I came home from school and she was fully dressed with her makeup in place and the house was clean. She behaved as if she hadn't abandoned Charley and I all that time, like it never happened. That same week she got a clerical job and life got better, but by then it was too late for all of us. Charley and I were robbed of the bond that so many of my friends had with their own mothers. At thirteen, I felt more like an adult, completely independent. And Charley felt more comfortable coming to me for things than our mother, who at that point felt more like a stranger. Since having my own children, my mother and I have grown closer and I can see her unfailing effort to be a good grandmother, as if she is trying to make up for lost time. I fear that Charley will never have a relationship with our mother, but then again, she doesn't have a relationship with anyone, with the exception of me, John and the kids.

"Thanks Mom. You shouldn't have," I say, placing my hands on the counter and feeling like I need its support to stay upright.

"I don't mind," she says and then she pauses, sets down a box and looks at me.

"What's wrong, Gwen? Are you okay? Maybe you should go lie down."

"I'm fine."

"Are you sure? Because Felicity told me I should check on you, but she wasn't sure why. And now that I see you, I'm worried. Should I be worried?" she asks, with her hand on her hip.

My head is spinning from all her questions. Maybe Felicity's not completely full of shit. That thought alone gives me the chills. But I certainly can't confide in my mother before coming clean to John and so I say in my most reassuring voice, "I'm fine, really. Max just had the stomach flu, maybe I'm coming down with it."

"Poor Max. You should really be taking probiotics. You could avoid these kind of things."

"I'll keep that in mind," I deadpan. "Ya know, I think I will go lie down. You're welcome to stay," I call out behind me as I make my way toward the stairs.

"I'll just put these things away for you and then let myself out. I'm having lunch with Susan Marcus and then heading back to the city. Feel better, honey."

I pause on the bottom stair and turn to look at her as she blows me a kiss. "Thank you. Bye Mother," I say with a subtle wave and then trudge up the stairs.

The next morning after school drop off, I drive to the clinic in Seaport, where Dr. Sheldan has set up my weekly appointments for my intravenous infusions. I'm relieved to not have to drive into the city every week for my treatment and I'm able to drive myself home afterward given the short three-mile distance. *It's easier to keep my secret this way*, I think, and I instantly feel sick to my stomach for being so deceiving, for lying to John. It's as if I'm having an affair with cancer, and for some reason I feel like it would be easier to confess having a secret lover then tell my husband the fatal truth.

I'm sitting in a comfortable chair, counting every drop of fluid as it is slowly infused into my bloodstream, and I am reminded of the grueling months of chemotherapy that I endured before. I always had John or Charley at my side to keep me company, but now I sit here alone, fighting back tears. I'm trying so hard not to feel sorry for myself, to stay positive, but then I think of the uncertainty of my future and I can't fight the devastation that I feel.

I picture Olivia's beautiful face and Max's soft, chubby cheeks to gain perspective. This is for them. *I can do this for them.* I pull my iPad from my purse and begin my online search for the best nutrition plan, homeopathic treatments, and tips on dealing with the side effects during treatment. I realize that I've been feeling out of sorts because I can't control this situation. But I feel a calm wash over me with every website that I research as I resolve to try *everything* possible, to do whatever it takes. After an hour of this, I type "how to tell your husband you have cancer" into the search engine. Surprisingly, there is an endless list of sites with advice for this very thing. Although it's comforting to read other people's struggles with cancer, it doesn't ease my fear of telling John.

My phone vibrates in my purse and I shift everything around until I find it and see Charley's name on the screen.

I say, "Hello," just in time.

"Whatcha doing?" she asks. Though she knows exactly what I'm doing. She was there when I made this appointment.

"Sitting on the beach, sipping a mai tai. You?"

"I really wish I could be there with you. I can't stand the thought of you sitting there alone."

"I'm fine. Really. You can't miss work every time I have a treatment."

"I know. You need to tell John, Gwen. This is getting out of control, all this sneaking around. Just tell him."

I let out a breath that I've been holding since she mentioned John's name.

"I know. I will, I promise. I just haven't had the right moment." Tears blur my eyes. *Why is this so damn hard?*

"There's never going to be the right moment. *Jesus*, Gwen. If you don't tell him soon, then I will."

"No," I say in a rush. There is no way that she can tell John. I just need more time. "Charley, you can't. It should be me. I'll tell him."

"Do it, Gwen. He should be sitting there with you right now, holding your hand."

Tears are now spilling down my cheeks and I can't speak, my emotions are balled up deep in my throat and one word will give them away.

Charley's voice is only a whisper. "Everything's going to be okay."

I am nodding even though she can't see me. And we stay on the phone until my treatment is through, each of us quiet as I listen to Charley work on the other end of the line, but her quiet presence is exactly what I need.

# 18

## *Charley*

I hang up the phone and look around to ensure that no one can see the emotion written across my face. I want so badly to be there for Gwen. It's killing me. I have picked up the phone so many times to call John and tell him the truth, but I can't betray Gwen that way. She needs me right now, and I'm going to be everything that she needs me to be just as she has done for me all these years. But, *dammit*, I wish she would tell him the truth.

I stare across the room at Grey's closed office door. I want to go to him. I am wound so tightly with all these emotions, I just need to lose myself in him, to feel free for just a few minutes. But we're at work, in the middle of the day, and I know the risk involved.

I jump when his office door opens abruptly. He steps out looking every bit the uber sexy businessman in a pastel purple dress shirt and charcoal dress slacks. He moves toward my desk and I notice that he has removed his tie since this morning, and the top two buttons of his shirt are undone with the sleeves rolled up to his elbows. His dark hair is a mess as if he has been running his fingers through it. His expression is intense as he approaches me and I can understand why the other assistants are so intimidated by him.

"Charley, can you make ten copies of this on letterhead?" he asks as he lays a sheet of paper in front of me, avoiding my eyes. I find myself biting down on the end of my pen, completely tied up in knots at the sight of him.

He walks back toward his office before I can respond and shuts the door. I go to the copy room and make the ten copies that he has requested. When I reach his office door, I knock lightly and step inside, close the door behind me and discreetly push the lock in place. I toss the copies on his desk and he looks up at me, his eyes meeting mine.

"Here are your copies," I say, swallowing the knot in my throat.

"Thanks," he says, running his hands through his hair.

I walk around his desk and push his chair back.

"What are you doing, Charley?" he asks, more annoyed than amused. "I'm in the middle of this proposal."

I kneel down in front of him and undo his belt and the button and zipper of his pants. He doesn't say anything. He only watches my face and lifts his hips when I tug at his pants and boxers. As I slip them down his thighs, he moves to the edge of his chair. I grip his length in my hand until he's ready and then take him slowly to the back of my throat, moving to the sound of his moans as I feel his fingers in my hair, guiding me. Just as I feel him start to lose control, he pulls himself out of my mouth and lifts me to his lap where I straddle him, my dress riding up around my waist. He moves the thin strap of my panties aside and lowers my hips until he's inside me. I moan at the feel of him and bury my face in his neck where I lick and kiss his skin, stifling the noise that I dare to make.

In a strained whisper, Grey says, "God, Charley you're so wet. What are you doing to me?" He guides my hips faster and faster until I melt around him, trembling in relief, relishing in the dizzy void that has taken over my thoughts. All tension from before is drained from my body. Seconds later I feel him empty into me, gripping me tightly as if he can't get close enough though our thighs are skin to skin, our bodies joined as one.

We stay like this while our breath evens out and then I stand and pull my dress back down over my hips and quickly walk to the small, adjoined washroom. I use the restroom and remove all traces of Grey, fix my tousled hair with my fingers and stare at my flushed face in the small mirror.

*What am I doing?* I ask myself. My emotions are all over the place, though my body is still behaving in the only way it knows.

I open the bathroom door and walk back into Grey's office. He is sitting behind his desk, his pants back in place, his hair in more disarray than before. My body hums at the sight of him, already in anticipation of more.

He just stares at me, his eyes dark and filled with lust and I can't get a read on what he's thinking.

"Well, I guess I should get back to work," I say, if only to break the silent tension in the room.

I turn to go but his voice stops me.

"Charley. What are we doing?" he asks, a genuine question.

I turn back to face him. And because I don't have the answer that he's looking for, I respond by saying, "Working. We're working. I just... I just needed you."

He only nods and then says, "Well, I'm here. Whenever you *need* me." He narrows his eyes at me as if he wants to say something more. But he must think better of it because he only smiles and says, "Thank you... for the copies." He picks up the stack of papers and begins to look them over. I take this as my cue to leave.

Stepping out the door, I mutter to myself with a smile, "You're welcome."

# 19
## Gwen

"I'm sorry, honey, I won't be home for dinner. Hal and I are meeting with a client for drinks. Tell the kids I love them."

"Of course. Be safe. Love you," I say into the phone where it rests between my chin and shoulder while I drain the cooked pasta over the sink. Steam rises up to my face and I turn my head away while placing the hot pan back on the stovetop to cool.

"Love you too," John says, his voice laced with regret as I slip the phone from my shoulder and end our call. He hates working late and missing out on our family time together in the evenings. I sigh, feeling a sense of relief to not have to face him. Maybe I'll be in bed asleep before he gets home. It's too hard to lie about my day and yet I'm not sure that I'm ready to tell him the truth. My fingers go to the bandage on the underside of my forearm, hidden by my sweater. The IV site is still tender to the touch. I'm not sure how long I can keep this from him.

"I'm hungry," I hear Max say from behind me, snapping me back into the moment, my task at hand.

"Dinner is ready. Why don't you go wash your hands?" I say. "Olivia. Dinner," I call out.

Moments later, the three of us are sitting around the kitchen table eating a pasta dinner, chatting about our day.

"It's down to me and Chelsea Hammitt for the lead role, Mom," Olivia says animatedly. She's trying out for the school play, a more modern version of the musical, *Annie;* she's been practicing for weeks.

"I'm so proud of you, Olivia. When do they announce the cast?"

"Right before Thanksgiving break, and rehearsals begin the first week of December."

"I'll keep my fingers crossed," I say, crossing my fingers in the air. I've already volunteered to help build and paint the stage set for the play, which will be performed at the end of the school year. I try to push the thoughts aside that creep into my conscience, the thoughts that wonder if I'll be here to paint the set when Max is in the fifth grade play, five years from now. *Five years.*

"How about you, Max? How was your day?" I ask, turning my attention to Max. He has pasta sauce dripping from his chin while he tries to stuff a huge noodle in his mouth with his fork. I smile and use his napkin to wipe his face.

"Travis pushed me down at recess and took my soccer ball," he says around a mouthful of food.

"Did you tell Miss LaBorn?" I ask with a frown. This isn't the first time that Travis has picked on Max.

"No. I played on the swing instead. I don't like Travis. He's mean."

"I know Max. Just use your words to fight back, not your hands and I'll talk to your teacher and see if we can get this straightened out, okay?"

"Okay," he says, so easy to please.

Hours later when the kids are in bed asleep, I grasp a hot cup of tea in my hand – one of the organic brands my mother bought – wrap a throw blanket around me and step outside onto the deck. The air is crisp, the dark sky remarkably clear and dotted with thousands of stars. I lay back on a lounge chair and stare at the stars. I trace the big dipper with my eyes and wish that I remembered more constellations, sure that I would be able to see them on this rare, clear night. I spot a shooting star; it happens so fast that I think I imagined it, but then I see another and another. *Amazing*, I think. And then I instantly wish that Olivia was awake to watch this. The thought occurs to me at the same time that I stand from the chair and before I know it, I'm running up the stairs to her room.

I shake her awake. "Olivia. Wake up sweetie," I whisper, breathless.

She stirs and then opens her eyes wide with shock. "What Mom?" she asks, still half asleep.

"Come here, I want to show you something," I say, taking her hand and grabbing the blanket off the end of her bed. I lead her down the stairs and out the backdoor.

"Mom, what are we doing?" she asks. She must think that I've lost my mind.

"You'll see." I guide us both down the grassy slope toward the water, the soggy grass is cold on our bare feet, the cold air biting as it blows off the bay. We sit in the white Adirondack chairs near the beach, pulling our knees up to our chests to keep warm. I wrap Olivia in her blanket and pull mine tighter around me. She watches me with curiosity, waiting quietly for an explanation. I lean back and look up and for a moment I think that we've missed it, but then I see a star shoot across the night sky and burn out in midair.

"Look," I say as I point to the sky and as she tilts her face up to the stars, they begin to explode one after the other.

"Wow," Olivia whispers, a smile stretched across her face. And rather than watch the meteor shower, I watch the awe and wonder on my daughter's face. Tears fill my eyes and slide down my cheeks one at a time, as if in slow motion, and I discreetly wipe them away with my blanket. And I think, *I'll never forget this moment*, as I store it away along with so many others. I reach over and grab her hand and she turns to look at me for a moment before glancing back at the sky. I see so much of myself in her. Her stick-straight blonde hair, big hazel eyes, and her quiet strength. My heart is overflowing with love and heartache all in the same beat.

And right then, I make a wish on a falling star, feeling the power of it so deep that it touches my cancer-riddled bones.

# 20

## *Charley*

I stare at the piece of paper that I just found in the back pocket of my jeans while sorting the dirty laundry. Ben had written down "Pedialyte, Gatorade, and Children's Motrin – 1 tsp" on a sheet of paper from his prescription pad. At the bottom he wrote, in his chicken scratch that I remember well, "Call my cell if you need anything" and his personal phone number. I had forgotten the business card and sheet of paper that were burning a hole in my pocket that day; I guess the stomach flu can distract you from these types of things. I had forgotten, until now. I am considering making the call if only to thank him for everything he did while I was sick. It's the polite thing to do, right? I grab my cell phone and sit back down on my bedroom floor, surrounded by piles of dirty clothes, and punch in his number. Suddenly my hand is shaking and my heart is beating like a drum in my chest. My finger hovers over the little phone icon as I consider what I'm going to say. And before thinking better of it, I hit call and bring the phone to my ear. It rings several times and just as I am about to hang up, I hear his voice.

"Dr. Roth."

I freeze, unable to find my voice.

"Hello," he says into the silence.

"Ben," I manage to say. "It's Charley."

"Hey, how are you feeling?"

"Better," I say. "I just wanted to say thank you for everything you did. You saved me."

"You were in pretty bad shape." He chuckles and the familiar sound brings a smile to my face.

"Yeah, well thanks," I say and then, "I'm still completely mortified that you had to see me like that." I bring my hand to my face in embarrassment even though he can't see me.

"It wasn't that bad. You didn't look much better twelve years ago," he teases.

"Hey," I warn. "You look the same but with less hair." He laughs again and it warms me from the inside out. He looks amazing but I'm not about to tell him that. He always had longer hair and now it's shaved close to his scalp, but it only makes his eyes more pronounced.

"When I walked into that exam room and saw you sitting there... well let's just say you... well, you took my breath away." His comment hangs in the air. It's almost too much. I'm not sure how to respond. "Charley, can I see you again? Just to catch up?"

My heart is thrumming so fast and hard, I feel as if he can hear it through the phone.

We both wait in silence for my response.

"Yeah," I finally say. And then add, nonchalantly, "That'd be great. We should... ya know... catch up." Although in my mind I have no intention of a chummy reunion of any sort. And yet, my heart feels achy and something else that I can't quite pinpoint. I rub my hand over my chest in an attempt to soothe the source of the discomfort I feel.

"Yeah, we should," he agrees.

Another beat of silence and I am suddenly desperate to get off the phone.

"Well, I have to run. I just wanted to say thank you."

"Well, you're welcome," he says.

"Bye, Ben."

"Bye Charley," he draws out my name with his breath as if he is reluctant to end the call. But I hang up before he can say anything more.

*You took my breath away.* His words replay in my mind as I stare at my phone. I wonder if he ever thinks of me. If all these years he has wondered about me? And if he does think of me, what is it that comes to mind? My betrayal? Or the three years that we spent together, happy and in love? I'm almost afraid to know the answers to my own questions.

Guilt is a vicious emotion and when I think of Ben, it nearly suffocates me.

It's Saturday night. I have somewhat avoided Grey this week. I managed to fill his schedule with client meetings outside of the office and I dodged his invitations for late night "booty calls," afraid that he would expect another sleepover. My emotions have been all over the place since Gwen's diagnosis and it's been screwing with my head in respect to Grey. I drew a line in the sand when this whole thing began and that line has been blurred.

I'm afraid that I'm giving Grey the wrong idea and I don't want his expectations about us to change. Nothing has changed. The space that I put between Grey and I these past few days has given me back my perspective. If anything I have less time and less motivation to be in a relationship than ever before and let's be honest, I have never before wanted or needed a relationship. So there you go. I need to focus on Gwen right now.

All these thoughts bounce around in my head as I try to calm my unexpected nerves about the evening. Grey is picking me up in a few minutes to take me to dinner. I have changed my clothes three times already. I want to look nice but not too nice. I don't want to send the wrong message. I don't want this to feel like a date, even though that's exactly what this is. I settle for a simple cotton black sheath dress with heeled booties. I pull my hair into a messy bun and finish the look with the right accessories. I admire myself in the mirror. Sexy but edgy. I throw my phone and tiny wallet into a clutch purse and down a glass of wine to drown my nerves. I hate waiting on someone. I should have met him at the restaurant. After a lipstick touch up, he finally knocks on my door. And I am suddenly nervous as hell.

I open the door and my breath catches in my throat at the sight of him. *Dammit, he is breathtaking.* Grey is wearing jeans and a dark button down shirt, untucked. His hair is still damp and I can smell his familiar clean, woodsy scent.

"Wow, Charley. You look incredible."

"Thank you," I say and I can feel my cheeks heat under his intense gaze. "Do you want to come in?" I ask. I'm not sure how this whole thing works; this is all new for us.

"Actually, I have a full night planned, so we better head out," he says with a smile.

"Okay," I say, feeling unsettled and then I mumble, "I don't know whether I should feel excited or scared."

"Maybe both," he teases as I grab my clutch and step out on the porch, locking the door with my key. Grey offers me his arm and I loop my arm in his, thankful for his warmth as we step out into the chilly night. It hasn't rained all day, which is a small gift this time of year. Grey leads me to his flashy car and opens the door for me like a true gentleman.

"My lady," he says as he helps me into the passenger seat and closes the door. I watch him round the front of the car and climb into the driver's seat and I remind myself to breathe. *It's just Grey*, I tell myself.

"So where are we going?" I ask while I pull my seatbelt across my lap and fasten it into place.

He shakes his head and says, "And ruin the surprise. No way."

"Surprise? I thought we were just two people sharing a meal, remember?" I'm intrigued now and loving his playful side, but my nerves are still balled up in my chest from the unknown.

"We are. Just relax. I promise I'm not going to propose," he says with a smile and then turns and winks at me.

And *dammit* if that doesn't make my stomach do a little flip as a full-watted smile stretches across my face. It's refreshing to know that Grey gets me and maybe his expectations aren't what I fear them to be.

He pulls into a valet-only parking lot just to the southeast of Pioneer Square. The valet attendant opens my door and I step out of the car as Grey pulls me into his side and guides me down the sidewalk, around the corner and into an old bar. I didn't catch the name, but it's old and sports-themed and Grey seems to know his way around as he leads me to the long bar in the back.

We sit in two empty bar stools and the mid-thirties bartender with dark hair and a matching beard immediately walks toward us, his eyes lighting up in recognition.

"Hey G!" he says, reaching out and shaking Grey's hand. "Haven't seen you in awhile." He looks at me and asks, "Who's the pretty lady?"

"James, this is Charley. Charley meet James. The best damn bartender in Puget Sound."

"Nice to meet you, James," I say and give him a little wave.

"Any friend of G's is a friend of mine. What can I get you?"

James looks and talks like your typical bartender and I smile at the way he calls Grey "G".

"Two shots of tequila," Grey says, holding up two fingers. James nods and steps away.

I turn to Grey and say, "If I didn't know any better, G, I'd think you were trying to get me drunk and take advantage of me."

"All part of the plan." He places his hand on my bare leg and spins my stool until my body is facing his. He leans in and kisses me on the mouth. My body instantly flushes with heat and when he pulls away I discreetly look around to see if anyone is watching us. PDA is really not my thing; I like to keep it behind closed doors.

James sets two full shot glasses down on the bar in front of us, along with a plate of limes and a salt shaker.

Without taking his eyes off me, Grey says to James, "Keep 'em coming."

I look at him, puzzled.

He hands me a shot glass and asks, "Salt?"

I shake my head and he picks up his shot glass. We are sitting close, our faces nearly touching and Grey says quietly, "*This* is to loosen you up. And it's not because I want to take advantage of you, although that will come later. If you're lucky." His smile sets my insides on fire. "It's because I want to get to know you, Charley. So cheers," he says as he clinks his glass against mine. We both raise our glasses to our lips and I pour the tequila to the back of my throat, feeling the burn. I set my empty shot glass down at the same time as Grey and grab a slice of lime. The sour taste erasing the flavor of the tequila just as James sets a fresh set of full shot glasses on the bar.

"Jeez, Grey. I'm not sure how many of these I can drink," I say, already dreading the next shot and the inevitable hangover it will bring.

"Okay last one," he says loud enough for James to hear.

We both pick up the next and, hopefully, last shot of the night and Grey asks, "What's your favorite song of all time?"

I stare at him, my mind drawing a blank.

"A song that no matter how many times you hear it, you never get sick of it and it instantly brightens your mood."

"'Jack and Diane' by John Cougar Mellencamp," I blurt out. It's the first song that popped into my head.

He pulls his face back and says, "Really?" as if he completely disapproves.

"Hey, you asked."

"You know he goes by just John Mellencamp now, right?"

"Whatever." I shake my head and then ask, "What's your favorite song of all time then?"

He thinks for a minute and then says, "'Fight For Your Right' by the Beastie Boys."

"Okay that's pretty solid," I say, picturing Grey yelling the lyrics in a crowded bar with his fisted hand waving in the air.

"See, a true classic," he says and then holds his glass against mine. "To learning something about you while we're still wearing clothes." He winks at me seductively as he clinks his glass against mine and I suddenly welcome this shot. His words settle in my gut, twisting it in knots as I begin to question his intentions all over again.

"One more round," I call to James as I slide my empty shot glass down the bar.

Grey smiles at me in approval.

The next round arrives and Grey turns to me and asks, "What's your favorite color?"

I set my full glass down and sigh. "Really? We're gonna do *this*?"

"Uh-huh." He nods, sets his shot glass down next to mine on the bar and spins my stool back toward him.

"How about, favorite position in bed," I say, cocking my head to the side playfully.

"How about I show you that later," he counters.

"Promise?" I say and bite down on my lip.

"Don't think I don't know what you're doing," he says as he smooths his thumb over my lip.

"What?" I ask innocently, getting lost in his dark eyes as the tequila goes straight to my head.

"You're trying to get out of these questions, out of dinner, this whole date by seducing me. You want me to throw you over my shoulder and take you back to my place and fuck you senseless." His tone is seductive and yet he is mocking me.

His words and the images they provoke make my thighs clench and at the same time the truth of his words makes my heart sink. Because without even realizing it, that is exactly my intention. I want something familiar, I want to keep this thing with Grey on my level. The way Grey is looking at me now, I know that although he is teasing me, he means what he said. And I feel somewhat ashamed. Surely I can have dinner with this man, or whatever it is that he has planned.

"As a matter of fact, I want to end this interrogation because I'm starving," I say but he only raises his eyebrows and looks at me like, *exactly*, misconstruing my words until I clarify. "For food. Are we actually going to eat on this date?"

He eyes me warily and then glances at his watch.

"Yes, dinner is next, I swear."

We both drain our glasses and then Grey throws a couple hundred-dollar bills down on the bar and calls out, "See ya James." James waves as we head toward the door. My body is feeling tingly and warm, my head a little dizzy from the tequila.

Grey takes my hand and laces our fingers together as we step outside. The cold air feels good on my flush skin, clearing my mind. We walk a few blocks until we are standing at the entrance to Safeco Field. Grey pulls his phone out and begins to text someone.

"What are we doing? You do know the Mariners' season is over, right?" I ask, wondering what in the world he has planned.

"Come on," he says ignoring my comment. He grabs my hand and leads me to the nearest closed gate.

A guy appears on the other side out of nowhere and unlocks the large iron gate, its hinges groaning in protest as he swings it open wide enough for us both to walk through.

"Hey Marco," Grey says as they hug briefly, giving each other a man-pat on the back. Grey steps back and ticks his head toward me, "This is Charley."

"Nice to meet you Charley." He holds his hand toward me.

"Nice to meet you too, Marco," I say, shaking his hand gently.

"It's all yours, I'll be in the office. Just let me know when you're ready to leave," he says to Grey as he turns the key in the gate, locking the three of us inside Safeco Field.

"Thanks, buddy."

I am silent as my mind runs through all the possibilities of why Grey brought me here.

He tugs on my arm and leads me down the corridor, down a huge staircase and through a door. We are suddenly standing on the baseball field, the bright lights glaring overhead in the eerie quiet of the empty stadium. Grey leads me out toward center field and I can see a blanket spread out near the pitcher's mound.

"What are we doing?" I ask.

"We're having dinner," he says, as if this is the most normal thing in the world.

When we reach the blanket I see a few paper bags filled with takeout food from a local restaurant. A large hooded Mariner's sweatshirt, a stack of blankets and a small cooler sit off to the side.

"Wow, this is some dinner," I say with a smile. Emotions overwhelm me but I tap them down. Grey did all this for me. Normally when men go out of their way to impress me, especially when it accompanies the intention of vamping up a casual fling into something more, it sends me in the opposite direction, a complete turn off. But *this* is different. Grey isn't trying to impress me. He didn't take me to a fancy restaurant or fly me to New York to see a Broadway performance on a moment's notice. He's trying to make me feel at ease. And although this evening feels extravagant, it is anything but fancy or pretentious. He has taken the fear away, he has made going out on a date with him fun and completely harmless. *He gets me*, I think again.

He motions for me to sit down and I do, tucking my legs up underneath me in a ladylike fashion, wishing that I'd worn jeans. He sits across from me.

"Are you cold?" he asks. As soon as he mentions it, I shiver and look up to see that the roof is open and the cloudless dark sky is above us.

"A little," I say. He snatches up the sweatshirt and pulls it over my head. I raise my arms in the air as he pulls the warm and bulky sweatshirt down into place. He grabs a blanket and wraps it around my bare legs and tucks it underneath me, snugly.

Better?" he asks as he leans over and kisses me on the mouth. I wrap my arms around his neck, pulling him closer and deepen the kiss, feeling the slow burn warm my insides.

"Mmm, much better," I mumble against his lips before I kiss him again. He pulls away and collapses on his side next to me, running a hand over my thigh.

"God, I want you so bad. But I don't want to give poor Marco a show," he moans.

"So how do you know Marco?" I ask while I run my fingers through his hair.

"Fraternity brother."

"At UCLA?" I ask as I recall reading his bio when I took the job. Undergrad at UCLA followed by an MBA from Seattle University, which is where he met John.

"Yeah, he owed me a favor." Grey smiles and I *know* there's a story there.

"Do tell."

He rolls onto his back and folds his arms behind his head. "Well, our sophomore year, he rode his motorcycle to meet us at a bar in this little beach town just south of Westwood. After we'd all had a few drinks, he decides he's going to ride his motorcycle back to campus and one thing led to the next and we were all daring him to jump his motorcycle off the top of this two-story parking garage. It was right next to the beach, so there was only sand below."

"Oh my God," I say in anticipation of the end of the story.

"Well he did it, lucky bastard barely had a scratch on him, but he buried his bike so deep in the sand dune, I thought we'd never get it out. The next thing we know a cop is laying down the law. Marco already had a few ticks on his record and I was sober by this point, so I took the blame. The cop let me go with a slap on the wrist, which wouldn't have been the case if it had been Marco."

"What happened to his bike?" I ask.

"We had to dig it out in the dark and park it. Wouldn't start. The next morning we drove our buddy's truck back and hauled it back to campus. His parents wouldn't pay to have it fixed." Grey laughs. "That damn bike sat outside the frat house for the rest of the school year."

"He's lucky he didn't kill himself," I say with a frown.

"Yeah lucky for us he's alive and still owed me a favor." Grey sits up and opens the cooler, retrieving two bottles of beer. He twists the cap off one and hands it to me and then opens the other and takes a long pull.

"You mean lucky for *you*, I bet you bring all the girls here." Images of Grey with other women cloud my mind, spiking a jealous burn. I know of his playboy reputation, but it has never bothered me before. *Until now.*

"Nope, just you." He takes another drink from the bottle and asks, "Hungry?"

"Starved."

He sets his beer down and rummages through the paper bags, pulling out cartons of Chinese food, plates, utensils and napkins. Everything looks and smells delicious and we both eat in silence for a few moments.

"You're different tonight," I say and then stuff a forkful of orange chicken into my mouth.

"What do you mean?" he asks, pausing just as he's about to take a bite.

"You're always so intense. Like in the office. And even in bed." My cheeks warm as I admit this.

"In bed?" he asks curiously.

"Yes. You are seriously intense in bed. And I mean that in the best way possible."

"And tonight?" he asks.

"And tonight, you're so relaxed and carefree, playful. It's nice to see this side of you."

"I'm always playful when I'm with you," he says a bit defensively.

"Sometimes, but not this much."

"Well this is what you get when you get to know me," he says, flashing me a mega-watt smile and opening his arms out to the side. "You like?"

I smile shyly and say, "I like."

He stuffs his fork in his mouth and chews, his smile still in place as if he's pleased with himself. And then he takes another pull from his beer.

"I'm the oldest of three boys, so I guess I'm a little intense by nature. My brothers are complete idiots so I grew up always looking out for them."

"Where are you from?"

"I grew up in the San Fernando Valley, just north of L.A."

"Where do your brothers live now?"

"Garrett lives in San Diego. He's a surfer by day and a bartender by night. And Graham's on his last year at USC film school."

"And your parents?"

"They both still live in the house I grew up in. My dad still runs Preston and Simms, although he says he's going to retire soon. But I'll believe that when I see it."

I sit up straighter. "Wait, your dad is Preston of Preston and Simms?"

"Yep."

Preston and Simms is the largest and most successful investment bank on the West Coast. I wonder how I never put that together. Grey is a financial genius, climbing the ladder to partner at record speed, the youngest at the firm. Everyone in the office talks about it. It all makes sense. Why did John not tell me?

"Wow, how did I not know that?" I ask out loud.

"Because it's something I don't like people to know," he whispers. I'm still staring at him in amazement as he picks at the label on his beer bottle. "Despite what people think, I got to where I'm at on my own. I work my ass off."

"I'm just surprised is all," I say.

"So what about you?" he asks.

I set my fork down on my plate and push it away. "What about me?"

"I know you're from Seaport, and I know you have an older sister, obviously. But what else? Is it just you and Gwen?"

I pick up my beer and take a sip, stalling although I'm not sure why. Maybe it's because it is just Gwen and I. And for as long as I can remember, that's the way it has always been. I don't like to talk about my family or my past for that matter. It hurts too much. It hurts to admit that I was never enough to make my father stay. It hurts to think that my own mother couldn't even look at me after he left, as if it was my fault that her life was falling apart; when in truth, she was the reason he left in the first place.

"Yep, it's just Gwen and I. My life's not that interesting," I say and then I start sifting through the paper bags, looking for something sweet.

Grey laughs and I look up. "What are you looking for?" he asks, slightly amused.

"Dessert," I say pointedly.

"In the small one," he says, pointing to a smaller bag behind the cooler.

I reach for it but he grabs it out of my hand before I can look inside. He stands up and makes a show of peeking inside the bag. "Aww, look what we have here."

"What is it? Is it chocolate?"

"Of course. You think I don't know about your sweet tooth? I pay attention, remember?" He raises one eyebrow and stares at me, waiting. I jump up and try to snatch the bag back, but he's too fast. He runs and dodges and I chase him until I'm breathless. I collapse on the field somewhere in the outfield and stretch out on my back, looking up at the sky. Grey walks slowly toward me and sits down beside me. He opens the bag and pulls out a small container. He peels back the lid and holds a brownie with chocolate frosting at my lips. "Want some?" he asks.

I nod and open my mouth and he very delicately feeds me a small bite and then another before devouring the entire thing himself. I lick the frosting from my lips and Grey leans over and kisses me softly. He tastes like chocolate. I bring my arms down from behind my head and run my fingers through his hair, pulling him closer until he's lying down next to me. I feel his hand slowly trail up my leg until he's gripping my ass underneath the fabric of my dress. Our breath becomes desperate, our kiss more heated as my body thrums under his touch. We lay like this for awhile, in the middle of the outfield, all hands and tongue, but nothing more.

Just when I feel as if I might explode if Grey doesn't take my clothes off and soothe the unbearable ache, he pulls away and mumbles, "Well at least I can say I made it to second base at Safeco Field."

I punch him in the arm but he only kisses me again.

"Grey, take me home. I need you," I whisper against his lips.

He slowly stands and grabs my hands, lifting me from the ground until I'm standing on my own two feet. He slips his arm around my shoulders and we walk slowly back to our picnic. I pack up all the garbage and stuff it into one of the empty bags while Grey folds up the blankets and grabs the cooler. I pull the thick sweatshirt off, feeling warm from chasing Grey all over the field, and fold it over my arm. We make our way back to the gate and he sends a text to Marco. Marco appears to unlock the gate.

"Thanks, buddy," Grey says as they do some kind of handshake.

"Anytime," Marco replies. "Nice to meet you Charley."

"You too. Thank you," I say.

We walk through the gate, Grey leading me with his hand on the small of my back and for most this would seem like the most natural thing in the world but I can feel his hand there, searing through the fabric of my dress, through my skin. Grey's presence colossal and intoxicating.

Marco locks the gate behind us and calls out, "Have a good night."

Grey waves his hand overhead as we continue to walk back in the direction we came. He reaches for my hand, intertwining our fingers and all I can hear are our footsteps until we get closer to the car and the loud noise of bar patrons fills the streets.

We're both quiet as we drive through the city streets and I wonder if Grey is driving to my place or his. But as soon as he turns onto Aurora Avenue, I know that he's taking me home.

He places his hand on my leg and says, "So... not so bad, right?"

I lean my head back into the headrest and turn my face toward him, feeling content and realizing for the first time since the night began that I actually had fun. I survived a date with Grey and I don't want the night to end. I'm not desperate to get home and wipe him from my memory but rather, desperate to get home and finish what we started on the baseball field.

"It was fun, Grey. Not so bad at all," I say quietly and I feel him squeeze my leg as a smile stretches across his face. And then I add, "Thank you."

We drive down highway 99 through the heart of the city in complete but comfortable silence as we pass the space needle, heading toward Green Lake.

Grey parks his car in front of my little house, just as tiny raindrops begin to dot the windshield.

He turns toward me and asks, "Can I talk to you about something? Inside?"

My heart literally drops into my stomach and I think, *Let it go Grey. Don't ruin a perfect night.*

"Sure," I say hesitantly.

He follows me to the porch where I withdraw my keys from my clutch and unlock the door. We both step inside and I slip my shoes off and flip on the lamp next to the couch.

We both sit down and he pulls me closer to him as if he needs to touch me while he says whatever is on his mind.

He starts by saying, "Don't freak out," and I immediately start to freak out, but only on the inside. After a long pause, he says, "I don't think we should work together anymore."

"What?" I ask, completely shocked. "We went out on one date and now you want to fire me?"

"No of course not. I would never fire you. I..."

"You want me to quit?"

"No." He tightens his grip on my leg. "You're the best assistant I've ever had, but I think that working together complicates things, not to mention that it's completely against company policy." He shifts nervously on the couch beside me and I'm very impatiently hanging on his every word.

"David and I are going to change things up a bit. Jenny will be on maternity leave starting the first of the month, so you're going to take over for her as David's assistant until we find something more permanent. Paul, our office manager, is going to be my new assistant indefinitely."

"What?" I picture David Stein in my mind. He's older and bald, round in the belly and a complete asshole to boot. His expectations are nearly impossible to meet. Jenny is the only person in the office who can tolerate him, which is why she's been his assistant for years.

"Why are you doing this?" I ask.

"We've been looking for Jenny's replacement for months and David asked for you. I actually think that you'll work well together." He smiles slightly and says, "You definitely won't put up with his shit. I see it as a great solution to our problem."

"Our problem? And what exactly is *our* problem?" I scoot away from him on the couch so that I can look him directly in the eye. I feel angry and hurt and whether these are relevant emotions right now or not is unclear, but I feel them nonetheless.

"Our problem, Charley, is that I really like you and I'm not sure what's happening between us but I don't want you to be my assistant anymore, because I want you to be part of my life outside of the office and you can't be both."

And just like that the walls are closing in all around me. I stand and walk away from him, needing to put space between us. I can't wrap my head around what he's saying.

"Let me get this straight," I say heatedly, pointing a finger at him. "*You* decided you want more from me so you made the decision to transfer me to another partner without even consulting with me first. You didn't even give me the choice to..." I stop short of finishing my sentence, suddenly aware of what I was about to say.

"The choice to what, Charley? Choose between me and your job?"

I nod and immediately regret it as I watch his face fall.

"See that's the thing Charley. Even if you were to choose your job, I couldn't work with you every day, knowing that I couldn't touch you or worse, knowing that someone else was. That's how deep I am into this thing with you."

We both just stare at each other from across the room, the air so thick with tension that I can hardly breathe. My heart feels heavy and unsure.

He breaks the silence and says, "Please don't be mad. This is all happening regardless and I wanted you to hear it from me before they tell you at the office on Monday."

"Wow. Thank you?" I say as a question, feeling so frustrated with the entire situation.

"I know you're scared, Charley. I am so much like you. I've been so focused on my career. I push people away, afraid of any distractions. But then you came along and well, something changed."

"You don't know anything about me," I say, blankly, folding my arms across my chest.

He stands and walks toward me. "I know that you push people away. That you use sex for intimacy and escape. I know that you have feelings for me but that you're so scared of them you can't even share something about yourself with me. You can't let me in. Hell, Charley, you can't even tell me your favorite color."

He moves closer to me and I take a step back.

"I think you should go," I say stoically, even though my emotions are welling up inside, tears threatening to exist.

"Charley, I'm not trying to pressure you. Just take some time to explore what you really feel for me. But don't push me away. Not like this." He pulls me into his arms and I straighten, every muscle in my body stiff as a board but I take a moment to breath him in. I can't let go of the anger though; it floods every part of me, drowning all other senses. I'm angry at Grey for making decisions for me, for redefining the simple arrangement we had, for wanting more from me when he knows I have nothing more to give. I'm angry that he thinks he knows me and a small part of me is scared that maybe he's right. I feel too much, as if I'm going to explode. I put my hands on his firm chest and push him back, hard.

"Go," I shout. "Just go." My lip is trembling and I feel like I might fall apart right in front of him.

He gives me one last glance, with defeat written all over his face as if he already knows he'll never win this battle and then he lets himself out. I quickly lock the door and move to my bedroom where I curl up in a ball on my bed and replay the entire night in my mind right up to the moment when I knew that it was time to let him go. A predictable conclusion and yet, I feel like my heart has shattered into a million pieces and I'm not sure why. And this uncertainty is possibly the most heartbreaking part of all.

# 21

## Gwen

It's early. Way too early on a Sunday morning for Charley to be knocking on my door, but she's here nonetheless. She called me late last night to tell me she was coming today, and I suspected that she was upset. A visit at eight o'clock in the morning tells me that my suspicions are correct.

I open the door, still in my pajamas, and Charley practically throws herself at me, wrapping her arms around my neck. "Hey Gwen," she whispers.

"Hi Charley. Good morning," I say, patting her on the back. She pulls back and I notice the dark circles under her eyes. Her hair is pulled back in a haphazard ponytail, strands falling out all around her face. "Coffee?" I ask her. She looks like she needs it even more than I do, as if she got less sleep than I did, which is saying something.

"Please." She steps all the way into the foyer and hangs her huge, puffy down jacket on the coat rack and then follows me into the kitchen.

"It's so quiet in here. Where is everyone?" she asks.

"John and the kids just left on a donut run. It's kind of their thing on Sunday mornings and I get to have a few minutes to myself," I say as I fill two mugs with steaming hot coffee, adding a hint of half and half to Charley's cup, just the way she likes it, and hand it to her.

She takes a sip and leans her hip against the counter. "You make the best coffee," she mumbles and then says, "It's colder then a witch's titty outside."

I shake my head at her, "God, you're so crude."

"Well it is. It's literally freezing outside. I had to scrape my windows this morning. You're so lucky you have a garage."

Her head snaps up and she looks at me apologetically as we both dwell on her word choice. *Lucky*. I'm anything but lucky. Charley is just making normal conversation but it's like everything she says takes on a new meaning.

"How are you feeling?" she asks.

"I'm fine," I say, with a shrug of my shoulder. What else is there to say? I'm not great, I'm not a mess – at least not this morning. I'm tired. I feel nauseous most days, like I did when I was pregnant with Olivia. A subtle sensation that neither has me throwing up nor sustaining a healthy appetite, just a gnawing ill feeling. Dr. Sheldan warned me about the side effects of the medication. He also reminded me that it could be worse.

"Have you talked to John?" she asks.

I shake my head and take a sip of coffee, averting my eyes to the dark liquid in my cup.

"Gwen," she says and I look up only to see the pity in her eyes. She sets her mug down on the counter and steps toward me. "Do you want me to take the kids out today so you two can talk?"

I just shake my head again. I can't even formulate words at this point. The guilt is eating away at me but still I can't tell him. He has asked several times if everything is okay, giving me the opening that I need. A chance to come clean. But I always brush it off, using the kids as an excuse. *I'm just tired* or *I feel like I'm coming down with something*. I can tell that he wants to push the issue. I can feel his hesitation, but he always backs down with a smile, massaging the tension in my shoulders, or kissing my cheek. Playing the supportive husband, a role that he does so well, and adding to the mountain of guilt I feel inside, a summit so high I may never rise above it. Tears fill my eyes and drip down my cheeks.

Charley embraces me and I lean my head against her shoulder, careful not to spill my coffee. And I am so grateful that she's here. I didn't realize how much I need her, how much I just need her here with me. It's funny how you spend your whole life holding someone's hand, walking them through life only to look up and realize that they've been holding you up just the same.

I hear the garage door open and I quickly pull myself out of Charley's arms and wipe the tears from my face. Charley wipes her eyes as well and reaches for her coffee cup.

Moments later, the kitchen is filled with laughter and harmless but persistent bickering, a complete contrast to the quiet from before. It sounds as if a circus has staked its tent right in the confines of this room but I welcome it. *This is my life*, I think.

The kids are hyped up on sugar from their chocolate rainbow-sprinkled donuts. I slip upstairs to change into warm clothes and then bundle the kids. We all retreat to the expansive back yard. It's cold outside but the sun is shining in the clear blue sky. John builds a fire in the fire pit near the beach and then we all gather on the soggy lawn for a game of baseball. More like John pitches to each of us until we manage to hit the ball and then we run around all the makeshift bases at lightning speed. It's more fun for Max this way. Laughter rings through the crisp fall air, dancing in the breeze like the fallen leaves and I feel happier than I have in weeks. Each time I glance at Max or Olivia, it's like my mind takes a snapshot of their smiling faces. Even John and Charley are laughing, so much at times that they can hardly run as they stand, doubled over, their eyes filled with tears. Every now and then, Charley gives me a look. A look that says, "isn't this great and I'm so sorry you're dying and by the way, you need to tell your husband," all at once. It's comforting to have her here, to know that she knows this isn't just some ordinary day. That today is a great day simply because I don't know how many of these days I'll have left. And in the back of my mind I can't help but wish that today was just another Sunday in a lifetime of somedays.

"Okay last pitch, Max," John yells. "It's lunchtime."

Max chokes up on the bat just like John taught him. His tongue is resting on his upper lip, his face drawn in serious concentration. John pitches the ball and Max swings just in time, smacking it over John's head as it flies through the air until it lands at the edge of the grass where it rolls into the tree line.

Charley and I scream in unison.

"Run Max," Olivia yells, jumping up and down.

John makes a big show of running across the yard, scooping up the ball and sprinting straight to home plate as Max runs his little heart out. John lets him touch home before he tags him with the ball and picks him up and swings him around.

"Safe," Charley yells. Max giggles, a huge, triumphant smile stretched across his face as John sets him down on his feet.

"Nice home run, little man," John says in a big burly voice, mussing Max's blond curls with his knuckle.

"Okay, who's hungry?" John asks.

"Me, I'm hungry," Max says, raising his hand in the air.

"Me too, Daddy," Olivia chimes in.

I start to walk toward the house to get lunch started, but John wraps his arms around me from behind and swings me around. I laugh, completely caught off guard by his playfulness.

"I got this," he says against my cheek as he kisses me softly. "Why don't you and Charley keep an eye on the fire."

"You sure?" I ask as he sets me down on my feet.

"Yep," he says and then calls out to the kids, "Okay guys, race you to the house."

The kids take off running as John growls and snarls, chasing Olivia and Max all the way to the house, their high-pitched squeals and bellowed giggles capturing my attention.

Charley and I watch until they reach the deck and then we sit down in the white Adirondack chairs that are set up around the fire pit.

"Wow, he's such a great dad," Charley says, drawing her knees up to her chest with a distant look in her eyes.

"Yeah, he is," I agree with a sigh and then shift gears. "So what's going on with you, anyway?"

"What do you mean?" she says but I know her well enough to know when she's evading my question.

"You seemed upset on the phone last night and you showed up on my doorstep at eight o'clock in the morning. So what is it?"

She looks up at me, taking a moment's pause before asking, "Why don't we ever talk about Dad?"

I wasn't expecting that question. Wasn't expecting Charley to bring up such a painful memory from our past. A memory that I had stored away all this time, locked it up tightly so that it would never resurface. And now I feel the ache in my heart, almost instantly.

"What is there to talk about, Charley?" Even I could sense the defensiveness in my tone.

"I mean, do you ever wonder about him?"

"No."

"I had a dream last night. It was so vivid, it was almost like I could smell him. Remember what he used to smell like? That salty, fishy smell when he came home from the docks?"

I remembered all too well. Only it wasn't just salt and fish, it was the whiskey too. Although it doesn't surprise me that Charley doesn't remember that detail. She was too young to understand.

"Yeah, I remember. But, Charley, what does it matter? There's no point opening old wounds."

"I just dream of him sometimes and it's like everything comes crashing back all at once. Sometimes I wonder what it would be like if he hadn't left. If Mom hadn't driven him away. If we had stayed a family."

I look at Charley and see the vulnerability that she tries so hard to mask. It reminds me of when she was young, scared like no little girl should be, her eyes so full of questions that I never answered. And maybe I should have. Maybe she wouldn't despise our mother quite so much. Or maybe she wouldn't dream of a father who was no more real than a fairy tale. But it wouldn't have changed our reality, wouldn't have changed the bad hand we had been dealt.

"Don't wonder about things that aren't real, Charley. Just focus on the present and all the good you have in your life."

"But where he is Gwen? Why have we never tried to find him?"

*Because I know exactly where he is.* I don't know why I still feel the need to protect Charley. I just can't stand the thought of shattering the image she has of our father, the pedestal that he still rests upon in her mind. At times, I feel jealous that I could never hide behind the naivety of a five-year-old. I was old enough to know the truth, never having any other image of my father than the one that he deserved.

"Let it go, Charley. He knows where we are and he's never come back for us. He obviously doesn't want to be found."

She sighs in defeat and stares into the dancing flames of the fire. I watch her expression carefully. I know she wants to tell me something and so I just wait silently for whatever it is.

"Don't you want to see him? Just once before, you know...?" Her voice trails off into a whisper, as if she's afraid to say the words. But we both know that just because she doesn't say the words, they aren't any less real. And my reality grips my heart once again. I absorb what Charley is trying to say, but deep inside I know for certain that I don't feel the need for any type of closure. I closed the door on that a long time ago, slammed it shut.

"I have no desire or need to see him," I answer honestly.

I hear John call out from the house, "Lunch is ready." I stand and stoke the fire with a long stick. The flames are slowly dying, the logs reduced to glowing embers.

"Come on, let's go eat," I say to Charley. She stands and we both trudge slowly up the extensive green lawn toward the house, and I wonder if her heart feels as heavy as mine.

The day has come and gone and after convincing Charley to stay the night, she is now camped out downstairs in the guest bedroom, even though she'll have to leave the house at the crack of dawn to drive back to the city for work. I could sense that she was reluctant to leave and, selfishly, I wanted her here as if she's some kind of buffer between John and I. A wall of protection between John and me and the throbbing truth that I have spun into lies so thick, I fear the truth may never surface. The evening was spent playing a mindless game of Monopoly with Olivia and Max; John playing the banker, of course, a job that he takes almost – painstakingly – too seriously.

I lie in bed staring up at the white ceiling, listening to John snore softly beside me. The steady rhythm of his breath soothing in its predictable way. The house is quiet, the wind the only sound as it blows off the shore and rattles the tall trees that surround the house. Every now and then, the French doors that lead from the master bedroom to the balcony rattle as if they might implode with each strong gust. Unable to bear the silence any longer, I step out of bed and tread quietly down the hall, stopping to peer into Olivia's room where I see her lying perfectly still on her side, her body barely moving with each shallow breath. She is so peaceful in sleep, as if she is still that tiny baby that I brought home from the hospital so long ago. My heart fills with familiar warmth as a smile tugs at my lips. These moments are my favorite, these quiet, stolen moments from which I could never tire. I softly close the door to Olivia's room and step across the hall to steal a similar moment with Max. The soft glow of his nightlight illuminates his face and my heart aches to reach out and touch his soft cheek. In contrast to his sister, Max is lying on his back, arms and legs sprawled out in every direction, blankets thrown to the floor as if he had a fit in his sleep. His tiny blue blanket with colorful silken tags of fabric surrounding the border – an attachment he formed when he was only four months old – is fisted in his hand as he hangs on for dear life. Although his body screams chaos, his breath is just as quiet and still as his sister's. I walk quietly to his bed and pick up the bedding from the floor. I cover him and tuck the edges of his blanket into the bottom corners of his mattress, knowing that it won't be long before the bedding is thrown to floor again. I kiss his cheek gently, careful not to wake him although nothing could wake this boy from sleep. You could set fireworks off near his bed and he would not stir.

I continue down the stairs and push open the guest bedroom door. Light seeps in from the hallway, lighting a path from the door to the bed.

"Hi," I hear Charley whisper in the dark from where she's lying in bed with the blanket pulled up to her chin.

"Couldn't sleep?" she asks.

"No. You?"

"No," she answers.

She peels back the bedding and I crawl into bed and lie next to her. She pulls the bedding snug around us as we both lie on our backs and stare up at the ceiling. And I am immediately taken back in time when we would do this very thing as children, after my father left and my mother locked herself away, out of our reach. A time when our safety net had been snagged out from underneath us and all we had was each other. Only it was usually Charley who would seek me out in the dark. Lying next to each other, I would take her hand in mine and we would whisper our fears under the veil of darkness, and it was as if nothing else existed.

Charley speaks first, her voice barely louder than a whisper, quiet as a breath.

"I think Grey and I broke up," she says.

I don't respond. I just wait patiently for her to explain.

"He transferred me to another partner because he can't work with me any longer. He wants more." She lets out a frustrated breath. I have heard this same story a million times, each different and yet the same. They always want more from Charley but she insists that she hasn't more to give, nor does she want to. But it's hard to miss the note of disappointment and longing in her voice.

"And you don't want more? With him?" I ask, although I think I already know the answer.

"I don't know."

I'm shocked by her uncertainty. That was not the answer I was expecting. Treading lightly, I ask, "It's different with him, isn't it?"

I hear her exhale loudly and then she says, "I feel something for him, but that scares me more than the thought of losing him."

I know that she only admits this because we're lying in the dark, whispering like the child versions of ourselves and she knows that I will never speak of it again. That whatever fears and secrets she confides will be kept in the dark, a silent pact that we made long ago.

"Maybe it's time to take a leap of faith. Maybe it's time to ask yourself if letting him go is more unbearable than the fear of holding on."

"The fear is crippling," she whispers. And I know exactly what she means. I know that kind of fear.

Charley is quiet for a long time. Her breath is even and calm, but I can feel her heart beating erratically in her chest.

She reaches over and wraps her hand around mine. It's my turn.

"I'm afraid to tell John. I'm afraid that what little strength I have will crumble and he'll see my weakness and I need to be strong for my family. I can't fall apart, Charley. It's like keeping this from him holds me together, keeps me strong. I'm afraid that once I tell him, I'll shatter into a million pieces and never be whole again."

Tears slowly trickle down my cheeks. It feels so good to say it out loud. My fears.

Charley remains quiet but squeezes my hand more firmly. Finally after what feels like hours, she says, "Maybe it's time you let go, Gwen. Maybe it's time you let us be the strong ones. It's okay to fall. John and I will be there to catch you."

A lonely sob escapes as if it has been locked away waiting for release.

"Remember when we used to sneak into Mrs. Dunmark's backyard?" she asks, conjuring images to mind from our childhood. I sniffle, wipe my eyes and take a deep breath, welcoming the distraction.

"Yes, that woman never mowed her lawn," I say, wiping my nose with the back of my hand. "We used to pretend we were in a meadow, like in *The Sound of Music*."

"Right. Remember when all the dandelions would turn from bright yellow to balls of white, cotton tufts?"

"We called it our field of hope," I remember with a smile, wondering where she's going with this trip down memory lane.

"We used to pull them from the ground one by one, close our eyes tight and make a wish before blowing the seeds into the air. You always wished to marry Ralph Macchio, remember?"

Charley laughs quietly to herself and then says, "God, you were so obsessed with *The Karate Kid*. I never thought he was that cute, but you dreamed of that guy."

I do remember. I remember covering the walls of my bedroom with pictures of him, cut out with care from magazines like *Teen Beat* and *Bop*. I guess some would call it an obsession, but it was more like a distraction, an escape. And Charley's right. I did love that movie, but more because it gave me hope, wishing for a Mr. Miyagi to come and take me under his wing.

"I would never tell you my wish. You would beg me to tell you, but I never did," Charley says.

"You were so stubborn like that," I say with a small smile as I picture a string bean of a girl standing in a field of weeds, arms folded across her chest in defiance as long brown hair whipped across her face in the wind. *So stubborn.*

"I was so afraid that if I told, it wouldn't come true. But you know what I wished for every single time?"

"What?" I ask.

"To be strong like you. You were my rock, still are. I wanted so bad to not be afraid anymore."

This confession pangs around in my heart, trying to find its place. I had no idea. I remember being afraid of everything, worrying about Mother, having clean clothes, what we were going to eat, how much money we had. Worrying about Charley, trying to be strong for her.

"My wish was never to marry Ralph Macchio. Well sometimes it was," I admit. "I usually wished to be fearless like you, Charley. You had this roaring confidence. Like 'what you see is what you get.'. You never worried what people thought of you, you were always yourself. You did whatever you wanted, whenever you wanted. You never worried about the consequences. I was worried sick about everything and everyone. I guess I still am. It's exhausting."

"I've never been fearless. Look at me, Gwen. I'm afraid to even throw out a receipt, just in case I want to return something. I can't even commit to a pair of designer jeans. I'm a complete mess."

"You're stronger than you think, Charley."

"So are you," she says. We lay in the dark, quietly, lost in our own thoughts. And the biggest fear I own bubbles to the tip of my tongue, begging to be told.

"I'm afraid to die," I whisper, so quietly that I think she may not have heard me.

But after a moment, she squeezes my hand and then I hear her whisper just as softly, "I'm afraid to die *alone*."

# 22
## *Gwen*

Well, Gwen, your scans look good. They look real good. The treatment agrees with you," Dr. Sheldan says as he looks over black and white images on a large computer screen. I can't make heads or tails of anything that he's looking at from where I sit on the exam table in a flimsy, cotton patient gown. My bare legs are hanging over the edge, swinging nervously back and forth, as I try to read more from his expression, his tone.

"How are you feeling," he asks as he glides toward me from across the small room on his wheeled stool, stopping just inches from the exam table.

I tell him I feel good, considering the circumstances but confide that the constant nausea keeps me from eating most days.

"You need to slow down and take care of yourself. You need your strength. Make sure you're resting. And try drinking vitamin enriched supplement drinks when you can't eat whole foods."

I agree to take better care of myself, feeling defenseless; I have no other choice. He puts his stethoscope nubs in his ears and stands, moving behind me as he peels open my gown and places the disc-shaped end of the stethoscope on the bare skin of my back. I flinch from the raw touch, the cold metal taking my breath away.

"You're not having any chest pain?" he asks. I think back to the previous days and weeks and can't recall having chest pain, at least nothing significant. I shake my head.

"Your heart looks a little enlarged on your scan and your lung sounds aren't what I'd like them to be. I'm going to schedule you for a cardiac work-up in the next few weeks just to be safe. Nothing to worry about. Okay?"

I nod. My mind is racing. All I can think is more appointments, more tests, more lies. It's getting harder and harder to keep this from John.

When my appointment is over and I am dressed and walking to my car, I pull out my cell phone and call Charley at work. I give her the update and we both agree that I have to tell John sooner rather then later and, most certainly, before the cardiac tests that will take me away from Seaport for another day. When I end the call, I am determined to tell John. I drive home practicing the words over and over aloud in the car. The words that I have feared telling John for far too long.

Hours later, after the kids are asleep, and John is in the shower, I sit in my bed with my back against the headboard. The television is on in the background, but my mind is focused on telling John the truth. My heart pounds in my head with anticipation.

When John finally emerges from the bathroom followed by a plume of steam, I am so twisted up inside; I think I might be sick. I watch him move to the closet in only a towel wrapped around his waist, taking in the cut of his abs and chest.

"You okay?" he asks as the towel drops to the floor. He pulls on a clean pair of white boxer shorts.

I realize from the metallic taste on my tongue that I'm biting down on my lip with my teeth, hard enough to draw blood.

I release my lip and my words hang suspended between us, just floating on air, out of my reach.

John walks to the bed and slides in next to me, lying on his side with his head propped up on one arm. He looks up at me, his brow deeply furrowed.

"Is it Charley? Because you haven't been yourself since you let her back into your life. Did she do something? Again?" His blue eyes are pleading.

I shake my head, stalling. My thoughts are a jumbled mess like a page of scrambled words as I try to make sense of the ones I rehearsed in the car. My mind is coming up short, empty.

"It's not Charley," I say, my voice catching on her name. I swallow hard and stare at my hands as they mindlessly pull at a loose thread on the comforter that is spread across my lap. I can feel John's gaze on me, so strong it's like he's burning a hole in the side of my face. "It's...I..."

In that second, I hear a blood-curdling scream from down the hall. It's Max. And without hesitation, I leap from the bed and run to his bedroom. I can feel John right behind me.

I push open the door and find Max sitting up in his bed, his face flushed red and wet with tears.

I go to his bed and sit on the edge, pulling him into my arms.

"Max, what is it?" I ask, drawing his face into my shoulder as I run my hand down his sweaty back.

"I had a bad dream," he mumbles through a chorus of sniffles.

John turns the bedside lamp on and says, "It's okay, buddy. There's nothing to be afraid of."

"There was a bad man and I was running away but I wasn't fast enough," he chokes out.

"It's okay. It was just a dream. There's no bad man," I say, my heart breaking.

"Can you sleep with me Mommy?" he asks, throwing his little arms around my neck and hanging on as if his life depended on it.

I look up at John as I run my fingers through Max's hair, his blonde curls damp with sweat. John nods with a small smile and I say, "Of course, Bubs. Come on let's get you tucked in."

I settle Max on his side and slide in behind him as John pulls the bedding up to Max's chin. He kisses each of us on the forehead and switches off the bedside lamp, bathing the room in darkness. Feeling Max tense, I put my arm around him, squeezing him tight, willing him to feel safe.

"Goodnight," John whispers as he leaves the room. I lie in the darkness with Max in my arms, listening to his breath until I feel his body slump and I know he's asleep once more.

I take a breath and blow it out, feeling restless with guilt as I realize how relieved I am at the interruption. I know I have to tell John, and, as ashamed as I am to admit it; I'm glad that it won't be tonight.

# 23

## *Charley*

The cold of winter has officially arrived, leaving Seattle bare and colorless. Golden leaves lay in soggy piles along the streets, the sky an endless sea of gray that nearly suffocates those who dare to mourn the sharp blue skies and vivid shades of summer. The damp cold pierces my lungs as if the air is made of tiny shards. I place my overnight bag in the back of my car along with two pies that I picked up at the bakery and a box of frosted sugar cookies shaped like turkeys for Olivia and Max. Gwen always hosts Thanksgiving at her house, where she cooks an amazing dinner and I tolerate my mother for a few hours. There are usually a few strays, friends of Gwen and John, who are alone for the holiday or sometimes she invites the neighbors. Whoever their guests might be, it is a welcome distraction from having to hold a conversation with my mother. But this year, I look forward to the holiday. I want to make it memorable for Gwen and the kids. I feel the urge to carve each moment in stone as if I might forget it otherwise. As if I don't know how many more moments, how many more Thanksgivings, how many more of anything I will have with Gwen.

I pull the car away from the curb and drive to the freeway, where I head north toward Seaport. I haven't seen Gwen since the day following my disastrous date and I feel anxious to pull her into my arms, to make sure that she's still here as if she might turn to ash and slowly blow away in the wind in my absence. I call her every Wednesday morning at nine and we stay on the phone until she is done with her treatment. I have become a pro at disguising our phone calls at work, my new boss not as tolerating as Grey.

*Grey.*

I haven't spoken to him, other than the cordial moments we share in the office. His phone calls and texts go unanswered. I'm not sure what I want. I miss him so much and yet the fear is stronger, sharper, obscuring all else. I see the look in his eyes, know the hurt that he tries so hard to mask when he sees me. And still I avoid him, stubbornly. I feel my own hurt, although I'm not sure where it stems from or who it belongs to.

I exit the freeway and drive by memory to Gwen's house hidden away down a long and narrow drive. As I walk to the front door, I can hear the seagulls call and the gentle waves lap at the shore, impervious to the cold or change of season. Reminding me that some things are constant.

I knock loudly and then let myself in, already knowing that Gwen is busy in the kitchen and John is most likely watching a football game in the family room.

Sure enough, I find Gwen wrapped in a fall-themed apron leaning over a hot oven as she bastes a large turkey.

"Hey," I call out as I place my bakery items on the counter.

Gwen stands, closes the oven door and turns toward me.

"Hey," she says and folds me in a hug.

I can't help but notice the swollen cheeks and the sharpness of her bones as I hug her. She looks puffy yet thin and frail at the same time. Overall the change is subtle, but I swallow the thick lump that has grown in my throat.

"How are you feeling?" I whisper.

"I'm good," she says as she wipes a trail of beaded moisture from her brow.

"And John?" I ask.

"Let's not talk about it today, Charley." She sighs. "I'm going to tell him tonight. I'm finally going to do it, I swear."

The look of resolve in her eyes assures me that she's telling the truth. She's finally going to tell him and maybe now we can both sleep at night. He's been worried about her and with the slew of tests coming up, including the cardiac workup; we both know that keeping it all from John will be impossible.

"Okay. Good. Well Happy Thanksgiving," I say in a pathetic attempt to change the subject.

"Happy Thanksgiving," she says with a smile. "Now grab that peeler over there and get to work on these potatoes."

"Yes, ma'am." I move to the sink and begin to peel the potatoes. "Where are the kids?" I ask, noticing for the first time how quiet it is.

"They're cleaning Max's room." I look at her in shock. "I know, but they built a fort in there yesterday and I refuse to clean it up. It's a disaster."

"Good for you."

She takes a peeled potato from my hand and begins to cut it in quarters beside me.

"Charley, I have to tell you some..." she starts to say something but Max and Olivia stomp down the stairs and interrupt her.

"Aunt Charley," Max squeals and wraps his arms around my legs. I put down the peeler and wipe my hands on a dishtowel before picking him up and planting a sloppy kiss on his soft, buttery cheek. "Hey Max. Hi, Olivia," I say as I pull her into my side.

"Hi Aunt Charley. Guess what?" she asks with eyes as big as plums.

"What?"

"I got picked for the lead part. I'm Annie." Her face is lit up like Christmas and I couldn't be more proud of her.

"Wow! That's amazing. I knew you could do it."

"You'll be there, right? In May, for opening night?"

"Of course. I wouldn't miss it. I can't wait."

She turns to Gwen. "Mom, can I watch TV in your room? Dad's watching football."

"Sure Honey," Gwen says. I set Max down on his feet and he runs out of the room, yelling, "See ya, wouldn't wanna be ya."

"Nice. Where'd he pick that up?" I ask.

"School," Gwen replies while she continues to cut the potatoes.

"Anyway, Charley..."

I hear a knock on the door and a moment later I hear my mother's voice. I inwardly cringe. "Smells wonderful in here. Hello Gwen," she chimes as she sets two large reusable grocery bags on the counter and kisses Gwen's cheek. "Hello Charlotte," she says and pats me on the shoulder cautiously.

"Hi Mom," Gwen says.

And I reply with a curt, "Hello Connie."

"Can't you just call me Mom?" she asks. *Here we go*, I think.

"Sure, when you start calling me Charley," I retort, straining to smile, reminding myself to remain polite. It's Thanksgiving.

164

"Fair enough," she concedes. "Now where are my grandchildren?"

"Olivia's upstairs and Max is in the family room with John," Gwen says and my mother walks into the other room as I hear Max yelling out, "Grammy, Grammy."

"At least someone's excited to see her," I say under my breath.

"Charley," Gwen warns.

"I know. I know." I let out the breath of frustration that I had been holding and try to figure out for the hundredth time why I can't get past my anger. When I look at my mother, I still see a bitter, helpless woman drowning in self-pity, as if she had been swallowed by grief. And yet, nobody died. I know that she's not that person anymore, but in my mind, she always will be.

Gwen tries to tell me something, *again*, but is once again interrupted by a strong knock on the front door. The expression on her face is of dread as she calls out to John.

"Coming," he says and I hear him open the front door.

"I tried to tell you. I'm sorry," is all Gwen says seconds before I see him standing in the kitchen, with John at his side, holding an expensive-looking bottle of wine.

Our eyes lock for what feels like forever, until John steps forward and kisses my cheek, breaking the trance. "Hey Charley. Happy Thanksgiving, I didn't hear you come in." I can hear Gwen speak to *him* as I watch her pull him into a hug. He hands her the bottle of wine and she thanks him.

John opens the fridge and pulls out two bottles of beer, handing one to him and I continue to stare. The air is thick and charged.

"Game's on," John states.

"Make yourself at home," Gwen says.

He steps toward me hesitantly. "Charley," he says quietly. And then in a whisper, "I tried to call you, to ask if it was okay." I feel all eyes on me and hear nothing but silence and the steady drum of my heart.

Despite feeling shocked, foolish and caught off guard, despite feeling a sense of relief to see him, to feel him this close, and despite feeling angry at the situation and at Gwen for that matter, I smile, wave my hand through the air and say, "It's fine. Happy Thanksgiving, Grey." I lean forward and kiss him on the cheek, inhaling greedily, filling my senses with him.

"Happy Thanksgiving," he whispers against my ear.

I step away and turn immediately back toward the sink and pick up a potato. I close my eyes and try to clear my mind – my heart – of the mess of emotions swirling like a storm inside. When I hear John and Grey retreat to the family room, Gwen is at my side.

"John invited him at poker last week. I tried to tell John that it was a bad idea, but he couldn't *uninvite* him. He was going to be alone for the holiday."

"It's fine, Gwen," I say, although it's hard to leave the anger out of my tone. I begin to peel the potato in my hand, slicing at it harshly until there is hardly any flesh left.

# 24

## *Gwen*

Dinner is ready, finally. Although it's more like Thanksgiving lunch given that it is only two o'clock in the afternoon. The timing is a tradition of sorts. This was supposed to be a good day. Yet all I feel is tension. Rolling off Charley in waves, building slowly in my mother's comments, hidden underneath Grey's unusual silence. The day is full of tension and I feel exhausted. So tired that I silently wish for a moment to sneak upstairs and lie down. My ankles and feet feel heavy and swollen from standing in the kitchen all morning, my back aches and my head throbs. But I put on my smile as Charley and I set all the prepared dishes on the table, including the Vegetable Tofu Bake that my mother insisted upon. Her vegan diet quietly crept itself into my traditional dishes. And honestly, I'm too exhausted to care. *Real butter, vegan butter – who cares?*

I call my family to the formal dining room table and everyone takes their place. John opens a bottle of wine and begins to fill glasses. I say a small prayer and then explain to Grey our tradition of sharing what we are thankful for. I begin.

"I'm thankful for my family and friends," I start. I try to keep the tears at bay and the emotion from my throat, but this year my words hold so much more meaning than those of the past. "I'm thankful for this day, for every day that we have together." Charley wipes a single tear from her eye, as she stares at her empty plate. I'm thankful that she doesn't look at me now, or I might not be able to hold back my own tears.

John goes next. "I'm thankful for my beautiful wife," he pauses and leans over and kisses me on the lips, "and for my two completely crazy children who I love more than this world!"

"I'm not crazy, Daddy," Max says with a giggle.

"You're the craziest," I say, reaching over and poking his side with my finger, earning a belly laugh that makes my heart ache. "Why don't you go next? What are you thankful for Max?"

"Um, I'm thankful for my house and the big giant turkey cookies that Aunt Charley brought."

Everyone laughs. It's hard not to.

Olivia looks deep in thought while we all look to her and wait for her to speak.

"I'm thankful for the lead part in the school play," she says triumphantly.

"Yay," we all say in unison and clap for her. She is absolutely beaming and I feel so happy for this moment.

"That's wonderful darling. I knew you could do it!" my mother says, shaking a closed fist over her heart.

Charley is seated next to Olivia and I watch her take a deep breath before she says, "I'm thankful for all this wonderful food and for everyone seated at this table." It's the same thing she says every year. I watch her glance quickly across the table at Grey and then pick up her wine and take a big gulp.

"Well," my mother says, "I'm thankful for this family and for our health." I look at Charley and Charley looks at me, our eyes lock for a moment before I turn away.

Grey clears his throat and says, "I'm thankful for all the amazing people in my life and for your gracious invitation. Thank you for having me." I am just about to raise my glass in a toast when Grey looks at Charley and adds, "And I'm thankful for you, Charley. For reminding me what I've been missing in life."

I watch all the color drain from Charley's face as the table falls silent.

"I'm thankful for Aunt Charley too," Max blurts out and you can see the relief in Charley's eyes as the moment is softened, the attention lifted from her and centered on Max.

"Thank you, Max," Charley says. Grey's eyes are still fixed on Charley while I watch her look at everything, anything, but Grey. I stand with my wine glass in hand and say, "Happy Thanksgiving everyone. Cheers. Now dish up."

"Cheers," carry on from around the room accompanied by the chime of crystal as everyone raises their glass in toast. Dishes are passed around the table one by one as conversation is sparked. John and Grey talk about the stock market as Mother and Olivia discuss the school play. Max is asking Charley, over Olivia's head, how many cookies he will get to eat after dinner and I sit and take it all in, feeling grateful yet utterly exhausted once again and unable to eat more than a few bites of the dinner that I spent the entire morning preparing.

I stand at the kitchen sink lost in thought as I watch John, Grey, Olivia, and Max in the back yard, fully engaged in a game of flag football. They run frantically back and forth beyond the glass doors, surrounded by white clouds of breath, completely oblivious to the wintry temperature.

"You okay?" Charley asks from behind me as she sets more dirty dishes on the counter. My hands are submerged in a sink-full of warm, soapy water as I mindlessly scrub the platinum serving ware that I use only on special occasions.

"Yeah," I sigh. She stands next to me, picks up a wet plate that I already washed and dries it with a blue and white striped dishtowel, as the backyard football game catches her attention.

"Doesn't it make you wonder about your future just a little bit when you see how good he is with my kids?" I ask quietly of Grey.

She sighs next to me and a moment goes by before she answers. "It makes me think about *his* future, Gwen, but not mine. I don't see a future with him."

"Come on, Charley. You don't watch him and wonder for just a second what it would be like to get married and have kids?"

"Wow. Married with kids? That's a stretch, don't you think?"

I start to open my mouth to say something but suddenly Grey is opening one of the glass doors. He steps inside, his presence almost too big for the usually vast space of my kitchen.

"Just grabbing another beer for John and me. Do you girls need any help?" Grey asks politely.

"We got it. Just keep those kids busy and I'll be happy," I say with a smile.

Charley is quiet beside me. She turns to put a dish away in the cabinet and bumps into Grey. I keep my back to them, giving them a little privacy.

"Charley, can I talk to you for a minute? In private," I hear Grey whisper.

"No, Grey. You've said enough today, don't you think?" Charley says quietly.

"Not nearly enough. We need to talk about this." Grey is still whispering and I struggle to hear while I continue to scrub dishes in the sink. Part of me feels like I should give them more privacy but the better part of me is too curious to leave the room.

"There's nothing to talk about," I hear Charley say more loudly and then I hear dishes clash and the slam of a cabinet door.

"Come on Charley. This isn't over, not for me."

"Yeah, well that's too bad because I've already moved on."

I'm shocked at how hostile she is toward him. I slowly turn around just in time to see Charley walk out of the room, leaving Grey standing with his hands on his hips and his head hung low. I can't help but feel sorry for him.

"I'm sorry Grey," I manage to say as I dry my hands on a dishtowel.

"Not your problem Gwen, but thanks," he says. He grabs two beer bottles from the fridge and heads back outside.

My mother walks into the kitchen at that moment, her hands spread out as she balances several dirty wine glasses between her fingers.

"Mom, can you finish washing these for me? I'll be right back."

171

"Sure, honey," she answers while setting the wine glasses one at a time on the kitchen counter.

I find Charley in the family room standing with her hands over her face.

"Charley, don't you think that was a little harsh, even for you?" She drops her hands and looks over at me.

"Stay out of it, Gwen," she snaps.

"No. It's Thanksgiving and Grey is my guest. He hasn't done anything wrong."

"No? This is *my* family and he's intruding. He shouldn't be here."

"We invited him, Charley. He's welcome here. Don't be rude."

"Rude? He should keep his mouth shut then. And yes, you're right, you invited him. Without even asking me if it was okay. You know how tortured I've been about this. Why would you do that?"

Charley is shouting at me and I've had enough of her selfishness. I'm too tired for this. I shout back.

"I can invite whoever I want. It's my house. I don't have to ask your permission, Charley. It's not my fault that you're so fucked up."

The minute the words slip from my mouth, I want to take them back. But it's too late. Charley's glaring eyes grow wide in shock, cementing the guilt in the pit of my stomach.

"Girls, what's going on?" my mother asks as she stomps into the room, looking back and forth between the two of us.

"Oh I'm *fucked* up now? Here we go!" Charley scoffs without missing a beat, as if my mother's sudden presence and her question do not exist.

"Charlotte, watch your mouth," my mother demands.

"Mother, stay out of it," Charley says, her eyes still directed at me, tiny slits spitting fire.

"I will not stay out of it. I am your mother."

Charley looks toward her then and says venomously, "Really? You could have fooled me. You want to know why I'm such a mess?" Charley looks back at me.

"Because my *mother* threw my father out and then pretended as if I didn't exist. Nothing like losing both your parents in one day. How's that for fucked up?"

I hear my mother suck in a breath from across the room.

"Charley, you're being unfair," I say, looking at the defeat in my mother's eyes. Charley knows exactly which button to push when it comes to our mother.

"I'm being unfair am I? I'll tell you what's unfair, Gwen. The fact that you lie to John. Every. Single. Day. You can't even tell your husband the truth and you have the nerve to stand there and tell me that *I'm* fucked up."

I flinch at her words. She starts to walk out of the room toward the front door. I follow her.

"Just walk out Charley, you're so good at that," I yell after her.

"Learned it from the best," she mumbles as she grabs her coat and purse and walks out the door, slamming it so hard that the walls rattle.

I am left shaking in anger yet instantly feeling guilty for allowing our fight to get so out of control. I could have easily apologized and smoothed everything over like I always do but instead something had snapped inside me. Tears start to fall down my cheeks and I suddenly feel exhausted, so exhausted that standing on my feet is almost too much to bear. Within seconds my head begins to spin and my breath feels labored, as if I can't get enough air. I move to sit down in the chair just a few steps away but I don't make it that far. I feel my knees buckle as I reach out with my hands, but all I feel is the cold tile against my cheek before everything is black and I am lost in a sea of nothingness.

# 25
## *Charley*

I slam the front door with every ounce of anger I feel and run to my car. The cold sea air is a shock to my heated body, tapping down the inferno flaring inside me. I climb into my car, throw it in reverse and back out of the driveway without another thought. My need to get far away from my family, from Grey, fueling my escape. I only make it as far as Tony's Tavern, on the edge of Main Street in the historical downtown Seaport. A local favorite dating back to the year before I was born.

I pull open the heavy wooden door and make my way through the dim-lit room to the bar where I plop down on a red vinyl barstool that has seen better days. The bar smells like stale beer and cigarette smoke even though no one has been allowed to smoke in here since 2005, but years of heavy smoking cling to the walls as a reminder of the past.

Tony, who has also seen better days, approaches me from behind the old mahogany bar. He has lost all his hair on his head but his gray beard and mustache grow as wild as his protruding belly.

"Well if it isn't Charlotte Brant. Something tells me you could use a drink?" he says with a wink as he wipes down the bar in front of me.

"Vodka tonic," I say, setting my purse down on the stool beside me. And then add, "Make it a double."

Without a reply, Tony sets an ice-filled glass on the bar and reaches for the good stuff on the back shelf. He pours until it nearly touches the rim, adds a splash of tonic and a lime wedge and slides the glass closer to me.

"Thanks," I say and then bring the glass to my lips.

Tony only nods and then moves on to the only other patrons desperate enough to be here on Thanksgiving. Three lonely men spaced out evenly along the bar. For a moment I imagine why these men are here, alone on Thanksgiving, and I feel a hint of guilt for abandoning my own family when I should feel lucky to have them, to have somewhere else to be for the holiday. But I'm still too angry to feel grateful. I'm angry at Gwen for inviting Grey and not warning me. I'm angry at Grey for showing up and pushing the issue of us when I can hardly stand to be in the same room with him. I'm angry at the pang of longing that hit me as I watched Grey in the backyard with Olivia and Max, catching me off guard. I'm angry at my mother for being the reminder of all the things I try so hard to forget. Overall, I'm just tired of feeling like there's a gaping hole inside me that I can't seem to fill.

I guzzle my drink down and order another, followed by yet another, burying my self-pity and my anger with each gulp. Welcoming the fuzzy, blurred edge of my reality.

In the vague silence of the bar, a song begins to play from the jukebox, louder and more obvious than the faded background music that was playing before. A song that I instantly recognize, a song that carries me back to a time long ago, back to a certain someone from long ago. I turn in my stool to the jukebox and nearly choke on my drink. Standing like a breath of fresh air, with his hands in the pockets of his jeans and a warm smile spread across his face is Ben.

He shrugs his shoulders and just stands there with those clear, blue eyes locked on my face while *our* song pipes through the speakers in the near empty bar. My head is trying to catch up to the shock of my heart as he walks toward me.

"What are you doing here?" I manage to say as he sits on the stool next to me. I can't help but glance at his left hand resting on the bar, noting the absence of a ring.

"Just finished a shift at the clinic. Thought I'd grab a quick beer before going to see my Mom. What are *you* doing here?" he asks.

I only shrug and turn back toward the bar and down the rest of my drink.

Tony silently brings Ben a bottle of beer and Ben nods toward Tony in thanks.

"Another please, Tony," I call out.

"Tough day?" Ben asks.

"You could say that," I respond. I feel intoxicated by the vodka, the song that still plays on the jukebox, and Ben's presence. Suddenly wanting to lose myself in more than the alcohol. Something or someone that could make me forget.

And as I finish another drink, and Ben sips his one and only beer like a responsible adult; we start to talk. We talk about his shift at the clinic, how he left New York to come home and care for his ailing mother, how it feels to be back in Seaport, and all the things that remain the same in this small town. We talk about him until the conversation eventually turns to me and by this time, I've had too much to drink and the words just pour out of me. About the day, my mother, Gwen telling me that I'm fucked up, about Grey. The words continue to pour out until I find myself empty of anger and filled with longing as I stare into Ben's eyes. The moment is charged as we both fall silent. Ben reaches over and tucks a lock of hair behind my ear, his finger grazing my cheek subtly. My heart beats heavy in my chest.

"I never forgot you," he says quietly. And I am all out of words. I have nothing to say, my insides churn, a lethal mix of regret, shame, and longing. I lean into him slowly until our lips touch and I feel his hand on my face, caressing my cheek. My body thrums as his warm lips work against mine, a familiar taste that sends me spiraling back in time. My eyes are closed and I crave more, wanting to get lost, to leave it all behind. But a phone ringing interrupts the moment. Ben pulls away and looks into my eyes, his lucid eyes glazed with his own longing.

He pulls his phone out of his pocket and glances at the screen. "It must be you," he says.

"Oh," I say in a daze, reaching for my purse. The ringing gets louder as I dig around in my purse until I find the source. I instantly see that I have several missed calls from my mother and her name is flashing across the screen.

"Hello," I say, holding the phone to my ear.

"Charlotte," my mother says, frantic. "I've been trying to reach you. It's Gwen." As soon as I hear Gwen's name, my heart plummets. "She collapsed. We're at Seattle General. Where are you?"

"What? Oh my God. Is she okay? Oh my God." My thoughts are racing. *The cancer. The cancer.* Is all I can think. "Mom, Gwen has..."

I try to tell her, but my mother interrupts me. "Charlotte just get here," she yells into the phone and hangs up.

The phone drops from my hand and I look up to find Ben's pleading eyes searching mine.

"I have to go. It's Gwen. I have to go," I jump up off the stool, nearly falling down on my intoxicated legs. I reach down and grab my phone, stuffing it frantically in my purse and search for my car keys. "I have to go," I keep repeating.

"Charley, slow down. What's wrong? Go where? Where do you have to go?" Ben says, reaching for my hands to steady me.

"Seattle General. It's Gwen. Oh my God. I have to go," I say again, nearly breathless.

"Tony, can we get a cup of coffee to go," Ben calls out. "Charley, calm down. I'll drive you. You've had too much to drink."

I nod as tears start to fall down my cheeks. Ben leaves money on the bar, grabs the cup of coffee and the car keys out of my hand. We walk to my car where he opens the passenger door and I mindlessly crawl inside. Within minutes we're on the freeway, heading toward Seattle, toward the hospital, toward Gwen. *Please let her be okay*, I keep repeating in my mind as I sit with my knees bent into my chest, cradling the hot cup of coffee that Ben is forcing me to drink. I can't stop crying as I think of the fight that Gwen and I had. *Please don't let that be the last thing I say to her.*

"What happened?" Ben finally asks.

"I don't know. Gwen collapsed," I say. And then I tell him the truth, unable to keep it inside another minute. "She has cancer. Stage four. She's been going through treatment to give her more time. But it's not good. No one knows but me." And this thought brings on a whole new realm of worry. "Oh my God, no one knows what's wrong with her. We have to get to the hospital," I say, frantic.

"It's okay. We'll get there. She's in good hands, Charley. Her records are all computerized. The doctors will have access to her chart. They'll know, Charley, they'll know."

"But John. Oh God, John. He doesn't know." I feel desperate. Desperate to be there, to be there when they tell John.

"He'll know soon enough," Ben mumbles. He doesn't ask questions. He just drives and places his hand on my knee when I begin to sob harder. The drive seems to take hours and all I can think of is Gwen, and what this means for all of us.

Ben parks in the physician's parking lot right in front of the hospital and I run inside following Ben's lead to the emergency room.

As soon as we walk into the waiting room, I see John pacing back and forth, his hand spread out over his mouth. And then I spot my mother sitting in the corner. With Grey. Olivia and Max are nowhere in sight. I go straight to my mother with Ben trailing behind me.

"Mom," I say as she looks up at the sound of my voice.

"Charlotte," she says and stands, wrapping her arms around me. I stand awkwardly, unsure of what to do. I haven't hugged my mother in years. She releases me and I start to approach John when a doctor walks out of the double swinging doors, grabbing John's attention.

"Mr. Porter?" the older physician says.

"Yes, I'm John Porter," John says, walking closer to the doctor as we all huddle around him.

"I'm Dr. Hoffwell. Your wife is suffering from congestive heart failure. We've stabilized her and we're doing everything we can to treat it. But sometimes the damage is irreversible. Only time will tell, we won't know anything for twenty-four to forty-eight hours."

"Congestive heart failure? I don't understand. She was fine just a few hours ago."

"Mr. Porter, this is a common complication of Gwen's treatment. Unfortunately the medication has weakened her heart muscle. Her heart's been working overtime and now her system is backed up."

"Treatment? What treatment?"

I step up and put my hand on John's back. "John, Gwen's been undergoing treatment for cancer. She wanted to tell you..."

"Cancer? What are you saying, Charley? How do you know this? What do you mean 'she wanted to tell me'?" He looks at me, completely baffled. His eyes grow dark with fear.

"John, Gwen has cancer. Again. She wasn't sure how to tell you because it's...it's..."

"IT'S WHAT, CHARLEY?" John yells impatiently. He's suddenly angry. My eyes flood with tears as all eyes are on me, even Dr. Hoffwell's.

"It's terminal," I manage to choke out.

John's face turns ghostly white. "What? I can't believe this," he whispers. No one else speaks. My mother is crying quietly with her hand on John's shoulder. Grey's expression is pained but even he is speechless. Only Ben speaks as he addresses Dr. Hoffwell, "Is she awake? Does she need surgery?"

"She's sedated to keep her comfortable. We have her on several medications to help increase her heart function and decrease her fluid levels. I don't feel that surgery is necessary; we caught it pretty early. For now, we just wait and give the drugs time to work in her favor."

"Can I see her?" John asks.

"She's being moved to the ICU as we speak. Just give the nurses about twenty minutes and then you can see her, but only one visitor at a time."

"Thank you, doctor," John says.

"Of course," Dr. Hoffwell says and then walks back through the doors to the emergency room.

"Where are Olivia and Max?" I ask, desperate to protect them from all of this.

"They're at Kristin's next door," my mother answers. "They didn't see Gwen, thank God, but they saw the ambulance. They're probably scared, but I just had to come. We didn't know what was wrong. I found her in the foyer right after you left." My mother brings her hand to her mouth in despair, tears streak her eyes and cheeks. "She was just lying there, face down on the tile. I tried to wake her and then I screamed for John."

"It's okay, Mom. You did the best you could," I say. But my heart is breaking. I did this. She looked so awful today, she looked so tired and then we fought. I did this.

John looks at me with tears in his eyes, "How could she not tell me, Charley? How could YOU not tell me?" And then he steps toward me and grabs me by the arms, his fingers pressing into my flesh. His face screams in agony and he shakes me in his grasp and yells, "How long? How long has this been going on?"

I flinch and whisper, "She was diagnosed over two months ago." He releases me and his shoulders visibly fall as if all the fight has left him in a rush, his face drawn in defeat. "I'm sorry John. It wasn't my place to tell you." But now when I think of the fact that we almost lost Gwen today, maybe I should have told John. Maybe letting Gwen keep this from him was the wrong thing to do. Maybe I was blinded by the bond that Gwen and I shared because of this. It was just her and I against the world, just like it used to be. Is that why I didn't push her harder to tell John? It was dangerous to not tell John, completely reckless. And pushing her today, arguing with her was selfish. I should have known better.

182

Too many emotions are boiling inside and the urge to flee overwhelms me. I make my way through the waiting room, through the sliding glass doors and step outside to stand in the cold.

"Are you okay?" I hear Ben's voice behind me.

"No. I'm not okay. I'm a horrible person. Gwen could have died today and it's all my fault," I cry.

I turn to face him. "What is wrong with me?"

Ben pulls me into his arms. I go willingly.

"Charley, this isn't your fault. Gwen's heart has been working too hard for a while now. And it's been failing because of her cancer treatment. Her body is reacting to the medication. This is not your fault. And for the record, people fight all the time. It doesn't mean that you love her any less. She's going to be okay, you'll see."

I bury my face in Ben's warm chest and shed tears of guilt and despair that I can no longer hold inside, knowing that despite Ben's reassuring words, Gwen's never going to be okay again.

After a few moments, I pull away and wipe my eyes. And when I look up, I see Grey watching us through the glass hospital doors.

Ben follows my gaze and says, "Is that him?"

"Yep."

"He looks pissed. You better go talk to him."

I look at Ben.

"And say what, exactly?"

"I don't know. That's between the two of you. Listen, I'm going to go see a friend who's on shift here today, see if I can hang at his place for a while." He holds my car keys out for me and I take them from his hand. "I can drive you back to Seaport when you're ready. That is, if you want me to. Otherwise I'll find my own way home. Just call me if you need anything, okay?" He rubs his hand down my back.

I nod. "Okay. Thanks Ben, for everything."

"Anytime. Good luck," he says and then disappears inside. A moment later I walk inside and approach Grey.

"Hey," I say.

"Hey," he replies, his hands are in his pockets as he looks down at me. "I'm sorry about today. I shouldn't have come. I didn't realize that you were with someone else." He looks so sad, so heartbroken.

"Grey. It's not what it looks like. That's Ben. He's an old friend."

"It's none of my business, Charley."

"He's just a friend," I say firmly. Hours ago I would have used Ben to push Grey away. But everything has changed with so much pain already swirling around us. I can't take the look in Grey's eyes. I can't cause any more pain today. "Thanks for coming, for being here for John," I say.

He runs his hand through his hair and lets out a loud sigh. "Charley, I came for you. I'm here for you. I wish you would've told me. I wish you would've trusted me."

"It wasn't my secret to tell. And... Grey?" I pause, looking him straight in the face to drive my point home. "I can't be the reason you're here. Please, let it go. There's nothing between us anymore." I beg with my eyes, beg for him to let me go, to make this easy.

"Charley." He says only my name and then runs his hand through his hair again. He leans down and places his hands on my arms. I look up into his eyes, a small flicker of warmth hitting me in the gut, and before I can clamp it down, he says, "I'm in love with you. Haven't you figured that out yet?" He looks at me expectantly and I suddenly can't breathe.

Seconds tick by as I stand, paralyzed by fear.

"I have to go," I whisper, averting my eyes to my feet. "I have to go," I say more assuredly as I slip out from under his hold and walk away. *I have to think of Gwen right now*, I scold myself. *I can't deal with this right now*, I tell myself. But deep in the crevices of my mind a tiny voice is whispering, *Why can't I just love him back? Why can't I let him love me?* And in the center of the fragmented voice is the heart of a little girl who just wants to be loved.

# 26

## *Gwen*

Small patches of light slowly pervade the darkness. It's hard to breathe as if I'm being held under water, fighting for every breath. I feel warmth in my hand and I wiggle my fingers slowly just to feel something real. I hear a constant *whooshing* sound and feel a hard plastic shell covering my mouth and nose, the source of the noise. I blink once, then twice, fighting against the sensation to float away, back to the darkness.

I feel the warmth in my hand grow tighter and then I hear his voice, distant at first but slowly progressing until I sense that he is here with me.

"Gwen? Can you hear me?"

I blink, opening my eyes cautiously and see him clearly in the bright light. John. He looks like shit but the sight of him still fills me with warmth.

I try to speak but there's not enough breath and my mouth is covered by plastic.

"Gwen, you're awake. Oh God, I love you so much. I thought I lost you." He buries his head in my side and I feel him squeeze my hand tighter. I try to squeeze back but I can't find the strength, so I wiggle my fingers again.

The light is too bright and I'm so tired. I feel myself slipping slowly back to the darkness, it feels so easy to let go, to gradually drift away until the warmth of his hand grows cold and I am lost once again.

# 27

## *Charley*

Hospitals require patience. Unfortunately a virtue that I never acquired. I have paced the entire perimeter of the ICU waiting room at least fifty times and we have not heard a word from John or the doctor. I silently wish that I was a smoker so that I had an excuse to ride the elevator down to the ground floor where I could stand outside in the cold air and ease my anxiety with a good dose of nicotine. It hurts to think about Gwen and what her body is going through. It hurts to think of her lying still in a hospital bed while her damaged heart works rigorously to keep up. Or to think that if and when her heart gets better, her body is still riddled with cancer. We might not lose her today or tomorrow, but one day we will and sitting here waiting for it to happen is our reality. It makes me feel angry, the thought of losing her.

Grey hasn't returned to the waiting room. It is just my mother and I. Neither of us speak. My mother flips casually through magazines that are strewn around the room and I continue to pace.

After what feels like hours, John walks out of the ICU. His hair is a complete mess and there are dark circles under his eyes. Time has escaped us and I have no idea whether it is day or night. But seeing John's face reminds me of how tired I feel.

My mother stands and I walk across the room to join them.

"How is she?" my mother asks.

"She's still sleeping. Although she did open her eyes a while ago. I'm going to stay here with her tonight." John looks at my mother. "Connie, do you think you can pick up the kids and stay with them at our house? I want them to sleep in their own beds tonight."

"Of course, John. What should I tell them?"

He sighs and rubs his hand over his face. "Just tell them that Gwen's sick and she has to stay the night in the hospital. I don't want to tell them too much until we know more. Once she's awake, I know that she'll want to see the kids. Maybe you can bring them into the city tomorrow."

"Alright," my mother says and then she wraps her arms around John. He hugs her back. "Make sure you get some rest, John, and some food. You need your strength."

"Mother, I can call Ben to drive you back to Seaport in my car."

"Okay, Charlotte."

"And John, why don't I sit with Gwen for awhile so you can get something to eat," I offer.

"Yeah, okay," he says, nodding his head repeatedly, looking every bit lost and unsure of basic human needs, like eating.

I dig my phone out of my purse and text Ben. He responds right away, letting me know that he's at his friend's apartment just a few blocks away and will be here shortly and that he would be happy to drive my mom back to Seaport.

I wait with my mother until Ben arrives, while John goes back to Gwen's room.

"Hey, I got here as soon as I could," Ben says as he walks into the waiting room, cheeks flushed as if he ran all the way here.

"Thank you for doing this," I say. I hand Ben my car keys and my mother gathers her things.

"Hello, Ben," my mother says, rubbing her hand down his arm while she cradles her purse in her other arm like a baby. "It's so good to see you. I didn't get a chance to thank you earlier for getting Charlotte here safely."

"It was no problem, Ms. Brant," Ben responds with his dimpled smile. "Are you ready?"

"Yes," my mother says and then turns to me and pulls me into an embrace. This time I hug her back and I feel her almost melt into me.

"See you in the morning, Charlotte. Take care of John and call me if there's any news."

"I will. Bye Mom. Thanks again, Ben." I raise my hand to wave goodbye, but Ben pulls me against him instead and I close my eyes, trying to draw from his strength.

"Bye," he whispers into my ear and kisses me tenderly on the cheek. And then they both leave.

I push through the double doors and find room number three. I walk through an open door, all glass, and pull back a privacy curtain that reveals my sister or someone who resembles her. Her unconscious body lies still and quiet as if she is just sleeping, so small and frail, drowning in a sea of tubes, wires, and pale blue fabric. Gwen's skin is colorless, ashen white. Her hair damp and matted against her head. It is jarring to see her appearance anything less than perfect. Her face is covered with an oxygen mask, thick green straps stretch across her cheeks to secure it in place. A machine is beeping continuously yet fading into the background against the wild beat of my heart. Several IV bags are hanging nearby, a maze of tubes running into one single line that drains into the vein in Gwen's arm. It's a dreary sight that instantly weighs on my heart. My attention turns to John, where he's sitting in a chair pushed up to the edge of the hospital bed, as close as it could possibly get. He's bent over with his head resting on Gwen's side.

"John," I whisper, taking slow, tentative steps into the room.

"Oh, hey," he says, sitting up and stretching his arms.

"Go eat. I'll stay here until you get back," I say around the lump in my throat.

"Alright, but call me if she wakes up," he says. He leans over, kisses Gwen's hand and whispers, "I'll be right back, Gwen." And then he stands and walks out of the room, leaving me in the still, eerie silence.

I sit down and reach for Gwen's cold hand. Tears sting my eyes and rather than fight them, I surrender. Sobs rack my body and I lay my cheek down on Gwen's arm.

"I'm so sorry. I'm sorry for the awful things I said. I'm sorry I wasn't there for you. I should have been there. Please be okay. Please be okay..." I repeat until my voice trails off.

I wake up with a jolt to find John gently shaking my shoulder. I fell asleep in the chair, bent over with my head resting on Gwen's bed.

"Hey," he says. "You should go home and get some rest. I'm going to need you tomorrow."

I stretch my arms above my head and yawn. Glancing at Gwen, I reach over and squeeze her hand.

"Are you going to be okay?" I ask John. I feel so guilty for not telling him, for how he must feel right now. Everything is crashing down on him all at once. I don't want to leave him here all alone.

"I'll be fine. I just can't... can't leave her." John brings his hand to his face and begins to sob. I've never seen him cry before and, to be honest, it's unsettling. I go to him and wrap my arms around his middle and he instinctively puts his arms around my back. And we stand like this for a while, John sobbing on my shoulder and me crying softly, trying to be strong for him. To be whatever he needs in this moment, a comforting shoulder, a supportive sister-in-law, anything he needs.

He finally pulls back and wipes his face, whispering, "I'm sorry."

"It's okay John. I'm here for you. We're family." I say this as if it is the most obvious thing to say, but for the first time I understand what this sentiment actually means. *Family*. I think of my mother and I, of John, sitting in the waiting room all day and night, together although worlds apart, our presence like a wall of protection for our own, for Gwen, for our *family*. Each of us a building block, part of a supportive structure, not just for Gwen, but for each other. For John, for Olivia and Max. A structure I hadn't known as a child. It's hard to build anything supportive when there are only two blocks. With nothing to connect the two, only one can support the other.

"Thank you," he says, taking the seat that I just vacated.

"Do you want me to stay for a while?" I ask, feeling that I could use the company almost as much as John.

"No, I'll be fine. Go get some sleep, it's late," he says.

"I'll be back in the morning, but call me if anything changes or if you need something." And then I add, "I'll call Mom and have her bring you a change of clothes and some toiletries in the morning, okay?"

"Okay." He nods and I turn to go.

"Charley?" he says. And I look back at him just as I'm about to step through the doorway. "Why couldn't she tell me? Why would she keep this from me?" he asks with desperation in his eyes.

"She was scared, John. I think keeping it from you... made it less real." I watch his eyes fill with tears as he nods several times before taking Gwen's hand in his. I stand and watch him for a moment, envious of the wealth of love he holds in his gaze as he looks at my sister. Like he would trade places with her in a heartbeat, give up his own life to save her. *Will I ever have that? Love like that?*

I quietly pull the curtain aside and leave the room. I ride the elevator to the ground floor and make my way outside. I feel the cold encompass me as I step outside into the moonless night. I spot an empty yellow cab parked off to the right and walk toward it, pulling my jacket tighter around me to ward off the chill.

194

"Need a ride?" I hear him say and spin around at the sound of his familiar voice. Grey is sitting on a bench, his hands buried in his jacket pockets, his cheeks red from the frosty air.

"What are you doing here?" I ask, shocked. I haven't seen him since he told me he loved me and I walked away. I can't imagine that he's been waiting here all this time.

"I came back to check on you and see how Gwen's doing. I didn't see anyone in the waiting room... so I was going to leave but here I am." He shrugs his shoulders and flashes me a half smile. "How is she?" he asks as he stands and steps toward me.

"No change," I say.

"How are *you*?" he asks, tipping his head slightly to the side, concern etched in his eyes.

I shake my head and shrug, glancing up at the streetlights to hold the tears at bay.

Grey holds out his hand and says, "Come on, I'll drive you home."

I hesitate for a fraction of a second before I take his hand, interlacing our fingers, and let him lead me to his car where it's parked in the covered lot across the street.

We don't speak as he drives through the practically deserted streets of Seattle. It's late on Thanksgiving night, nearly morning now, and the city is quiet. I stare out my window as building after building blurs by, wanting so badly to just close my eyes and make it all disappear.

Grey parks in front of my house and we sit in silence while the engine is still running. I glance at him, his face illuminated by the streetlight in the otherwise dark interior of the car. One glance and all I see are his dark eyes, burning, hungry and, though I know I'm undeserving, I lean in and brush my lips across his. Drawing in a deep breath, he wraps his hand into my hair and pulls me closer. My subtleness turns raw and bold at his hands. And I am lost, nearly begging for escape.

"Come inside," I breathe out against his lips.

Without a word, he kills the engine and removes the key from the ignition. We break apart in the same moment and step out of the car, the slam of the car doors echo through the sleepy street. We walk quietly to my stoop where I unlock the front door, push it open, and step inside. Grey doesn't waste anytime. He shuts the door behind us and pulls me to him in the dark. He kisses me so deeply; I ache everywhere. He walks me backward toward the bedroom while he slips my jacket off my shoulders and then peels my shirt off over my head. By the time we stumble into the bedroom, we're both wearing only our pants. But those don't last long either. Completely naked, we fall back onto the bed, where Grey takes his time with me. And even when I beg him to go faster – harder – he continues to move steady and tender, generating more emotional turmoil rather than driving it away like I need, like I crave. But when my body finally erupts, I am molten, flowing, burning hot as I clutch Grey's bare skin in my hands, holding on so tight that my fingernails are digging into his flesh. He thrusts his hips achingly deep, drawing out every last ripple of pleasure until I feel him empty into me, his body a burst of shudders and pants, until we are both melting into one another and I continue to hold onto him as if he is my life raft amid a tropical storm. Once our breath slows, I feel him pull out of me and roll to his side where he cradles my back to his chest with one hand and tucks my wild hair behind my ear with the other. Normally, I would feel uncomfortable with this level of intimacy, a combination of the cuddling, Grey's tenderness, and the heady emotions from the day but I am so utterly exhausted that instead I close my eyes and drift off. But even in my last moments of consciousness, I can't ignore how good it feels to be in Grey's arms or how relieved I am to not be alone.

I open my eyes slowly, feeling disorientated, until I feel my own quilt under my chin. I draw in a deep breath, relieved that I'm in my own bed as I let my head sink back into my pillow. The room is bathed in darkness and I glance over at the clock to see that it is morning, but too early for the light of day. It is then that I remember falling asleep in Grey's arms and a quick glance around the room confirms that he is no longer here. His clothes are gone. I instantly feel a sense of longing which confuses me more than anything. Sadness lingers on the periphery, but from what? *Did I want him here when I woke up? Did he leave because he knew I wanted him to or because he wanted to, needed to?* I should feel relieved that he's gone, that I dodged the awkwardness of waking up next to him and having to make excuses of why he should go. This is the way I like my relationships with men. Easy, uncomplicated, clear. But my feelings for Grey are anything but uncomplicated, anything but clear. It's as if my head and my heart are conspiring against me, taking advantage of my vulnerabilities, kicking me while I'm down and so focused on Gwen that I can't see straight.

Which makes me think of something else that's bothering me. Visions from my dream last night dance through my mind, a recreation of real life moments that have resurfaced in an unfamiliar setting, the way that dreams sometimes do. I try to make sense of them but all I can see is the back of my father's truck as he drives away for the last time. I can feel Gwen's arms around me like I'm there in that moment, my heart breaking into a million pieces.

Her voice in my ear, muttering, "It's okay Charley. I'll never leave you. I'll never leave you." I can't recall if Gwen ever actually said those words to me or if that's part of the dream, the illusion. I can't recall how I was so sure that he wasn't coming back. Bits and pieces of memories have flooded my mind lately, haunting my dreams and filling me with the strangest sense of nostalgia for a time that was so long ago, I'm surprised that I remember anything at all. All I have are these fragmented images and sensations and no matter how hard I try to piece them all together, I'm still left with more questions then answers. But one thing is always constant, a bubbling resentment toward my mother. And that seems to be the one thing that I hold onto, the only thing that makes any sense. For years, Gwen and I never talked about my father, or the past, and I certainly don't discuss it with my mother, the one person who seems hell-bent on sweeping it all under the rug. But now it's all coming back, the past crashing head-on into my present like a highway collision. I can't ignore the feeling of helplessness that weighs on my heart, as if I'm a casualty in an ageless war, reminding me that eventually everyone leaves.

# 28

*Gwen*

I slowly peel my eyes open and the first thing I see is John's face. The room is dark with the exception of a small fluorescent light on the wall behind the head of the bed. John's eyes are open, staring into mine with an unreadable expression. I've never had to guess what John's feeling, as if his eyes were a direct window to his heart; I've always known instantly. I know that when he's sad, his eyes droop slightly and he gets this extra crease underneath. Or that when he's angry the dark rim surrounding the blue of his eyes morphs into a thick, black line and when he laughs, when he's happy, the gold flecks stand out more, lighting up his eyes with a kaleidoscope of color.

But his eyes are silent.

Seated in a chair, bent forward with his elbows sinking into the side of the bed and his chin resting on the back of his hands where his fingers are interlaced almost in prayer, he says nothing. Just continues to stare directly into my eyes. I reach up and pull the hard, plastic mask from my face and set it aside. The room instantly grows quiet without the noise from the flowing oxygen. I feel my breath grow heavy and I'm not sure if it's from the loss of the oxygen or from the sudden awareness that John knows. *He knows*. I can see it in his eyes now. The pity, the sadness, the fear... the anger. It's all there.

Tears well in my eyes as I watch him cup his hands over his mouth and take a deep breath. But rather than exhale, he releases a sob as tears spill down his cheeks. He lowers his face to my chest as he reaches over and grabs my hand, interlacing our fingers. His body shakes against mine and I feel all his emotions mixed in with my own feelings of guilt and shame. I reach my other hand up, with difficulty, and rest it on the back of his head, my fingers slipping through his blond hair in comfort. Tears stream down my face quietly, but I hold back my own sobs, giving John this moment. He needs it more then I do.

When he finally looks up and shifts back in his chair with red-rimmed eyes framed by dark circles, I take a deep breath and whisper through a dry throat, "I'm sorry." And then, unable to hold it back any longer, I gasp and begin to sob like a child. I cry for all the moments I felt scared and alone, feeling regret for not telling John sooner, overwhelmed by the relief I feel now that he knows. I cry for the reality that I won't always be here for John and Olivia and Max. The fear gripping my heart so tightly that I can hardly gain a breath. *I don't want to leave them. I don't want to die.* I cry for that as well, the unfairness of it all. The fear of the unknown, the fear of the pain, the end. I let it all out. Everything that has built up inside me for months now, everything that my denial has suppressed.

John strokes my hair back and holds me until I begin to cough and my breath becomes raspy. He reaches for the oxygen mask and places it back over my nose and mouth. I inhale greedily for a few moments before moving it aside again.

"Why didn't you tell me?" he asks, his eyebrows pulled in as he continues to stroke my hair.

I shake my head and bite down on my lower lip, my eyes still wet with tears. I don't even know where to start, my guilt stealing my words.

"Dammit Gwen," he says, choked with emotion as he sits back in his chair, the muscles in his jaw pulled tight.

"Why can't you let me help you? You don't have to do everything yourself. You don't always have to be the strong one." He runs his hand through his hair and leans forward again, closer to my face and whispers, "I love you, Gwen. You should have told me... you should've told me."

"I was scared," I mumble through my tears.

"I'm scared too," he admits, shaking his head side to side as tears well in his eyes once again. "But, dammit, when are you going to trust that I can handle it. That I'm here for you. That it's okay for you to need me. Huh, Gwen? When?" He's getting angry but trying so hard to be in control.

"I do need you," I say in a breathy rush. And as the words leave my lips, I realize that I have never told him that before. And I can't recall ever actually thinking it, but it doesn't make it any less true in this moment. I do need him. I always have and I need him now more than ever. Another sob bursts out of my chest.

John sits back again and says angrily, "I'm right here." He points to himself, slapping his fingers hard against his chest. "I'm right here, Gwen," he says again louder, nearly shouting, as tears fall down his cheeks. I flinch. "We're a team. I've always been here for you. Why can't you trust that?" he asks with such hurt in his expression that my heart breaks a little more. He draws in a deep breath, composing himself as he leans over and reaches for my hand, bringing it to his lips and kissing each one of my knuckles.

"I do. I'm sorry. I'm so sorry," I whisper in between my choking sobs.

And all I can think of is why after thirteen blissful years of marriage does it come down to this.

# 29

## *Charley*

I force myself out of the warmth and comfort of my bed where I want to stay and sleep the day away. In need of caffeine, I stumble to the kitchen and start a pot of coffee. As I pour myself a steaming mug from the carafe, I spot a note on the counter from Grey.

*I'm picking you up at eight and driving you to the hospital, no arguments.*

He signed it "G" which reminds me of the bartender the night he took me out. *Is that what people call him? His close friends, his brothers?* I wonder if we have reached that point where we know each other well enough to call each other by a nickname. I have memorized every inch of his body, every cut, every dip, every scar and yet I feel an unfamiliar nudge in my chest from one simple alphabetical letter written in his handwriting.

After two cups of coffee and a shower, I feel a little more like myself as I sit on the sofa and stare out the window at the dreary morning. I'm anxious to get to the hospital and yet I dread it at the same time. I just want Gwen to be okay. I called my mother earlier this morning to check on Olivia and Max and ask her to bring John a few things when she returns. I think of Olivia and how scared she must be, old enough to be completely aware that something is wrong and smart enough to know she isn't getting the entire truth about her mother. I vow to be strong for her and for Max. That's what Gwen would do and what she needs me to be. There is a part of me that still feels like a five-year-old little girl, needing to lean on someone, waiting for someone else to tell me that everything is going to be okay. To take care of me. But another part of me knows that I need to be that someone for Gwen and John and the kids.

I hear a soft knock on the door, startling me from my thoughts. I hadn't even noticed anyone walking toward the house but now I can see Grey's flashy car parked at the curb out front.

I scramble to the door, pull it open and feel the air get sucked out my lungs at the sight of him. He's freshly showered in faded jeans and a navy sweater, a white T-shirt hangs over the top of his waistband from underneath, and he's wearing a pair of Converse tennis shoes. He looks so incredibly young and much less intimidating.

"Hi," I say shyly.

"Hey," he says and hands me a paper cup from a local coffee vendor. "Tall, skinny latte with one packet of Splenda?"

I look at him, again shocked that he would know how I take my coffee.

"I pay attention, remember," he reminds me as I take the warm cup from his hand.

"Thanks," I say and then step back so he can move in from the cold.

"Let me grab my jacket. I'm anxious to get to the hospital," I say as I walk back to the bedroom to get my things. My head is a whirl of emotions, like an assortment of objects swirling around in a tornado. I can't fixate on any one thing and that makes me feel jittery, nervous.

I find Grey standing in the living room, peering curiously at framed photographs that I have displayed on a sideboard table near the door. Pictures of Gwen and I at her wedding, school pictures of Olivia and Max that Gwen has given to me already adorned in the frames. He looks up when he hears me.

"Ready?" he asks.

"Yep," I say as I slip my coat on and sling my handbag over my shoulder. The air feels awkward between us after last night. Grey's hand is on the doorknob but I feel like I need to say something before we get in the car. The idea of sharing such a small, confined space with him and this tension fills me with unease.

"Grey," I say quickly before he opens the door.

He drops his hand to his side and turns to face me.

"I... last night..." I am at a loss for words. I stand there, frozen, fumbling for words like a complete idiot.

He walks toward me, draws me against him as I stare up at his face and places his finger against my lips. "Ssh... focus on Gwen right now. We can figure out the rest later."

His hand falls back to his side and he presses his lips gently against my cheek before he releases me and walks out the door. It takes me a moment to collect myself. The tension has lifted but I'm left feeling like I don't deserve him; I don't deserve Grey's kindness. I follow him out to the car, knowing that I'm going to break his heart, but feeling drawn to him like a drug addict looking for a fix. And like an addict, I take what he gives without care of the destruction that I might leave in my wake.

The hospital is quiet on this Friday morning, much like the car ride with Grey. Grey insisted on waiting in the ICU waiting room, while I go inside to see Gwen and John.

I find John sprawled out in the chair asleep and Gwen lying in bed awake. Her face lights up when she sees me, but I can't ignore the pale, waxy look to her skin or the sunken dark circles around her eyes. The large oxygen mask has been replaced by a nasal cannula, delivering oxygen through tiny tubes in her nostrils. She places her finger against her lips and whispers, "I don't want to wake him."

I nod and walk around to the opposite side of her bed and sit on the edge, drawing one leg up underneath me. I swallow the lump in my throat.

"How are you feeling?" I ask.

"I've been better," she says with a slight smile. I know that she's trying to spin the situation with humor, putting on her armor of strength, but I can see the pain in her eyes.

Tears well up and spill down my cheeks without hesitation and I say, "I'm so sorry, Gwen. I didn't mean..."

"Neither did I, Charley. We're good," she says, as she reaches over and squeezes my hand. "We're good," she says again with tears in her eyes.

"Are you going to be okay?" I ask her hesitantly, almost afraid of the answer. I let my purse slide silently to the floor and peel my jacket off my shoulders.

"The doctor said that my fluid levels are down and my heart is already getting stronger. The medications are working. He thinks I should be able to go home by the end of the weekend. I'm supposed to have some scans today and Dr. Sheldan is coming by to discuss treatment plans, so we'll see," she says with a sigh. "Can you call Mom? I need to see Olivia and Max. I just need to feel them in my arms, ya know?"

I nod and say around the knot that has formed in my chest, "Yes, I'll call her." I lie down on my side and snuggle in beside her without another word and we both lie in silence as I listen to her wheezy breath draw in and release, while John snores softly on the other side of the room. Gwen whispers, "I'm so glad that you're here."

And I find myself thinking back to my dream and Gwen's voice as she whispered, "I'll never leave you." I whisper those same words to her now, so softly that only I can hear.

We lay like this for a while until John's snoring fades and he clears his throat. I sit up slowly and Gwen says, "Honey, you should go to Charley's and get some real sleep. I'm not going anywhere."

John stretches his arms overhead and says, "Well, I could use a shower."

"I'll call Mom now and have her bring Olivia and Max and John's things," I say as I stand slowly and kiss Gwen on the cheek. I turn to John and add, "And John, my place is yours for whatever you need."

"Tell her to pack me a bag too, would ya?" Gwen says. "Something comfy to wear when I spring out of here." Gwen wears her signature smile but it doesn't reach her eyes and I have to turn away before she sees the heartache that I am trying so hard to mask.

"I'll tell her," I assure Gwen as I bend down to pick my purse up off the floor. "I'll be right back," I say to both John and

Gwen as I step out into the hallway and make my way back to the waiting room to call my mother.

I see Grey first. He's sitting in one of the chairs in the tiny waiting room, bent forward scrolling through something on his phone. He looks up and sees me, standing abruptly as he tucks his phone in the pocket of his jeans. "How is she?" he asks as I walk toward him.

I shrug. "She's awake and seems better than I was expecting, but she looks terrible and it sounds like a truck is idling in her lungs," I say.

"I'm sorry," he says, running his hand down my arm. I shake off the wave of chills his touch invokes.

"I need to call my mom," I say as I pull my phone out of my purse. "Give me a sec." I step away and dial my mother.

She answers on the first ring as if she's been waiting by the phone. I give her a quick update on Gwen.

"Oh thank God," she says, relieved that Gwen is finally awake. I repeat John and Gwen's requests and she assures me that she'll be here as soon as possible.

"How are Max and Olivia?" I ask.

"Max seems fine. Olivia is upset and anxious to see her mom," she says.

"That's understandable," I say mindlessly, staring out the window, feeling sick with worry for both the kids and Gwen. For all of us.

I say goodbye, toss my phone back in my purse and turn to Grey.

"You don't have to wait around for me. My mom's bringing my car and I'll most likely be here all day."

He doesn't argue as he says, "Okay, but please call me if you need anything and tell John the same. Okay?"

"I will," I answer, nodding my head. And then add, "Thank you."

"I'll check back in later then," he says in a questioning tone.

I only nod again and watch as Grey makes his way toward the elevator, wondering what happens when the weight we carry becomes more than we can bear.

# 30

## *Gwen*

I feel out of sorts with the way everyone is fussing over me. I feel completely helpless, lying in this bed with barely enough strength to raise my head. I've had a series of tests and scans already this morning and John, Charley and I sat at full attention as Dr. Sheldan explained that due to the toxicity of my heart, we have to stop treatment. He suggests we wait a month, monitor my heart and when I feel stronger begin a new treatment, an oral medication that is less aggressive but still effective. My scans still showed promise, meaning the cancer has not grown or spread since we started two months ago. I don't feel any sense of relief from this news. He explained that my heart is not pumping blood efficiently, the muscle severely weakened and damaged, and went over a list of medications that I will have to take in order to treat this condition. I listened to Dr. Sheldan, hanging on his every word but my mind was screaming, *Why is this happening?* It all feels like a dream. John asked a thousand questions: How will this effect my daily life, my routine? Can I drive? How do we know that I won't have another episode? Does the new treatment change my prognosis? Questions that I would not have thought to ask and could not articulate in the moment. Dr. Sheldan answered each one clearly: I should feel like myself in a few weeks; No driving until he gives me the okay; As long as I am taking my meds and getting plenty of rest, I shouldn't experience another episode, but that I need to listen to my body, extreme fatigue, shortness of breath, dizziness are all symptoms that need immediate assessment; and the new treatment offers a similar prognosis - a hopeful five years but longer if we're lucky.

*Lucky.* I'm feeling anything but lucky.

As if to disorientate me further, it seems that Charley, of all people, has assumed my usual role. Once Mom arrived with Olivia and Max and two separate packed bags for John and I, she sent John to her house for a shower and sent Mom and the kids to a coffee shop down the street where she swears they serve the best cinnamon rolls in Seattle. I tried to argue as I was desperate to see the kids, but Charley insisted that I freshen up a bit so that my appearance wouldn't scare Olivia and Max. Now she is brushing the tangles out of my hair and helping me brush my teeth. All difficult tasks when you're lying on your back with your head elevated only thirty degrees. She washes my face with a warm cloth and applies a light moisturizer. I'm not sure if I look much better, but I sure feel better.

After what feels like forever, John reappears in my room looking freshly showered and clean-shaven. He looks tired as hell but I'm glad that he's here.

"Ready for the munchkins?" he asks as he bends down and kisses my cheek.

I nod, feeling anxious. John and I decided to tell the kids that I have cancer. We aren't going to tell them what that means for all of us, agreeing that we should keep things simple and easy.

"Technically, they're not supposed to be in the ICU, but I did some schmoozing and they can both come in for awhile," John says.

"I'll go get them," Charley offers. "Be right back."

Moments later, I see their heads poke in from behind the curtain that is pulled closed across the open doorway.

I try to sit up a little straighter, ignoring the pain in my chest and my labored breath.

"Hey," I say. "Come here you two."

"Hi Mom," Olivia says first as she steps into the room followed by Max who is distracted for a moment with all the gadgets around us.

I pat the empty space next to me on the bed and Max runs and leaps up beside me, hugging himself tightly against my side. I wince at the pain but wrap my arms around him.

"Mommy," he says into my chest.

"Hi Bubs," I say around the lump in my throat as tears sting my eyes.

I watch Olivia as she hesitates, unsure of the situation. "Come here, Love Bug," I say and motion for her to join Max on the bed. She sits beside me stiffly, opposite of Max. I run my hand down her back and brush my fingers through her hair. "How are you?" I ask her.

I watch as she tries so hard to be strong but I see her bottom lip tremble before she bursts into tears. I pull her to me and John walks over, leans down and embraces us all and we stay like this, as if time is at a standstill, even if only for a few moments.

I feel Max trying to wiggle out of our group hug and so I clear my throat as I reach up and wipe my tears away. We all disengage and John sits next to Olivia on the bed.

"So Daddy and I want to talk to you about why I'm sick." I look to John for reassurance and he nods and places his hand on Olivia's shoulder for support. "I have cancer. It's like a bunch of bad cells that spread in my body, taking over the good cells. I can't get rid of it, it's something I'm always going to have, but I have medicine that will help stop the bad cells from growing. I don't want you to worry though. Everything's going to be okay."

"But if everything's okay, why are you sick?" Max asks, innocently.

"Well... I was taking the wrong medicine before and my body didn't like it and that's why I had to go to the hospital, but now I'm going to have the right medicine."

"Are you going to die?" Max asks bluntly with his eyebrows pulled in tight.

"Well..." I look at John, unsure of what to say.

"Not for a really long time, Buddy," John says and reaches over and musses Max's blond curls. This seems to placate him.

"I don't want Mommy to die. Who's going to cut the crust off my sandwiches? Who's going to tie my shoes in double knots, the way I like it?" I smile at the simplicity of his thoughts but my heart breaks at the same time.

"So you're going to be okay?" Olivia asks hesitantly, much less confident than Max with our answers.

"Yep. I'm going to be okay. I have to take it easy for a while until my body heals from being sick, but after that, everything will be back to normal," I say, squeezing her hand.

"Promise?" she asks, her eyes so big I am reminded of her face as a toddler. I hesitate for the briefest moment, not wanting to make a promise that I can't keep, but knowing that I need to reassure her, that it is my job to protect them both from the horrible truth, the crippling fear of my death; I lie.

"Promise." The physical ache in my chest morphs into a stabbing pain that takes what little strength I have to contain. John and I exchange a look and then he gives me a slight smile. I feel exhausted all of a sudden and John must sense it. He stands up and says with more energy than I can muster, "Who wants a hamburger?"

"Me," Max cheers.

Olivia's not buying John's enthusiasm, she sits still and stares at me as if I might disappear the moment she turns her head.

"Go eat, Love Bug," I say. "I'm just going to rest for a while."

She stands up, albeit reluctantly, and follows John and Max out the door.

I exhale the breath I'd been holding as a flood of suppressed tears pour down my cheeks and a choked sob echoes in the abrupt silence of the room. I give in to the pain as I wonder how much more my damaged heart can endure.

# 31
## *Charley*

After leaving Olivia and Max with Gwen and John, I lingered outside the door to Gwen's room, just waiting. I'm not sure how much time has passed when John and the kids finally step into the hallway, moving so slowly, it's as if their feet are weighted down with bricks.

I quickly muscle a smile and say, "Hey guys, where to now?"

"We're heading across the street for a burger," John says. "Wanna come?" he asks almost as an afterthought. Knowing he needs some time alone with Olivia and Max, I decline.

"You guys have fun and I'll see you in a bit," I say. Neither Olivia nor Max respond. John pats my shoulder and then I watch the three of them walk away, hand-in-hand.

I poke my head into Gwen's room, but she seems to be asleep and I don't want to wake her.

I watch her chest rise and fall for a moment, trying to imagine how hard this must have been for Gwen, putting on a brave face to tell her children that she's sick. I worry about Olivia and Max and how this moment changes the course of their lives, thrusting an unfair dose of reality into their naïve world that no child should have to face.

I leave Gwen and return to the waiting room.

I spot my mother sitting alone in the corner with her back to the only window; a small pool of light shines through like a halo around her face. Her eyes are vacant as she stares at nothing in particular, her fingers fanned across her lips. I sit down in the chair next to her and several minutes tick by before she acknowledges me, as if her mind had to travel back from some distant place before it could land here in this bleak reality.

She drops her hand from her mouth and says my name.

"Hi Mom," I say. Her mouth lifts on one side in a half grin as if a full smile requires too much energy or happiness.

She turns her body toward me and takes my hand in both of hers. I look at our hands and note how similar they are, small and thin with long, spindly fingers. It feels strange to hold my mother's hand, intimacy has never really been our strong suit.

We both stare at our hands, our heads tilted so close to one another that I can smell her strawberry scented shampoo. Her voice is quiet and soft as she says, "I keep going back in my mind to when you and Gwen were young and I keep asking myself if things would be different if I would have handled it all better. I look at the both of you and I'm so proud of the strong, competent women that you've become, but over the past few days I've seen firsthand the cracks in your foundation and I can't help but feel that it's my fault."

I look up at my mother's face; her eyes are fixed on our hands as if she's afraid to look into my eyes. Tears slowly trickle down her cheeks and she reaches up with one hand to wipe them away. I don't know what to say. We've never talked about the past or our feelings or anything else involving matters of the heart. I have always blamed my mother for my issues with relationships and intimacy and anything else that seems to go wrong in my life. But I have to wonder what "cracks" she is referring to. The part of me that seems hell-bent on spending my life alone rather than risk my heart? I know that love can lift you up and make you feel invincible but I also know how vulnerable it can leave you. The higher the high, the harder the fall and the more violent the shatter, scattering a million tiny shards of your heart into a thousand different directions. I don't know how many falls a heart can take before there is nothing left to put back together, but I have never wanted to find out. And Gwen? What "cracks" does she have? The fact that she couldn't tell her own husband that she's sick? That she felt she couldn't rely on someone else? I've never thought of Gwen as anything but whole and strong, shatter-proof and well... perfect, really. But my mother is right, Gwen has her own deep-rooted issues but she hides them better.

"I'm sorry Charlotte," my mother says quietly. My heart is in my throat, choking me. I feel shocked that she has uttered the words after all these years but I feel angry at the same time. I'm angry that she has not said them sooner, I'm angry that she feels this way now, that it took a family tragedy for her to admit she was wrong.

"It's a little late, don't you think," I mumble, pulling my hand out of her grasp. She looks up at me; tears are flowing steadily down her face now.

"I guess I deserve that," she says, reaching into her purse and retrieving a tissue that she uses to wipe under her eyes and nose. A few uncomfortable moments pass as my mother sniffles beside me and I pick at my cuticles, trying to rein in my anger. Part of me wants to leave her sitting here to wallow in her self-pity, escape this emotional confrontation while I still can. But instead,

I stay rooted in my chair wanting desperately to know what else she has to say, starving for some sort of emotional connection that I didn't realize I even wanted or needed from her. From the corner of my eye, I see her pull her slouched shoulders back and straighten her spine, sitting up tall in her chair as she gains her composure.

"Let's take a drive. There's something I want to show you," she says, as she pulls my car keys out of her purse and stands.

"Where are we going?" I ask, suddenly very curious as to what she feels I need to see right this very minute.

"You'll see," is all she says as she makes her way toward the elevator, leaving me no other choice but to follow her.

A few minutes later, she is driving my car out of the hospital parking garage, heading deeper into the city. My nerves are frayed as my mind flashes through all of the possibilities and, with each turn she takes, I wonder where on earth she could possibly be taking me. We are driving into the bowels of the city, a darker part of Seattle where I would never willingly go. She finally pulls over and parks the car on the side of a deserted street. We're underneath the freeway and the noise from the passing cars overhead fills the quiet space around us. I look at my mother, waiting for her to tell me what the hell we're doing here.

She turns to me and says, "Do you see over there?" as she points across the street. My gaze follows her finger to where a group of homeless men are huddled around a small, make-shift fire trying to keep warm in the chilly winter day, the freeway overpass protecting them from the elements. There are a few battered tents set up nearby as well as the cliché cardboard shelters. The men are dirty and dressed in layer upon layer of ripped and faded clothing. Knit stocking hats, fingerless gloves, and worn shoes. *So my mother wants me to appreciate my life more? Brought me here to show me how blessed I am in comparison?* Because it's working. I am just about to ask her this question aloud when one of the men turns and looks in our direction. One minute he looks like every other hopeless man on the street, dirty and broken and the next minute I recognize the knit hat he's wearing. It's so thin and faded that I have to look extra hard to be sure that my eyes are not deceiving me, but I recognize the thick blue stripe framed by thin bands of white and green. A Seahawks stocking hat that my mother made during her knitting phase, a hat my father wore religiously in the cold mornings on the boat. I remember it vividly, and once my eyes confirm that it is, in fact, the same hat, I now see the hazel eyes directed my way and recognize my father's face. Through the overgrown gray beard and ragged skin, the tired eyes and yellowed teeth, through the overall haggard appearance, I can see my father. I gasp and feel my mother's hand on my shoulder, grounding me. *Why did she bring me here? Why would she want me to see what has become of my dad? How could she know that he's here, living this way and not do something, anything? How can she live with herself, knowing that she did this to him?* Every part of me is frozen except for my mind, which is firing questions so rapidly it's like an AK-47 is discharging in my head.

I try to recall the image of him that I keep on file in my mind, what he looked like the last time I saw him. Side by side, it seems inconceivable that this is the same man, but there is no mistaking the eyes. As if all at once my body thaws, tears make their way down my cheeks as I reach up and spread my hand out against the cold passenger side window and whisper, "Daddy." *He's been so close all this time.* I always pictured him living far away in some exotic place, living far too good a life to come back to ours. Fishing on a big boat in the middle of paradise, anything, but not *this.* I hear my mother's voice and like hearing fingernails on a chalkboard, I cringe.

"I thought that it was time you knew the truth."

Without taking my eyes from the man who looks like nothing but a stranger yet somehow the same man that I have loved and yearned for all this time, I ask, "What truth?"

"Why he left?"

I wait, knowing that she will blame him, make herself a victim, that is just her way.

"Charlotte, you were too young to remember and I was always grateful for that. I let you blame me, hate me even, because I thought that it would help you cope. And there were times I hated myself, so it seemed rightfully deserved." She stops and blows her nose and I stay fixated on the man across the street who is now looking through a deserted trash bag. I swallow a mix of shame and longing, pity and resentment, swallow it down until I feel like I might be sick. My heart is beating so hard I fear that it will march right out of my chest and then keep going like the *Energizer* bunny banging on its drum.

"The truth is that the boat was leaving the dock every morning but your father wasn't on it, not in the end anyway. He was a drunk, still is. He was always a good man though, Charlotte, always. In his heart, he had good intentions; I believe that. And he loved his girls. He loved you so much. But Lord knows, he loved the bottle too and in the end he couldn't give it up. And he couldn't risk hurting you. So he left."

Flashes from the day he left cloud my vision. My mother yelling at my dad. She was angry, but she had tears in her eyes. My dad kneeling down and hugging me close, kissing my temple as he said, "I'm sorry, Charley," in a voice so thick I hardly recognized it as my father's. I didn't understand at the time what it was he was apologizing for, but I remember that feeling in my gut, knowing that something bad was happening, something significant.

I can remember watching the screen door slam and then running after him, screaming, "Daddy, don't leave. Take me with you. Don't leave me, Daddy." He kept me at arm's length, holding me back while he threw his green canvas duffle bag into the cab of the truck and climbed inside. The sound of the ignition turning seemed to echo down the street, followed by the roar of the engine as he slowly pulled away from the curb. I ran as hard as my little legs would carry me, feeling certain that he would stop, that he would change his mind. I had never felt pain like that. The unbearable pain I felt inside, like someone was driving a hammer into my chest, when his truck finally disappeared at the end of our street. When I realized that he was gone.

And to think he left that day to *spare* me.

I finally turn to face my mother, my eyes are so blurry with tears that I can hardly see her face.

"But... why... why didn't you tell me this before," I cry. "Why did you shut us out? Why did you leave me too..." I choke out, now sobbing uncontrollably.

"Oh, Charlotte, don't you see?" she says as she reaches up and cups my cheek with her soft hand, wiping away my tears with the pad of her thumb. I can see the regret in her eyes and the pain even after all these years. "He left me... he left me too. I'm so sorry for all that time we lost. For not being there for you and your sister. I have to live with that every day. But I was broken. I'm not as strong as you and Gwen." She drops her hand from my face and swipes at her eyes and nose and then looks me deep in the eye and says, "I brought you here so that maybe you can stop blaming me for everything, but more importantly, I want you to stop blaming yourself. You're so good and so strong and you deserve to have love in your life. Do you hear me, Charlotte? You have so much love to give and you deserve to be loved." She places her fingertips under my chin and gently lifts my face until

I'm looking her directly in the eye and then drives her point straight into my heart, "Do you hear what I'm telling you?"

I nod through my tears and then she pulls me into her arms tightly and I go willingly, as I sob against her green cotton sweater.

"You and Gwen are my whole world. I'm so close to losing Gwen and I can't lose you too, Charlotte. I can't lose you," she mumbles against my temple where her lips rest. A storm unleashes inside my soul, a fury of emotions, like each of my memories are being rewritten in fast-forward motion, leaving new imprints on my heart in their wake. I sob and find comfort in my mother's embrace; a scene that I once yearned for but had long since given up on. We stay like this for a while, until my tears dry on my cheeks and my breath evens out. My mother releases me and I look out my window at my father once more before we leave. I so badly want to open the door, run across the street and confront him. A part of me wants to see the look on his face when he sees me, after all this time. *Would he recognize me? Would it change anything, if he knew I was here?* But the man I see is nearly a shell of the man I once knew and my heart can't take any more disappointment.

As if reading my mind, my mother says, "He's not your father anymore. He's not the same man. You have to let him go."

I take her words like a punch in the gut. I steal one last look, my heart filled with grief for a man whose soul may be dead but who is still very much alive. Such a contradiction between my head and my heart.

# 32

## *Gwen*

I sit on the edge of my bed, grateful to be home after spending several days in the hospital. I stare at the bathroom door that stands a mere ten feet from where I sit, but it might as well be miles because there is no way I can get there on my own. I have to pee. It seemed like such a simple task when I first sat up in bed, but apparently my body has other ideas. I know I should call for someone, for John, to help me but I just want to do something on my own, to not feel so helpless. The doctor said that I should have my strength back in a week or two, but I was hoping I was the exception and that it would take only a matter of days to feel like myself again or at least enough to use the bathroom on my own.

I stand on my feet slowly and attempt to take a step but my legs are shaking violently and the room begins to spin. I slide my back down the side of the mattress and as soon as my butt hits the floor with a subtle thud, I feel a release of warmth. I actually piss myself right on the floor of my bedroom. Before the mortification has time to seep in, there is a light knock on the door and then Charley's face peeks in from the hallway.

Seeing her face while I'm sitting in my own pee because I can't even go to the bathroom on my own, completely undoes me. I sob into my hands, unable to even look her in the eye.

"Gwen? Are you okay?" she asks in a panic, rushing to my side. "What happened?"

"I peed my pants... so sorry... couldn't make it to the bathroom," I manage to say through my sobs. She is quiet for several seconds and so I look up from my hands. And she is holding back a smile, I can tell.

"You scared the shit out of me!" she says with her hand over her heart. And then she plops down next to me, stretches her legs out in front of her and laughs. She laughs so hard that she's crying and I find myself laughing through my own tears. And it feels so good to laugh, to let go of everything that I've been holding inside. The sadness, the frustration, the anger – I let it all go. After a few moments of ridiculous laughter, Charley says, "And I thought I was a mess." And I laugh even harder until my stomach hurts and my breath becomes labored.

"Okay, Gwen, enough," she says holding her side, breathing heavily. "Don't make me get your oxygen tank."

We both sigh as we catch our breath. I feel better. Hard to imagine while I'm sitting in my own pee, but I do.

"How about a shower?" she asks and nothing has ever sounded better.

"I would love a shower," I say. Charley stands and puts her hands under my arms, pulling me slowly to a standing position. I put my arm around her and we walk together to the bathroom. She helps me strip off my wet clothing and step into the shower until I'm sitting on the tiled bench in the large stall.

She starts the water and sets the perfect temperature, making sure that my shampoo and body wash are within reach and then she says, with a small smile, "I'm going to step out and give you some privacy, just yell when you're ready to get out."

"Okay," I say and then as she is turning to leave I add, "Charley, thank you."

She only smiles and steps out of the bathroom, leaving the door slightly ajar. Whether she realizes it or not, she has given me the perfect gift, a few moments alone with the ability to wash my hair, to feel like I can do something, *anything*, for myself. The warm water feels great on my skin and I feel as if I've gained a small sense of dignity back now that I have clean hair. I sit with my eyes closed and let the water spray over my face.

I never thought that I would ever say this but Charley has been a godsend. She has been amazing with the kids. In fact, she spent most of the weekend here at the house with them while John stayed with me in the hospital. And when John carried me into the house this morning, we were greeted with a huge "Welcome Home Mommy" banner that hung from the banister courtesy of the kids, but no doubt facilitated by Charley. The house was clean, spotless in fact. She has taken the week off from work to stay and help out, alongside my mother which is no small feat. It's as if aliens have abducted my sister and replaced her with this other grownup, more responsible version. And yet, inside she's still Charley – evidenced by her ability to make me laugh over the fact that I wet my pants. Something only my childlike sister could do.

"How's it going in there?" I jump at the sound of Charley's voice.

"I think I'm done," I say, noticing that the water is beginning to run cold.

She reaches in and turns the water off, handing me a towel instantly. I dry my skin, ring the water out of my short hair and wrap the towel around myself. Charley helps me stand and walks me into the bedroom. I can smell disinfectant and know that she has rid the floor of my mess and remade the bed, turning it down to look fresh and clean. She helps me sit on the edge of the bed and then rummages around in my closet until she finds a pair of black sweatpants, a light pink T-shirt and comfy underwear.

"This okay?" she asks, holding out the three items.

"Perfect," I say while I pull the T-shirt over my head and then she helps me stand and slips on my underwear followed by my sweatpants. She helps me crawl into bed, tucking me in on propped pillows.

"Are you tired? Do you want to sleep?"

I think for a moment and then say, "No, not really." My body feels tired from all the moving around but I feel refreshed.

"TV?" she asks, nodding toward the flat screen mounted on the wall above the fireplace.

"Yeah, maybe for a little while."

She hands me the remote and then disappears into the bathroom, emerging seconds later with a brush in hand.

"Here, sit up," she says and I do. She slips behind me and starts brushing my hair. It feels so good that tears sting my eyes. The quiet way she takes care of me, securing every shred of my dignity that she possibly can, brings me to tears.

"Remember when you used to brush my hair?" she asks as she moves the bristles though my short, thick strands.

I wipe my eyes with the back of my hand. "Yeah, it seems like yesterday, doesn't it?" I say, remembering that time in our life clearly.

"You were always there, taking care of me..." her voice trails off and she sighs, setting the brush down.

"What is it, Charley?" I ask, scooting to the middle of the bed until we are sitting side by side, propped up by loads of euro pillows.

"Nothing," she says shaking her head, but I know that look. She wants to say something.

"Just say it, Charley. I may have pissed my pants, but I'm still your sister, I'm not going to break."

This rewards me a small smile from her and then she asks, "Did you know about Dad? Did you know all along that he's living under the I-5 bridge?"

I take a deep breath, completely caught off guard and say, "Yes, I knew."

"Why didn't you tell me?"

"Well, at first you were too young to know the truth. And I don't know, I guess after sheltering you from it all for so long, it just seemed easier to let you think what you wanted about Dad... and Mom... about the whole thing. It was hard to keep track of him, he moved around a lot. First it was small apartments in the city and then he crashed on other people's couches until eventually he ran out of options. Mom always seemed to keep tabs on him."

Charley's a grown-up but she always seems so fragile. I've always protected her from this truth as if it would be too much for her, but maybe she should've known the truth all along. Maybe it wasn't right to keep it all from her, like the way I kept my cancer from John.

"What about Mom? She said that she was broken when Dad left and that's why she shut us out, but why didn't she fight for him? Why did she give up so easily?" Charley sounds like that little girl that I remember. In so many ways, when it comes to her emotions, she still is a little girl. And maybe that's my fault.

"His drinking had been spiraling out of control, getting worse by the day. Mom and Dad were fighting constantly and he was always angry. Some nights he didn't even bother to come home. The night before he left, he came home late. I heard him stumble in and then heard Mom and Dad arguing. I opened my bedroom door to see what was going on and I could tell he was drunk. He could hardly walk and Mom was beyond upset. She was screaming at him and... he hit her, Charley. He actually hit her."

I bring my hand to my cheek, lost in the memory, picturing my mother's tear-streaked face and the shock written in her expression. I watched her raise her chin slightly in defiance, but before she could respond, my father pushed her back against the wall where she hit her head and fell slowly to the ground. I wanted to run to her, overcome with a fierce protectiveness, but I was scared, rooted in my spot where I watched it all from my bedroom doorway. Watched my dad morph into a stranger, become someone I didn't know. I just stood there and watched when he kicked her in the stomach over and over as she was lying defenseless on her side, all the while he was muttering things about how she never respects him, how tiring her nagging has become, and what a terrible wife and mother she is. I tell this all to Charley now in excruciating detail.

"Is that the man that you wanted Mom to fight for?" I ask.

Of course, I also remember, minutes later, when it was over, my father was full of apologies and almost terrified of what he had done, and my mother was no fool, told him in the most heartbreaking voice that he couldn't stay unless he got sober. That enough was enough. I knew then, that it was the first and last time he would ever hurt my mother. At least with his fists.

I can feel myself getting angry. All those nights I heard my Mom crying. All those nights I listened to Charley dream about him coming back for her. I never wanted him to come back. I felt relieved that he was gone. I felt guilty for feeling that way, knowing that his absence caused both my mother and Charley so much pain but I was relieved.

"I didn't know," Charley whispers, looking down at the brush in her hands, fingering the course bristles.

"Mom gave him a choice, Charley. His family or the booze and he chose... well you know what he chose. He left us because he's a coward. He wasn't strong enough to choose us. Mom was devastated. She loved him so much. She would've done anything for him, but she wasn't willing to risk our safety. She did it for us, made him choose, but she couldn't handle the fact that he left. She struggled with depression. She could hardly get out of bed for months and I held us all together. I bought the groceries, bathed you, took you to school, cooked our meals. I did it all. And then came all the men. And they all left too, one after the other..."

"I'm sorry Gwen, I didn't know," she says, shifting around until she's facing me on the bed, a single tear sliding down her cheek. I watch her reach up and wipe it away. Her hair is messy and falling in her face, her skin flawless. Her beauty sometimes catches me off guard, seeing the woman that she's become.

"I know. I didn't *want* you to know."

"The part that I can't let go of, the part that's eating me up inside is why someone would choose that life, choose such a lonely and cold existence when they could be surrounded by love?" Tears are flowing steady down her face, breaking my heart again. She sniffs and then says, "Because I would've loved him, Gwen. I would've loved him so much."

"I don't know why," I whisper, shaking my head. "It's funny... well not funny... but I sometimes find myself asking the same question about you." I look into Charley's eyes to gauge her reaction.

"Me? What does one have to do with the other?" she asks, confused.

"Is it not the same? I worry about you and why you always choose to be alone over love. I try to tell myself that you just haven't met the right person, but come on, we both know that's not it."

She's quiet for a moment and I worry that I've said too much.

Her brows are pulled in tight as she looks from her hands to my face.

"You think I'm a coward, like him? Is that what you're saying?" Her voice is quiet and hoarse.

"I don't think you're a coward, Charley," Gwen whispers. "There's a big difference between being afraid and being a coward. But yes, I think you push people away because you're afraid. And Dad? Choosing the easy road makes him a coward." I think of my father, leaving without even trying to change, without even giving it a shot.

"You think being homeless is the *easy* road?" Charley asks, clearly not seeing what I see.

"I think getting clean and trying to be a man worthy of a family, worthy of love was too daunting a choice for him. So, yes, living alone with no one depending on him, drinking away the regret of his choice, having to answer to no one, feeling nothing – that was definitely the easy way out."

I take a breath and fight the emotion churning in my gut. I've never said all this aloud. I've always felt this way, but I've never actually said it. It triggers so many memories, so many different feelings. Part of me wants to feel sorry for my dad, because it is all so sad when you think of it. And then I feel angry again, because as sad as it is, he made his choice. Some people might argue that addiction is a disease not a choice, but I disagree. Cancer is a disease, an affliction that selects you at random, bears you no choice. It seems unfair that my father could waste his precious life this way while despite all the right choices I have made, my life is being taken from me. I think of Charley and her choices and the difference between my dad and my sister. In so many ways, she reminds me of him. The good things, the things I remember about him before he lost himself. Like his honesty. Charley is blunt, straight to the point, no-nonsense. Just like he was. And her laugh, it's infectious. And God, my dad could laugh, always finding the humor in everything. But she is not him. She is so strong, she just doesn't see it and maybe I haven't wanted to see it. But I see it now.

A steady stream of tears rolls down my cheeks, leaving a salty taste on my lips.

Charley is quiet, taking it all in. We have never really talked about the past and it's a lot to swallow all at once.

"Charley, I get that you're afraid. But don't let Dad's choices define you. Not everyone's a coward." I am about to add that not everyone's going to leave her, but I hold the words back, suddenly struck by the fierce truth, that while not everyone will leave her, I most certainly will and sooner than we both want. Instead I say, "Not everyone is going to turn away from love. From you."

She wipes her face on her shirtsleeve and looks up at me. Her eyes, the mirror of my own, are childlike as they search my face for more answers. But I have nothing more to say.

"I know that," she finally says, her voice barely a whisper. "I don't know what's wrong with me. I get close to someone and I just freeze up, like there's nothing inside me to give. Like nothing I have will be enough. And then I make a mess of everything. And I don't know how to do it any differently."

I reach out and squeeze her hand and say, "I wish you could see what I see."

She only nods and squeezes my hand back.

After a moment, she says, "I'm so sorry, Gwen. You're taking care of me again and I should be taking care of you."

"I actually feel normal for the first time in days," I admit. "This is what we do, you tell me about the mess you got yourself into and I tell you what you should do. I almost forgot that I peed my pants." I laugh, despite myself and then add, "I'm not going to break, Charley, so don't treat me like it."

She wipes her eyes again and says with a halfhearted smile, "Okay."

I clear my throat, feeling like we could both use a break from all the revelations. "Now, can you grab me something to eat? Something full of fat and sugar? Like a donut... or maybe a cookie. I've been choking down Mom's green smoothies and I can't take it any more. The woman is obsessed with my diet."

Charley looks up at me, attempting a real smile. *Mission accomplished.* "They're not that bad. She has Olivia and Max drinking them too. But I'll grab you a donut from earlier. Be right back," she says as she slips off the bed and starts for the door.

"Hey Charley," I call out after her.

She stops and turns back toward me. "Yeah?"

"Let's not tell anyone about... ya know, the incident," I say sheepishly.

"Just don't piss me off," she smirks and disappears through the door. I take a deep breath and let it out slowly, feeling drained suddenly from the whole conversation.

# 33
## *Charley*

I walk out of Gwen's bedroom, my mind reeling. I couldn't get away fast enough. Stepping into the hall, I slide my back down the wall and sit with my knees pulled into my chest. I can't believe the flood of information that my mind, as well as my heart, is trying to process. Like the fact that my dad hit my mom. It's hard to wrap my head around the idea of him as a violent man, even if the alcohol changed him into something he wasn't. But more jarring is my mother's silence. She's never said a word. All the hurtful accusations that I have spewed at her over the years come back to me now full force and I can't help but feel guilty, ashamed even. The image of my father that I held in my heart for so long is slowly crumbling, fading to nothing.

Lies. All of it.

And I am gripped by the notion that I could be more like my father than I care to admit. *Maybe there's something wrong with me. Maybe I can't love the way my mother loved my father or the way Gwen loves*

*John. Maybe I'm incapable of love.* I think back to the one time that I was sure I was in love, with Ben. But I screwed that up. *And if it was really love that I felt for him, would I have purposefully hurt him?*

I think about what Gwen said. *Is it easier not to let anyone love you, to dodge the disappointment and expectations, to live alone? Is that what I've been doing? Choosing the easy road? Letting my fear choose my path?* Although somewhere I think my subconscious believed this all along, my heart is just catching up.

I see my father again in my mind, or at least the fragmented man that remains of him, and I think about the choices he made and where those choices have led. And I feel sorry for him, an overwhelming pity taking root. *Is that what I want? To be like him?* I don't want to be a coward. I don't want to be alone. And then I think of my mother and the fact that she's alone, that she never remarried. *What does that say about her choice? Shutting us all out because she couldn't deal. Was it easier to not deal with it all?* And then it occurs to me. She did choose love, her love for her daughters, even though she was too broken to show it. It's as if I see everything now through a different lens. As if I finally see my life's portrait the way it is meant to be seen.

I grip my hair in my hands, wanting all the thoughts to stop. It's almost too much to think about on top of almost losing Gwen. I stand and walk to the bathroom, where I splash cold water on my face and comb my fingers through my hair, securing it in a bun on top of my head. As I make my way down the stairs, the doorbell rings and I yell out, "I'll get it." I swing the door open and find Ben standing there, hands in the pockets of his jeans.

"Ben," I say, stunned to see him in the flesh when his face was all I could see in my mind just a few minutes ago.

"Hey Charley. I wanted to check-in and see how Gwen's doing. And to see how you're doing..." He smiles and my heart catches. I step outside, into his personal space and look up at his clear blue eyes, taking me back in time to when I once saw my whole world in their depths. Something comes over me, nostalgia maybe, or maybe something more. That familiar need to erase what I'm feeling, to make it all stop. My heart is beating loudly in my chest as I shift my weight to my toes and raise up to meet his lips. I kiss him softly and then feel his hand in my hair as he pulls my face closer, parting his lips. And I lose myself for a moment, reveling in the euphoria that clouds all other thoughts. The heavy pull in my gut, flush of warmth, the budding arousal expanding...

"Charley?" I hear his voice, startling me, pulling me from whatever moment I was having with Ben. My heart sinks, clearing out the arousal in a quick beat. Ben and I step away from each other at the same time, leaving a clear view of Grey standing behind us, holding a bouquet of lilies – Gwen's favorite – his jaw pulled taut and a murderous look in his eyes.

"Grey?" I take another step away from Ben, an awkward vibe snaking its way between us. As if to emphasize this, I hear Ben clear his throat.

"Is this you figuring it all out?" Grey asks with an injured tone that's hard to miss.

"Grey..." I start to explain but truthfully I'm not sure what to say.

"Honestly, Charley, I don't know what else I can do or say," he scoffs, shaking his head from side to side. "Can you give these to Gwen?" He hands me the bouquet of lilies and I feel him almost flinch when his hand brushes mine. Our eyes meet for an instant but he tears his gaze from mine abruptly and walks away, his long strides carrying him out of sight before I can utter a word.

"Grey..." I call out as I start to run after him, not even sure what I'm going to say, but it doesn't matter; I'm a moment too late. I stop when I see him reach his car and climb inside. He glances at me one last time before he backs out of the driveway and I can't deny the sinking feeling in my gut. It was only a matter of time before he realized the truth, before he realized that there wasn't anything about us that needed figuring out, so why do I feel sick to my stomach?

I blow out a breath, feeling my shoulders sag, and walk back to the porch. Ben is standing there, watching me. He runs his fingers over his lips and tilts his head to the side, waiting for me to say something.

I fold my arms across my chest, hugging myself in the cold. "I'm sorry..." I whisper, looking down at my feet. I don't know what else to say.

Ben sighs and hangs his head. "Don't be mad at me for saying this, but you haven't changed a bit. All these years and you're still avoiding the obvious." I look up at Ben's face as he says, "I can't do this again. Give my best to Gwen." I stand and watch Ben walk away, following the same path as Grey but without the urgency. I'm left surrounded by my own destruction, a swirling vortex of debris. It feels like the walls are closing in all around me. As if my chest is being squeezed so tight that it hurts to breathe, my entire world pressing into me from all sides. I'm losing everything. I'm losing Gwen. I've lost Grey. I don't really have any close friends. I've held my mother at arm's length nearly my whole life. And for what? So that I won't ever feel the way I feel right now, in this moment. Utterly alone? All those years ago, I pushed Ben away so that I wouldn't have to feel the pain of him leaving me, so that I wouldn't have to watch him walk away. And yet, he still left and it still hurt like hell. Only I had no one to blame but myself.

I look up to keep the tears at bay. It's the middle of the day but the sky is painted with dark clouds. I can't go back in the house and face John or my mother or Gwen. I set the bouquet of flowers inside the door, grab my jacket off the coat rack and, after closing the door behind me, I walk down the driveway, toward nowhere, breathing in the fresh air, hoping to clear the shit-storm raging in my head.

I've wandered around for hours, the rain started a while ago, but it didn't deter my need to keep walking. I'm soaked to the bone, my Converse sneakers full of water and still I keep walking until I find myself standing in front of Ben's old house. I see his car parked in the driveway and recall him telling me at the bar that he moved back to Seaport to care for his mother after his dad passed away. My feet are pounding the pavement faster than my heart is hammering in my chest, but I suddenly have so much to say to him, so many things that I never got the chance to say. I feel as if I *need* to say them.

The sky has grown completely dark and the rain is beating down hard and steady. I step up to the porch, nearly jump when the censored light turns on and then I knock on the door. I wait but there's no response. Just as I'm about to go, the door flies open and Ben stands there in jeans and a T-shirt, barefoot. My eyes are drawn to his bare skin, veins weaving around his sculpted arms like thick chords.

"Charley? What are you doing here? Did you walk here?" He glances behind me to the street before looking back at my face.

"I'm sorry, Ben. I'm so sorry..." I start to choke up but the words pour out of me and I am unable to stop them. "I was scared. I was so scared. I loved you so much and I didn't want you to leave... I couldn't bear the thought of you leaving." Tears are making their way down my face and I feel my body begin to shake, either from the cold or my confession, I can't be sure. Ben's expression is unreadable but he just stands there, searching my face silently, with his hand on the door. "I never meant to hurt you," I say, shaking my head from side to side. "I never wanted to hurt anyone. I just thought... I just thought... if I was with someone else it wouldn't hurt as much. But I was wrong. I was so wrong. Hurting you... was the worst part and I was completely heartbroken when you left."

I feel the rain dripping off me like the words falling from my mouth. I process them at the same time as Ben, not realizing until I said the words aloud how I felt.

"Come here," he says as he pulls me inside and shuts the door. I am sobbing and shaking, a complete mess. But he pulls me into his arms and holds me close, my drenched clothing soaking his T-shirt.

"I know all this, Charley. And I'm not going to lie, you crushed me. It took me a long time to get over you, in some ways I'm still not over you. But once I got over my anger and my bruised ego, I realized why you did it."

"I'm sorry..." I start to apologize again but he pulls back slightly and puts his fingers over my lips.

"It was a long time ago... water under the bridge," he whispers. I look into his eyes through my tears and he stares into mine; we stay like this for a beat. I slowly lean in and press my lips to his and he kisses me for the briefest of moments before he pulls back and rests his forehead against mine, closing his eyes.

"As much as I'd love to see where this goes..." He smirks and whispers, "Trust me I've thought about being with you like this since I saw you in my exam room. But this really isn't about me,

Charley. It's about *him*. I saw it in your eyes, the way you look at him. I know because you used to look at me that way. We both know you're running away, but what are you afraid of this time, Charley? Because it doesn't look like he's going anywhere."

I can feel our hearts beating against each other as he holds me tightly. Every part of me is touching every part of him, our faces so close I can smell a faint trace of beer on his breath. It occurs to me how intimate this is, yet it feels safe and familiar. His eyes are open now and I stare into them, knowing that he's right. About everything. Maybe I've always known that there was something different about Grey, something that set him apart from all the others, something that threatened my simple existence. Ben's question lingers in the air like smoke after a fire. *What am I afraid of?*

"I don't know," I answer, my voice only a whisper.

His fingers trail down my cheek as he says, "I guess our time has passed, huh?"

I sniffle and say, "I guess so."

"Charley, if you feel for him, the way I think you do, then don't screw this up. We only get so many chances at love."

I throw my head back slightly and smile. "God, when did you get so philosophical?" I groan.

"I've screwed up a few chances of my own, so I'm speaking from experience," he says with a smile as he loosens his hold on me, putting more space between us.

"Is that so?" I ask, curious as to what he's been doing all this time.

"Yeah, unfortunately." He steps back and nods toward the living room down the hall. "Come in, I'll get you a towel."

I slip my wet shoes off and follow him down the hallway and take a seat on a bar stool at the kitchen island. I look around, a flood of memories rush me all at once. Being here with Ben and his parents. So envious of how close they all were, how wholesome they seemed. And feeling lucky to be a part of it. I loved them. Ben. His mom. His dad. Being in this room, remembering it all, I know without a doubt, I loved him. Ben hands me a towel and I squeeze the excess water from my hair.

"Is your mom here?" I ask, all at once longing to see her.

"No, she lives over at The Cliffs in assisted living. I moved her there last spring. I didn't like leaving her here alone during my long shifts at the clinic."

"I'm sorry. That must be hard." I feel awful that I never visited all these years, but I was so ashamed of what I had done.

He shrugs. "Thanks, it's not easy. Sometimes I wish I had a sibling to ease the load, ya know. Do you want some dry clothes?" Ben asks.

"Maybe just a ride back to Gwen's, if that's okay. I think I have a lot of things to sort out. It's been a crazy day."

"Are you sure I can't convince you to stay?" he asks, followed quickly by, "As a friend, of course."

"Maybe another time," I say, seeing Ben for the good friend that he always was. My best friend, in fact. And maybe that's why it hurt so much.

He nods and grabs his wallet and car keys off the counter. I follow him back toward the front door, slip on my soggy shoes, and step back into the rain. Ben drives me home in silence, although I meet his gaze each time he glances at me, like we're speaking without saying anything at all.

When I reach Gwen's door, it's locked and I have to knock. I realize how late it is and instantly feel guilty that no one knows where I've been. John, eventually, opens the door.

"There you are," is all he says as he steps aside and I walk though the doorway. And then he adds, "You're soaked."

"Yeah, you could say that," I say. "Sorry that I snuck out without telling anyone."

"We didn't worry too much. We found the flowers with a card from Grey; it wasn't much of a mystery. We knew you were with him." John closes the door and turns the dead bolt into place. I hang my wet jacket on the coat rack, slip my shoes off and follow John into the kitchen.

"That's not exactly how it went, but it doesn't matter. I'm back," I say and then ask, "How's Gwen?"

"She's sleeping. She seemed pretty wiped out today." I think back to our conversation and how much that must have taken out of her. John pours a glass of red wine into an already used glass on the counter and then asks, "Do you want some?"

"Sure," I say and then tell him just a small glass. I'm freezing and need a hot shower.

He takes another wine glass from the cabinet and pours until it's only half full, handing it to me. "Thanks," I say and take a sip. I notice the lilies from Grey arranged in a vase on the kitchen table and my heart sinks.

"I'm not even going to ask what you've been doing," John says with a smirk.

I roll my eyes at him. "Trust me, it's not what you think." I take another sip of my wine. "Are you doing okay, John?"

He sighs and then says, "I think so. I just wish she would let me help her more. I feel like I have to constantly ask her if she needs something and I can tell that she's getting annoyed but I don't know what else to do." He lifts his glass to his lips and takes a big gulp, and then sets it down on the counter.

"I know what you mean. Give her some time, John, she'll come around. You and I both know that Gwen is not good with giving up control."

"Yeah, I know. This is just all so... so fucked up," he says, shaking his head as he rakes his hand through his hair. He folds his arms across his chest and leans back against the kitchen counter.

"I'm sorry, John. It isn't fair."

We both stand in silence sipping our wine until I drain the last sip and say, "I'm going to shower and turn in for the night." And then I ask, "Where's my mom?"

"She went to bed a while ago," he says.

"Okay, well goodnight."

"Goodnight," John says and I head upstairs. I'm sleeping on an inflatable mattress in the office while my mother is sleeping in the downstairs guest room. It's strange to think of us all under the same roof again and yet comforting at the same time. I peek into Gwen's room at the end of the hall and my hand instantly goes to my heart as I take in the scene. Gwen is lying on her back, fast asleep with Max snuggled in on her left side and Olivia sleeping on her right, Gwen's arms are wrapped around them both. Tears spring to my eyes as I draw in a breath and release it, easing the knot in my chest. All I can think is that there is more love in this house than I have ever known.

# 34

## *Gwen*

It's Friday. I wake up feeling better than I have since Thanksgiving. It's amazing what a week in bed will do for recovery. I take slow steps to the bathroom, having mastered this task a few days ago and freshen up, taking care not to wake John. I dress in a clean pair of yoga pants and a sweatshirt and slowly make my way down the stairs with a death grip on the handrail.

I look around the house to find everything is in order. I'm not sure what I expected to find. I guess I was expecting pure chaos in my absence. John has been home the entire week and my mother and Charley have been staying here as well. Between the three of them, life has been continuing on without me. The kids are fed and driven to school with homemade lunches in tow. According to Max, Grammy cuts the crust off his sandwich almost as good as I do. Homework, soccer, play practice – it's all happening without me. Charley even attended the PTA meeting on Wednesday, taking detailed notes for my benefit. It's as if they don't even need me.

This morning I'm determined to make the kids breakfast and give them a warm send-off for school, one where I'm standing vertical rather than lying in bed like a corpse. I see the look in their eyes, and it's killing me. They need to see that I'm going to be okay.

I open the bottom cabinet and slowly bend down to retrieve the waffle iron. My vision turns dark and I sit on the kitchen floor immediately, afraid that I might pass out. I close my eyes and wait for the dizziness to pass. When I open them a moment later, I realize that the waffle iron is not in the cabinet where I keep it. I swallow back an overwhelming sense of anger.

*Is it too much to ask to put things back where they belong?*

I grip the edge of the counter and pull myself back on my feet and begin to open one cabinet after another, slamming each one harder when I discover that it does not hold the waffle iron. By the time I get to the last cabinet, I slam it so hard that it wakes John. I hear him thumping down the stairs, two at a time. He steps into the kitchen while I'm slumped over the cold marble countertop, trying to catch my breath. My frantic search has sucked whatever energy I thought I had.

"What are you doing?" John asks quietly as I hear him approach.

Without turning to face him, I say rather calmly, "Making breakfast."

"Come back to bed, Gwen," he says, stepping closer. I feel his hand on my shoulder. I recoil at his touch and am shocked at my cold-hearted reaction. John flinches and removes his hand immediately, as if I physically shocked him.

"Come on, honey," he whispers.

"I'll be up in a minute, I just want to make breakfast," I say through clenched teeth. I'm so angry. I feel it pulsing through my veins but I can't seem to rein it in. It's spreading, consuming me like a raging fire that I can't contain.

"*I'll* make breakfast, Gwen."

I turn and face him, leaning back against the counter for support.

"I think I can manage to make breakfast for my kids, John. If I could just find the fucking waffle iron, everything will be fine." I hear the tension in my voice, I'm not quite yelling but I want to. I want to unleash the fury. I look at John, standing in front of me in only his black boxer shorts and a white T-shirt, his hair unruly. A look of disbelief and pity on his face, which only fuels my anger even more. I almost hate him in this moment. *Almost*, I think. The way he's been hovering over me all week, asking me what I need every five seconds, like I'm some kind of invalid. The way he's been creating a buffer between Olivia and Max and me, like he needs to protect them from their own mother. I'm not dying, *not yet anyway*. It all makes me so angry. My heart is beating erratically in my chest as John and I stand in the kitchen staring at each other, like a showdown in an old western movie, each of us waiting to see who will draw their gun first.

Apparently, he's braver than I in the moment, because after what feels like forever, he points to something beyond my right shoulder and says in a clipped tone, "It's on the counter, behind you." And then he turns and walks away. I hear him thud back upstairs and then I slowly collapse on the floor. Angry tears fill my eyes as I sit in my own pool of pity, feeling so much resentment toward John. His bitter last words taking what I wanted; he won't even give me the satisfaction of telling him off.

I hate him but I hate myself more.

A week later, after Charley and my mother have gone home, the kids and I are curled up on the sofa in the family room, watching Saturday morning reruns of *iCarly* while John cleans the breakfast dishes in the kitchen.

After a while John steps into the room and tells us that he's going to take a shower. Olivia is the only one who acknowledges him verbally. Max is too absorbed in the television and I'm still too angry to break my silence. The tension is palpable. I can hardly stand to be in the same room with John. I've been snuggling with Max and Olivia in our bed most nights, forcing John to sleep in Max's room. I feel like everything is spiraling out of control but I don't know how to stop it.

Max shifts around on the couch when the episode ends and knocks over a bowl of dry Cheerios in the process, spilling them all over the floor.

Max looks at me hesitantly and says, "Uh-oh."

"It's okay Bubs, I'll get it," I say without a moment's pause. I slide to the edge of the sofa and stand slowly, make my way to the hall closet and retrieve the vacuum. I plug it in on the far wall and push it closer to the couch. It takes all my strength to push the ottoman out of the way which leaves me frustrated that such a small task has left me breathless. I stand and catch my breath and then say, "Feet up," and watch the kids pull their legs up underneath them on the couch. I flip on the vacuum and start to push it back and forth over the carpet. It feels much heavier than I remember, but I concentrate on the puddle of Cheerios on the carpet and the ping of each one being sucked into the vacuum.

My breathing becomes ragged and before long, I can hear my own wheeze as I struggle to drag in a decent breath. My vision blurs and I feel the room begin to spin. I slide down until I'm sitting on the carpet, the vacuum still running.

I can vaguely hear Olivia as she says, "Mom, Mom, Mom," repeatedly. I try to reach my hand up to her, to reassure her that I'm okay, but I can't muster the strength. I hear her yell, "Max, go get Dad, hurry." The vacuum is still whirling away as I'm still struggling to breathe. Slowly, the air comes and my wheezing fades, the room stands still once again. I see John and Max walk in and John immediately flips the vacuum off and the room is suddenly bathed in silence.

"Gwen, honey, are you okay?" I hear John ask, his voice frantic with worry.

I nod my head slowly as if it's made of lead. I manage to whisper, "I'm okay."

John kneels down next to me, places his hands under my arms and drags me up until I'm sitting on the couch.

"Honestly, Gwen, tell me, do I need to take you in?" John asks, sitting beside me.

I catch my breath and say, "No. I'm okay. It's passing. I just got winded." I lean back on the couch, now drawing in big breaths, feeling almost normal again.

"Kids, Mommy's fine. But I need you to go upstairs for a bit, okay," I hear John say.

They both hesitate for a moment, watching me, but I say, "I'm fine. Go on," and I wave them away.

When the kids are out of earshot, John says quietly, "What were you thinking, Gwen?"

"What do you mean?" I ask, feigning ignorance.

"With the vacuum. It could've waited. You could've asked me to do it."

My anger is brewing, even though I know he's right. I should've waited.

"It was no big deal. I just got winded," I say.

John leans forward and rests his elbows on his knees, rubbing his hand down his face.

"Gwen, it's more than that. It's your heart. You need to wait until it gets stronger."

"I said I was fine, John," I say through clenched teeth.

"You're not fine, Gwen. I almost lost you. Dammit, why do you have to be so stubborn?"

Something snaps inside me and all the tension and anger breaks free and I can't stop it even if I were to try.

"Maybe if you'd stop hovering over me, treating me like a child, maybe I wouldn't have to be so stubborn. Jesus, John, it's like I can't breathe without you needing to know about it," I yell.

He stands up and paces in front of me. "Maybe if you would just once, ask me for help. JUST ONCE. It's not that hard. Like, 'Gee, John can you get me a glass of water?' when you're thirsty instead of trying to get it yourself. Then maybe I wouldn't have to ask you if you're thirsty every five *fucking* minutes."

"I can get my own water, John. I don't need you to wait on me," I snap back.

"Exactly. You don't need me. That's the whole problem here, Gwen. You couldn't even tell me you were sick. Who does that? Who doesn't tell their husband they have cancer? Do you have any idea how that makes me feel?"

I watch John rake his hand through his hair, dragging in long, frustrated breaths and blowing them out through his nose. The volcano of tension has erupted and I fear the aftermath. He's right. I was wrong to keep it all from him, but where does that leave us?

"I want to be so mad at you Gwen, but it seems like such a waste of time. I refuse to live like this another day. You have to stop hating me for loving you, for wanting to take care of you, for wanting you to need me." He sits down next to me and holds my hand between both of his. "I don't know how much time we have left and that scares the shit out of me," he says calmly with tears in his eyes. "But you have to let me in. You have to let me take care of you, Gwen. Being in a relationship, being in a marriage is about being there for each other, especially in the worst of times. You have to let me be there for you."

I hear what he's saying. I cry at his words and the pain in his voice. *Why is it so hard for me to let him take care of me? Why is it so hard to admit that I need help?*

I cry harder, shedding all my anger when I feel John's arms around me. I lean into him completely, letting him hold all my weight, hoping he feels the significance.

I fully surrender.

"I love you, John," I say through my sobs. "I'm sorry. I don't know what's wrong with me." I look up into his eyes and he wipes my tears away with his fingertips, leaning in and kissing me on the lips.

"I love you too," he says, pulling back just enough to tuck my hair behind my ear, reminding me of all the reasons I fell in love with him in the first place.

That night, after John tucks Olivia and Max into their own beds, he climbs into our bed beside me and kisses me madly and then makes slow, sweet love to me. And I forget that I'm sick, I forget that we were fighting, I forget that I was ever angry. I forget my own name.

And in my postcoital bliss, I vow to be a better wife, to tell my husband everything, even when it makes me feel weak. I know that he'll be there to raise me up and love me strong. I vow to show him every day how much I need him. Because at the end of the day, in sickness or in health, I *do* need him.

# 35

## *Charley*

"It's snowing," Max squeals from the glass doors that lead out to the back deck. "Aunt Charley, come look," he calls. I make my way over to the window, cup my hands around my face and look out. Sure enough, fluffy white flakes are falling softly from the dark sky. It hardly ever snows in Seattle. I get caught up in the idea that the snowflakes falling outside the window are some sort of Christmas miracle.

It's Christmas Eve and we are all under the same roof again, at Gwen's house. This is the first Christmas in a long time that I can remember feeling like a real family. My mother and I have slowly been getting closer. Gwen has completely recovered from her episode. She is starting her new cancer treatment the first week of January. John and Gwen have been acting like long lost lovebirds, it's almost enough to make me sick, but it beats the crazy tension from before. My job has been going well, so well in fact that I just received a big, fat raise. The end of the month will mark the longest I have stayed at the same job in three years. It feels like a small triumph. Especially when working in the same office as Grey has been awkward to say the least, tempting me to jump ship every time that we are in the same room. I don't do awkward. But I've hung in there. Avoiding Grey at all costs. We haven't spoken since the day he saw me kissing Ben. Evidently, the scene was the final knife in the back that he needed to cut me loose for good. I'm not proud of myself. I'm heartbroken. I realize what I felt, or still feel, for Grey is significant, but I just don't know what to do about it. So I do nothing. I haven't been seeing anyone else either. For once, I've been alone, spending time with my family. Denying my need to escape every time I feel something, denying the need to run into the arms of a man.

I actually feel like everything is going to be okay. For all of us. For now.

"Can we go outside?" Max asks, his enthusiasm infectious.

I turn around and raise my eyebrows in plea at Gwen who is standing in the kitchen, drying the last dish from dinner with a festive red dishtowel. My mother is standing beside her in a bright green Christmas sweater, wiping down the counter and John is putting the clean dishes away behind them.

Olivia runs over to the window and looks out. "Can we, Mom?" she begs.

"Of course, but we're *all* going. Grab your coats and gloves."

"Woohoo," Max and Olivia holler in unison as they run to get their coats.

I walk toward the entryway to grab my own coat and watch John pull Gwen into his arms and plant a kiss on her lips as I pass. It brings a smile to my face but makes me long for Grey, which surprises me. I know that he's in California with his family, and according to the memo I read at work, he won't be back until after the New Year. I think of him now, picturing him in a huge house on a steep cliff in the warmth of California. His mother and father are probably wearing matching Christmas sweaters, as they all sit around a piano and sing Christmas carols. Grey, his two brothers and doting parents. They probably go to church too. Midnight Mass, they're probably Catholic. The scene runs through my mind as I realize how little I know about Grey.

Outside on the back lawn, we stand in our warm coats, hats, and gloves and marvel in the white magic. The air is still, an eerie quiet, creating a sanctum of serenity that is ours for the taking. The snow is starting to accumulate on the ground but not enough to roll around in it. With arms out and faces turned up, we watch the snowflakes as they float down from the night sky. They seem to be falling in slow motion. Max tries to catch them on his tongue and, before long, we're all trying to catch snowflakes on our tongues. We look absolutely ridiculous but I couldn't care less. I feel so happy in the moment that I could cry, but I don't. Instead I laugh. And it must be infectious, because soon we're all laughing, even my mother. And it's hard to ignore the urge I have to take a picture and send it to a certain someone with a caption that reads "White Christmas."

Later, after John has read "Twas The Night Before Christmas," in front of the fire and Max and Olivia have left cookies and milk on the mantel for Santa, I sit by the fire with my mother while John and Gwen put the kids to bed.

"Do you remember your dad reading that same story every Christmas Eve?" my mother asks.

I shake my head, unable to recall the memory.

"Well, you were pretty young. Gwen probably remembers. He loved Christmas. Always made a big deal about everything. Bought you girls extravagant gifts that we couldn't afford." She pauses and then laughs. "He even littered the front yard with reindeer poop one year when Gwen started questioning things."

"Huh, I don't remember," I say, wishing I had more good memories of my dad, of my childhood. And then I ask, "Why didn't we ever talk about Dad before?"

"I just thought it would be too hard. And I think I was afraid of the questions you would ask, if I opened that door." I understand what she means. She didn't want the truth to come out. But now that the lid has been blown off that can of worms, I guess nothing is off limits.

And then I ask, "Mom, how did you know that you loved Dad?" A simple question that every daughter probably asks their mother at some point, and for the first time I feel like we can share a typical mother-daughter conversation.

She scoots closer to me on the sofa and considers my question in silence. And then she says, "I think what you really want to ask is how you'll know if you're in love with Grey. And I think that only you can answer that. But let me ask you this. Tonight, when you stood outside catching snowflakes on your tongue, I saw something in your eyes that I haven't seen in a long time. You looked at peace, almost... dare I say, happy. Were you thinking of him? Did you wish to share that moment with him?"

I don't answer her. I just look into my mother's eyes. I feel like for the first time, she really sees me and I realize that, despite our distance, she knows me, like a mother should know her daughter. I lean the side of my face against her shoulder and she grabs my hand and holds it in her own.

And then she whispers, "That, my dear, is love."

My heart hurts in my chest the minute she says it, and I know the truth right then. Maybe I've known the truth all along but didn't want to see it. Maybe I was afraid of what it might mean, afraid to even admit it to myself. But I know now, without a shadow of doubt.

I'm in love with Grey.

# 36

## *Gwen*

I walk into the family room and see my mother and Charley having a moment on the couch. Part of me is happy to finally see them getting along, to no longer have to play referee to their constant bickering, but another part of me is somewhat envious. I have never been close to my mother. I love her and I know her in a way that Charley never has, but we've never confided in each other or had any kind of intimate relationship. It seems in the past few weeks that Charley has grown closer to our mother than I have in the ten years since I reconciled with her after Olivia was born. I'd be lying if I said I didn't feel left out.

"Come here Gwen, sit with us," my mother says, holding her hand out to me when she notices me standing in the room.

I plop down next to her on the couch and she pulls me closer and holds my hand.

"We were just talking about how over-the-top your father was about Christmas. Do you remember that year he broke his arm? Charlotte, you were probably only two."

I remember. "He fell off the roof, putting the Christmas lights up," I say.

"Not just the lights. He had bought a light-up Santa with a sleigh and all eight reindeer. I told him to set it up in the front yard, but he insisted it be on the roof for the full effect."

"Our house was lit up like *National Lampoon's Christmas* that year," I say remembering how magical it looked at night when my dad would flip the switch.

It's quiet for a moment and then my mom says, "Charlotte, here, just realized that she's in love with Grey."

"Mother, seriously," Charley scolds.

"So the question is, what are you going to do about it?" I ask. I knew that Charley felt something real for Grey, but I also knew that she had to realize it on her own. I just hope that it's not too late. Grey doesn't seem like the type to sit around, pining for a woman.

"I don't know," Charley says quietly. I sit forward and glance at her. She looks terrified, sitting on the other side of my mother, gripping her hand with her bottom lip between her teeth.

"Well we could get drunk," I suggest.

"That sounds like a marvelous idea, Gwen," my mother says.

"Wine or liquor?" I ask, as I stand to grab something from the kitchen.

"Wine and I'll get it. You sit and relax, Gwen," Charley says as she hops up and heads for the kitchen. I sit back down and cuddle up next to my mom. She pulls my hair aside and kisses me on the forehead, an endearing gesture that I find myself reveling in. "I love you Gweny," she whispers, squeezing me against her side tightly.

The way she calls me by the nickname she gave me during the early years melts something inside me and I whisper back, "Love you too, Mom."

Charley's back in a flash with an uncorked bottle of red wine and three glasses. She pours each of us a loaded goblet and then we clink our glasses together as she says, "Merry Christmas."

We drink, we laugh, we reminisce. I can't remember ever feeling so connected to my sister or my mother. When Charley gets up to grab another bottle of wine, John comes in wearing a Santa hat with his arms full of presents.

"Partying without me I see?" he says with a wink as he sets the gifts down in front of the Christmas tree.

"Oh, honey, you already wrapped all of these? Why didn't you tell me, I would've helped," I say.

"I know, but I didn't mind. You already did so much today. Do my wrapping skills meet your approval?" he teases.

And then Charley says with a slur, "Perfect John. It looks like Santa's elves wrapped them." She punches him in the arm playfully and nearly spills her wine. John takes the glass from her hand and finishes off what's left in it.

My mother and I laugh. I get up and arrange the presents under the tree, the same way I have for the past ten years.

We finish off another bottle of wine before we decide to call it a night. I know that the kids will be awake at the crack of dawn and anxious to open their gifts from Santa Claus. My mother hugs me goodnight, holding on for an extra beat before kissing my cheek and letting go. Such a subtle gesture but one that leaves a lump in my throat.

I follow everyone out of the room, flipping off the lights along the way except for the white lights on the Christmas tree. I glance back from the stairwell, admiring the soft glow from the tree, the smoldering logs in the fireplace, the stockings that hang from the mantel each with the kids' names embroidered in red at the top. I want to hold on to the moment just a little bit longer, to revel in the warmth of the room, the way it fills my heart to the brim.

"You coming?" John whispers from a few stairs above me. I turn and follow him upstairs, to our bedroom.

When John and I finally crawl into bed, he leaves his bedside lamp on and hands me a small box.

"What's this?" I ask with surprise.

"Merry Christmas," he says.

I pull the lid off the box and lift a small black velvet case from its confines. I glance at John and he nods toward the case. I open it to find a stunning diamond and platinum ring. The center gem is a nearly three-carat emerald cut diamond surrounded by a halo of smaller stones. The delicate band is adorned with diamond accents, giving the ring a glamorous effect. It is the most exquisite ring I have ever seen.

"It's beautiful John... I don't know what to say. I love it." I'm stunned as I pull it from the box and hold it up to the light. It's nearly blinding.

"Your wedding band is so small, I just thought it was time for an upgrade."

"I love my wedding band, though," I say, holding up my ring finger and admiring the simple gold band set with a beautiful solitaire diamond, a much smaller affair. But it reminds me of where John and I began, in a small apartment in the city, eating dinner on the sofa because we couldn't afford a dining table. So young and crazy in love.

"You could wear it on a chain around your neck to make room for your new ring," John suggests.

I slip my wedding band off and slide it on my right hand and then slip my new ring in its place. Perfect fit. "This thing is humongous," I say, holding up my hand to admire it. "I love it," I squeal with a huge grin on my face. We both lie back on our pillows, facing each other. "Thank you," I whisper.

"There's a tiny inscription on the inside," he says and I immediately pull the ring off my finger and examine the inside of the band. In tiny cursive letters, so small one would never see it unless they knew it was there, it says, "beyond forever."

Tears spring to my eyes at the significance. "Oh John, I love you," I say, slipping the ring back on my finger and pulling him close.

"Gwen, I mean it. I will always love you, no matter what," he says with tears in his eyes. "Always. It will always be you."

I nod through my own tears. I know exactly what he means. We don't talk about the inevitable, but it's always there just on the periphery. And John's promise to love me forever now holds a new meaning than it did on our wedding day.

I hold his face in my hands and I kiss him. I kiss him with all the words that we leave unspoken. And I pray to God that this is the first of many more Christmas seasons in my new forever.

"Mommy, Mommy, Santa came. He came," Max yells in my ear as I slowly open my eyes one at a time. A smile stretches across my face as Max's excitement comes into focus.

"Okay, I'm getting up," I say, rubbing the sleep from my eyes. I feel John stir beside me and slowly climb out of bed.

"I'll start the coffee, you get everyone else," he mumbles. I sit up and stretch, while Max throws my robe at me and runs out of the room yelling Olivia's name. I pull my robe on and catch sight of my new ring as it captures the light streaming in from the hallway. I take a moment to admire it, practically giddy with happiness.

I go to the office first and wake Charley. She mumbles a few obscenities at me but eventually gets out of bed with my promise of hot coffee. When we make our way downstairs, my mother and Olivia are already in the kitchen with John and Max. We take a few minutes to sip our coffee and nibble on the pumpkin bread that I made yesterday for this very occasion, all the while warding off Max's insistent pleas to "hurry up." Olivia is less excited this year, and I wonder if the magic of Christmas, more specifically Santa Claus, is wearing off. But as we move into the family room and take our places around the Christmas tree surrounded by more presents then she has ever seen, I see her face light up and I know that we have made it through another year with her childlike innocence still in tact.

As John begins to pass out gifts, Charley plops down on the couch beside me.

"Woah," she says, grabbing my hand and holding it up to the light. She admires my new ring and says, "Nice job, John."

"Right?" I agree. "I love it."

"Well, it's beautiful," she says, letting go of my hand and squeezing me into her side.

I lean into her and feel my mother's arm go around both Charley and I as she whispers, "I love my girls." I lean forward and smile at her before my attention is snared by both Olivia and Max as they begin tearing through the wrapping paper on their gifts.

It is a perfect morning. The kids are ecstatic as they open their presents. Max opens his Xbox and Olivia unveils her very own iPad filled with a long list of downloaded ebooks. I may have gone a little bit overboard given the circumstances, but by the look on their sweet faces, it was well worth it.

I sit surrounded by love and warmth, taking it all in. Never has my heart felt so full. A single tear escapes, sliding slowly down my cheek and I look up to find John staring at me from across the room, his own eyes filled with unshed tears. There are no words to describe what it feels like to look into his eyes and know for certain that he gets exactly what I'm feeling, right now in this moment. From the look in his eyes, I know he feels it too. We both nod in understanding and my eyes flood with tears. I know from this point on, every moment will be like this, a bittersweet recognition. A beautiful moment marked with a note of thankfulness and tinged with sorrow. But most importantly, these moments will never be taken for granted. Because I'm thankful for every, single one of them.

# 37
## *Charley*

It's New Year's Eve. After three days of relentless begging from Michelle, the new receptionist in our office – barely of the legal drinking age and still in that college party-mode – I agreed to join her at an upscale club downtown. She's a petite thing with pale skin and short blonde hair, and the biggest brown eyes I have ever seen. She looks like the girl next door and has the personality to match. She rallied a group of her college girl friends for the occasion and scored us a huge corner booth, a rarity on the busiest night of the year. Also seated at our table are Victor and Sienna both from our office, Victor's boyfriend Marcus, and Stacey – the tattooed, pierced barista from the coffee shop in the lobby of our building. It's an eclectic mix of personalities but makes for a fun evening. I normally love to celebrate New Year's Eve, the thrill, the mystery of where the night will lead, but I can't muster even a trace of excitement this year. Instead, I find myself regretting my decision and wishing for the alternative – an evening at Gwen's where she's hosting a small party with their friends, kids included. But Michelle was insistent and I thought it would be a good distraction. The truth is, I miss Grey. He's still out of town and I'm still out of answers to the questions that are swirling around in my head. I promised myself that the moment he's back from California, I'll tell him how I feel. But the fear of the unknown is terrifying. And so, dressed in a new black backless dress and heels, I sip a dirty martini and watch the mingling crowd around me in hopes of shedding Grey from my mind for at least one night.

The members of our table are all on the dance floor, all except for Marcus who claims that he doesn't dance. A band is playing an eighties remix, too loud for Marcus and I to indulge in conversation. The majority of the crowd appears to be in their thirties, rather than the twentysomethings from my table. Receding hairlines, tailored suits, designer dresses with red-soled shoes – a dead giveaway. In a quiet pause between songs Marcus leans over and asks if I'm having fun.

I shrug as the band starts up again.

Marcus leans in closer and yells in my ear, "Not really my scene either."

I smile and turn my face closer to his and say, "It makes me feel old." Even though I'm younger and more unattached than most of the people on the dance floor, I can't seem to muster enough energy to join them.

"I know what you mean," he mouths.

Marcus is attractive with smooth dark skin, strong, defined cheekbones and straight black hair, not to mention that he's dressed to kill. He doesn't look a day over twenty-five but I laugh anyway.

I focus my attention back to the dance floor as I finish my drink, pick up the drink stick from my empty glass and pull the olives off one at a time with my teeth. I glance over my shoulder in search of our waitress when I see him.

Grey.

He's sitting alone at a table nearby and staring right at me. I nearly choke on my own breath as our eyes lock. He doesn't turn away. I have not laid eyes on him since before Christmas and now, seeing him just a few feet away gives me an actual physical pain in my chest. He's wearing a bright blue dress shirt, unbuttoned at the top with the sleeves rolled up to his elbows. His hair is glistening with product and his dark eyes are piercing, so beautiful I am instantly lost in a sea of Grey.

It's as if a veil has been lifted, a veil of the past that I allowed to color every part of my life and now I finally see everything more clearly. I see *him.*

Just then, Michelle bounds into my line of sight, breaking the trance.

"Whew, it's getting hot in here," she yells over the music as she plops down in the booth beside me. I manage a small smile and watch her guzzle down her fruity drink, but my mind is on something else, someone else.

I feel like I need to do something, say something. I want Grey to know how I feel but I don't know how to do this sort of thing. I can't just blurt it out. I can't just walk over there and pick up where we left off. *And what if he rejects me? What if I'm too late?*

I reach into my small clutch purse beside me, push around the lipstick and breath mints until I feel my phone in my hand. I pull it out, holding it in my lap under the table and type a short text to Grey. It is the only thing that I can think of in the moment. The only thing I am comfortable saying right now. I can only hope that it's enough.

*My favorite color is blue.*

THE WORDS WE LEAVE UNSPOKEN

A minute goes by, maybe two, before I turn to glance his way when there is no response. I suck in a breath as I watch a tall, long-legged blonde sit down at his table. He pulls her chair closer and places his arm around her back as she nestles into his side and whispers something into his ear. I watch as he tips his head back a bit and laughs. The knife finally hits its mark when I see him turn his face to hers and gently kiss her lips. My face burns like fire and my heart breaks apart. I allowed myself to feel something for a brief moment and already the vulnerability has exposed me, let the enemy breach the fortress of my heart. *How could I have been so stupid?*

The club feels too small, too crowded. The beat of the music is pounding in my ears, too loud.

I grab my purse and slide out of the booth, leaning in and telling Michelle that I'm not feeling well. I race to the door, pushing through the crowd quickly until I feel the cool night on my skin. I gasp for air as if I couldn't breathe while inside. My chest feels like a raw piece of meat, filleted and bleeding. The cold wind licks at my bare skin and the light drizzle wets my face. I hear Michelle beside me, saying my name.

"You okay?" she asks.

"I don't know," I answer honestly. "I think I'm gonna to call it a night."

"Are you sure? It's only eleven o'clock." Michelle's eyebrows are pulled in, lines creasing the skin between them.

"Yeah, I'm sure. I'll grab a cab."

"Well, happy New Year." She leans in and gives me a swift hug.

I hug her back, wincing from the pain of brief contact as if my ribs are bruised and say, "Thanks for the invite."

"Thanks for coming. Goodnight girl," she says and then disappears through the door and into the sea of bodies inside.

Two yellow cabs are parked along the curb in wait. I walk to the nearest one, pull the car door open and slide into the backseat.

"Where to, miss?" the cabbie asks with a strong Middle Eastern accent, his dark eyes and bushy eyebrows appear in the rearview mirror as he waits for my destination.

I rattle off my address, complete with the nearest cross street.

The cab pulls away from the curb and darts into traffic. I release a heavy breath of relief and fight the stinging tears that threaten to exist.

Twenty minutes later, as we zoom down the main drag along Green Lake, I watch swarms of people gather outside pubs and restaurants. I see crowds of people pouring into the small mid-century homes in the neighborhood, all anxiously waiting to ring in the New Year. I feel hollow inside as the realization that I'll be alone at the stroke of midnight settles in. I regret leaving the club so suddenly. The old me would have shrugged off the threatening scene and buried myself in another man's arms with a vengeance. There were plenty of appealing offers that I had politely declined. But as the vision of Grey's mouth on the blonde's perfectly painted lips flashes through my mind, a dull ache settles into my gut and I know that I made the right decision. The cab pulls up outside my bungalow. I slip a twenty-dollar bill to the driver and exit the car. My usually quiet street is filled with voices and music echoing from nearby house parties. I unlock my front door, step inside and slip off my shoes. I melt into the sofa and let the night wash off me with a sigh. Turning on the television to drown out the quiet, I find the New Year's Eve special in Times Square, the countdown showing thirty minutes until the drop of the ball.

Before long, the seconds are ticking by on the television screen with one minute to go. A sudden knock on the door startles me. *Who in the world could that be?* I peek out the front window but cannot see a car that I recognize on the crowded street. I open the door with the chain still in place and my heart stops when I see Grey's face. I close the door and pull open the chain before opening the door all the way. Grey steps inside, invading my space just as I hear the countdown in Times Square chiming from the television. *Ten, nine, eight, seven...* seconds tick by although it feels as if time has stopped completely. I hear fireworks on the television simultaneously with the crackle of fireworks outside, most likely coming from the Space Needle in Seattle Center.

Grey whispers, "Happy New Year, Charley" and then engulfs me in his arms, lifting my feet inches from the floor as his lips crash against mine. My hands go to his hair as I pull him closer, breathing him in, relishing in his familiar scent and the feel of his body pressed against mine. He takes another step inside without letting me go or interrupting our kiss, I hear the door slam closed as "Auld Lange Syne" plays in the background. I pull away when I remember the blonde and her painted lips.

"What are you doing here?" I ask, looking into Grey's warm eyes.

He shrugs his shoulders, his arms still around me. "I got your text."

"What about the blonde?"

"What about the tall, Antonio Banderas?"

I smile. Marcus kind of does look like a younger, taller Antonio Banderas.

"You first," I say.

"Last minute date. It never would have worked out," he says with a sexy grin, still so close to me I can smell peppermint on his breath.

"Gay," is all I say in return, staring into his eyes.

"So, where does this leave us?" he asks. His easy tone is underlined with so much more.

I stand on my tippy toes and press my lips back against his as I slip my hands up underneath his shirt, feeling the smooth, cut planes of his back with my fingertips. Grey's hands are running down the bare skin of my back, where my dress leaves me exposed.

"God, this dress. Are you trying to kill me?" he murmurs against my lips as he walks me backward toward the bedroom. Once we are inside the door to my room, he slips the dress from my shoulders and steps back to watch it fall to my feet, leaving me standing in only a pair of black lace panties. He takes a moment to admire me but I can't wait another second. I practically lunge at him, kissing his cheek, his neck, as I unbutton his dress shirt. I slip it from his shoulders, down his arms and let it fall to the ground. He undoes his own belt and slacks, letting them fall and then he steps out of them all while I kiss him senseless.

He pushes me back on the bed and crawls over me, kissing his way from my belly to my lips, slowly. That familiar dizzy high comes over me as I anticipate what is going to happen next, but then I find myself with my hand against Grey's chest, holding him back as my eyes shoot open and look into the depth of his own.

"Grey," I whisper. All at once, I want him to know what this means to me. That this isn't like before. I want him to know what I feel for him. I can't lose him again. But once I'm staring into his eyes, the words get caught in my throat. I am so far out of my element, I'm not sure what to say or do. My heart is thrumming in my chest as his eyes search mine, questioning.

My heart is full of so many words that I long to convey, but they remain unspoken, as if they are trapped inside, locked away with no will to escape. I avert my eyes, feeling on the verge of tears.

Grey gently, sweetly presses his lips to my temple and whispers against my ear, "I know, Charley." And then he kisses me. And it feels weighted with a promise, loaded with meaning. Grey draws out every touch, every kiss, taking his time and I stare into his eyes as he takes me to new heights and, for the first time ever, I feel like we're making love, something I have never experienced before. A new high that leaves me so full that I feel like my heart might burst. Such an obvious contrast to the dizzy void, the emptiness I normally crave.

When we are done, Grey pulls me close and tears roll one by one down my cheeks. Overcome with emotion, I lay in Grey's arms in silence until I feel his breathing even out and his arms grow limp around me. I watch his sleeping face, memorizing every detail, and before I can stop them, the words, "I love you, Grey," tumble softly from my lips. It surprises me that they come with such ease, but then again, Grey's asleep. I close my eyes and nestle my head into the crook of his neck, feeling so content in his arms.

A few moments later, just as I'm about to drift off to sleep, I feel Grey tighten his embrace and then he whispers, "I love you too, Charley." For a moment I think that I imagined it, that he really didn't hear my words or say his own. But I feel his lips lift into a smile against my temple as he presses his lips there softly.

I wait for the fear to settle in, take its hold and darken the blinding light that is exploding inside me like the fireworks that lit up the sky at midnight.

But all I feel is love.

# Epilogue: Five Years Later

## *Gwen*

The horn of a ferryboat bellows in the distance as I watch it glide across the dark blue waters of Elliott Bay. The sun is high in the clear sky, the rising temperature breeding beads of sweat along my brow. Escaping the heat of the balcony, I step back inside the cool, air-conditioned hotel suite as I raise my phone to my ear just in time to hear Charley's voice chime, "Leave a message." The same words I have heard nearly twenty times in the past hour. *Where could she be?*

I hear a knock on the hotel room door and scurry across the plush carpeting, hoping it's Charley at the door.

I find John and Grey in the hallway wearing only their black pants and white dress shirts, their ties and suit jackets missing.

"Any luck?" John asks as they step into the room.

"No, nothing. She's not answering her phone," I say. I glance at Grey, armed with an apology at the concern etched into his brow.

He holds his phone up, showing me the screen. I stare at it, dumbfounded, until I recognize the map of downtown with a flashing red dot, pinpointing Charley's location.

I look up at Grey then, my mind full of mixed thoughts. Relief that we have found Charley at last, but disappointment that Grey has the ability to track my sister like a lost dog.

The disappointment must have won over the expression on my face because Grey shrugs and says a bit defensively, "You do realize that your sister loses her phone more than anyone I've ever known."

A small smile forms on my lips as I realize that Grey's tracking app has nothing to do with trust and everything to do with Charley's absentmindedness. I snag the phone from his hand and try to make sense of the address. She is somewhere close to the hotel, but nowhere with a distinguishable landmark.

I step away, slip on my heels and grab my purse.

"Where do you think you're going?" John asks.

"To get my sister," I say with my chin up, stepping around both of them toward the door with Grey's phone still clutched tightly in my palm.

Grey grabs my arm gently, holding me back from the door. "Whoa, don't you think I should be the one to go?"

I turn to look at him and say as lightly as possible, "No offense, but I've talked her off way more ledges than you. I'm going."

John clasps his hand on Grey's shoulder. "She's right, man. Let Gwen go find her."

I pause while Grey releases my arm and then add, "Don't worry. She probably just needed some air. We'll be back in time, you'll see."

Grey reaches into his pocket and hands me a valet ticket. "Here, take my car." I take the ticket from his hand and rush out of the room, trying to ignore the look on his face. The look that says what my heart fears.

As I wait for the valet to bring Grey's car around, I send out a silent wish. I wish for this to be some crazy misunderstanding with a very logical explanation. Like maybe Charley ran out to pick up a last minute gift for Grey. Or maybe she had a sudden craving for Mexican food from a street vendor downtown.

I slip behind the wheel of Grey's sporty car, feeling cramped in the small space, a strange feeling in comparison to my oversized SUV. I follow the signal from Grey's phone as it leads me south along the waterfront, deeper into the city. I pull the car over on a rundown street, beneath the freeway. A yellow cab is parked nearby and I can see Charley in the backseat. She turns and spots Grey's car and I watch the initial shock register on her face. A moment later, she is walking toward me wearing a long, white terrycloth robe with the hotel's logo on the breast pocket and flip-flops. She climbs into the passenger seat, closes the door and lets out a loud breath through her mouth.

"What are you doing here, Charley?" I ask, clicking the door locks in place as I take in our sketchy surroundings. Her eyes are scanning a crowd of homeless men and women that are lurking a few yards away.

"I just wanted to see him," she says. And immediately it hits me. She came here to find our father. My eyes instantly settle on each face in the distance, frantically searching the crowd for him. I don't see anyone I recognize, but it's been so long. *Would I know him? Would I recognize his face after all these years?*

"You're not running away, are you?" I ask, needing to know what's going on in her head. "Because Grey loves you so much, Charley. It'll break his heart if you don't go through with it."

She turns to look at me and I can see the tears pooled in her eyes.

"He's not here," she says. "I just thought if I saw him again, I would know what to do."

"What do you mean, Charley? Are you having second thoughts? I thought you wanted to marry Grey? I thought that you were finally ready?"

"I was ready. I mean... I *am* ready. But I just don't know... I don't know if I can do this." She turns away from me, scanning the crowd again.

I take a deep breath and twist my body in the small seat until I'm facing her side of the car. "Charley, Grey loves you. He's not going anywhere. I know that you're scared but he's been waiting for you, waiting to marry you for *five* years. Trust me. Trust in Grey."

"I'm pregnant," she blurts out as she faces me again. As soon as the words leave her lips, her tears slip down her cheeks.

I'm stunned but elated all in the same breath. "Oh, sweetie," I gasp, reaching out for her and drawing her into my arms. "That's a good thing."

"I'm scared, Gwen. I'm so afraid that I'm going to screw this up," she mumbles against my shoulder. "I don't think I can be somebody's mother."

I pull back and grip her shoulders. "Look at me," I say and she looks up at me with sad, puppy dog eyes and swollen lips. "You're going to be an amazing mom. And you're not alone. You have Grey. And you have me. And you have Mom. You have a full support system." Tears are pouring down her cheeks and she closes her eyes. I gently shake her. "Look at me, Charley. You are not *him*. You are nothing like him."

She sniffs and nods and we look at each other, our eyes locking as if a silent pact passes between us.

"Now let's go get you ready. You're getting married today," I say with a smile, my mind whirling with Charley's pregnancy news. An odd sense of relief lodges itself in the pit of my stomach knowing without doubt that Charley is going to need me now more than ever. I almost feel ashamed at the things that bring me comfort. "Okay?"

"Okay," she whispers. I hand her a tissue from my purse, rev the engine, and take off back toward the hotel. I glance at the clock on the dashboard, thinking that we just might make it in time.

I stand stiffly in my long dress; its light, sheer fabric blowing in the breeze as I watch Olivia and Max walk down the white carpeted aisle toward the arch where Grey and Charley will be exchanging their vows shortly. The bay sits in the background, bustling with sailboats, creating a view so sharp and flawless it's as if someone painted it for this very occasion.

Olivia's blonde hair is swept up off her shoulders, showcasing her olive skin and the sharp angles of her arms and back. She looks beautiful and so grown-up in her steel-blue dress that matches my own. It calls to mind the passing of time.

Time has slipped away, although I can't say that it has gone by unnoticed. Each morning I wake and take in my surroundings, thankful for another day. It hasn't been easy. Illness looms constantly; a simple cold lands me in the hospital for days. I endure blood tests, scans, doctor appointments, and the sixteen prescription medications that line the counter in my bathroom, out of my children's sight. But I do it all for them, and I'd do it all over again if I had to. I move forward, taking one day at a time with the notion that none of us know what lies ahead. Anything could happen to any one of us at any time. And so I do whatever it takes, whatever buys me another day or another year to watch my kids grow, to be with John.

I've learned to let go. To ask for help. To love without condition. To say aloud the words that I normally would keep to myself, knowing that I might not get the chance to say them tomorrow.

Olivia and Max reach the front and veer to their respective sides. I can see the hint of Max's dimples as he straightens his tuxedo jacket and gazes over the small crowd that has gathered to witness this special day. Even at ten, Max seems grown up, older than his peers, and every bit as handsome as John. Olivia stands confident, holding her small bouquet of lilies.

Mrs. Preston walks down next, flanked by Grey's brothers, as they escort her to her seat beside Grey's father. John follows, escorting my mother to the front row, where she sits alone but without care. My mother has never looked more exquisite, happiness replacing the fine lines that once carved out her features like a road map of her past. As if the truth really has set her free.

"Ready?" I hear from behind me and turn to face Charley. She is gorgeous in her white strapless gown that gathers tightly around her tiny waist, hugging her flowing curves at the hips where it bells slightly and stretches elegantly to her feet. She is radiant, timeless really, with her hair swept up save for the few curled tendrils that fall gently around her face. Although I see the fear in her eyes, the uncertainty that lies beneath her beauty, the vulnerability.

"You look amazing, Charley."

"Thank you," she says, blowing out a long, shaky breath through pursed lips. I watch her eyes flash past me and something settles over her face. An ease, a confidence that was not there moments before. And when I turn to follow her gaze, I see Grey standing under the arch with John beside him, fulfilling his best man duties. Grey is beaming at Charley with liquid eyes and Charley is wholeheartedly gushing. And all at once it hits me that Grey is Charley's home. She has finally found her constant, her star to guide her, her true self. A lone tear slips from the corner of my eye as I feel the curve of a smile stretch across my face. Standing here, watching everyone I love bathed in happiness on a beautiful, sunny day fills me with a sense of peace, a fulfillment that I find hard to describe.

I reach over and grab Charley's hand and whisper, "I love you," not wanting to hold anything back, wondering if I have ever told her.

I feel her squeeze my hand and whisper back, "I love you too." And then on cue, I grasp my bouquet, step forward and begin my walk toward everything that I love, feeling overwhelming gratitude that I'm here, that I get to be part of this day, that I am surrounded by so much love.

# FOUR YEARS AFTER THAT...
## *Charley*

The end came two weeks after Harper's third birthday. As hard as Gwen fought, it was a moment of utter peace. Knowing the end is coming and the actual second that it does are two very different things. We are all holding up as best as can be expected.

I see Gwen with each glance in the mirror, as if her hazel eyes are staring back at me. The one feature we have always shared, our one physical link. In the end, I struggled with the guilt of moving forward, the guilt of feeling so much happiness in my life, a life that was only just beginning when Gwen's own life was slowly fading to an end. Knowing that Gwen was fighting so hard to freeze time, to live in the moment, to never think of what lie in wait around the bend. But I see now that guilt is useless, a waste of time. Instead, I try to harness Gwen's strength and live each day like she would, to be the kind of mother to Harper that she would be proud of.

And when I feel as if it is all too much, I remember Gwen's wish, to be fearless. And I imagine her flying in the wind, arms outstretched without a care in the world, feeling many things but none of them fear. And I think, *I can do this. I can be strong for her.*

I've come to realize that love comes in all different sizes and shapes, all different faces. For my mother it looked like an ultimatum, a choice, a sacrifice. For Gwen, it came in the name of courage and surrender. And for me, it came through forgiveness. It came when I needed it the most, and fought it the hardest. They say that sometimes you don't realize your own strength until you come face to face with your greatest weakness. I believe this to be true. Love came when I was most fragile, lifted me up and made me whole. I was wrong about love. It doesn't rob you of your strength, tear you down, and leave you vulnerable like I had feared for so long. Love comes from within, builds you up. Love is my strength and I feel stronger than ever.

# NOTE FROM THE AUTHOR

This story was never intended to be about Gwen's cancer or her battle with the disease but rather about what happens behind the scenes. It is about how people react and change in the face of devastating circumstances. Although I researched Metastatic Breast Cancer and different forms of treatment, Gwen's experience is a fictional account and any mistakes are my own. I have met so many women, many of them young mothers like Gwen, who are fighting cancer or in some instances, living with it. I am in awe of their strength and their positive energy. And I am always surprised when I learn their story, because from the outside you would never know their internal battle. Out of respect for these women and anyone battling a life-threatening disease or accepting a terminal one, I leave that part of Gwen's story to them. Because it isn't my story to tell.

# ACKNOWLEDGMENTS

I feel so blessed to be able to write every day, to give a piece of myself to each and every character. It has allowed me to know myself better, to dig deep where we tend to hide our darkest fears and our biggest wants. And I feel so grateful to all my readers, to all the bloggers, to all the authors that I have met along the way for their support and love of books. None of this would be possible without someone out there, willing to read and share the stories I tell. So thank you! Special thanks to Ena Burnette with Swoon Worthy Books and Enticing Journey Book Promotions – your enthusiasm for *Gravity* and your determination to make sure that EVERYONE reads it is amazing, YOU are amazing! I can't wait for the day when I finally meet you in person, although I feel like I already know you! To Aestas, I can't thank you enough for your support of *Gravity*, your words reached so many people!

To my loyal beta readers: Kristin Gentry, Debbie Bayley, my sister, my mom. Thank you for taking the time to read this book in its early stages and for answering all my neurotic questions.

To my editors at BubbleCow, you never disappoint! Thank you for being part of this journey for the third time around! Seriously, you guys rock and I have learned so much from you!

To Eric and the two little people who have stolen my heart, Ryder and Ivy May – you bring me a happiness so great, it almost feels as if I don't deserve you! Thank you for supporting me, loving me, and giving me purpose.

# CONTACT THE AUTHOR

L.D. Cedergreen loves to hear from her readers. She can be found on:

facebook at www.facebook.com/AuthorL.D.Cedergreen
or Twitter: @LDCedergreen
or Instagram: LDCedergreen

Please consider leaving a review on Amazon.com or Goodreads!

www.ingramcontent.com/pod-product-compliance
Lightning Source LLC
Chambersburg PA
CBHW021217250626
47155CB00008B/2839